RUTHLESS LOVER

The Institute Series

A.K ROSE
ATLAS ROSE

Copyright © 2023 by A.K Rose

All rights reserved.

No part of this book may be reproduced in any form or by any electronic or mechanical means, including information storage and retrieval systems, without written permission from the author, except for the use of brief quotations in a book review.

ONE

Alexi

Now...

THERE WAS pain in her eyes before they closed. A cruel pain... a cutting pain.

Pain I caused.

"I hate you." Her voice shook as though deep down she didn't believe those words at all.

Still, I played her game. "I know you do."

Her jaw clenched with the trail of my finger along the edge of it. Muscles flexed under my touch. She felt this. The heat of my breath on her cheek. The hardness of my cock. My betrayal. One she wore on the side of her face.

I caressed the deep purple bruise as disgust grew inside me. It was a cold, dark empty pit, filled with the demons of my past. I'd existed in that pit for what felt like forever, fighting those beasts with teeth and claws, desperate to survive. Never once stepping into the light...*until I met her.*

Then I fucked it up, didn't I? In the worst possible way.

I skirted the deep purple edge, then trailed down her throat. Her breath caught; panic filled her eyes before she swung.

Slap.

My head jerked with the blow. Heat followed, searing through my cheek. Her lips curled; sparks ignited in her eyes. I took that rage. *I needed that rage.* Because it was better than not having anything at all. It was better than not having *her* at all. Agony consumed me at the thought, my heart pounded harder. Still, I forced myself to focus, to be consumed by the sting in my cheek and the disgust in her eyes. She was real and alive, safe with me, even if she thought otherwise.

Her screams filled my head.

Gut wrenching screams. *Hopeless screams.*

The screams of agony and betrayal.

The sight of that man on top of her, holding her down while she fought. My throat thickened and I glanced to the purple outline of her jaw. All because I used her family to get myself out of this fucking mess...a mess that almost killed her. *She's alive...she's alive and that's all that matters.*

Everything else I'd handle...

Even if it meant a bullet to the brain.

My touch trembled as I trailed down her throat to the hollow at the base of her neck. Her blow came again, this time curled into a fist. I moved, catching her feeble blow with my other hand.

Hard commanding breaths consumed the space between us. The sound raspy and ragged. I captured her fist, dragged her hand over her head, forcing her spine to arch, jutting her breasts upwards.

With my other hand I gripped her wrists, pinning them in place before I turned my attention back to her. Her chest stilled, a shudder tearing free as I grazed along the edge of her dress over her breast.

Her hips bucked from the bed in a surge of desperation. "Get the fuck off me, you *lying piece of shit!*"

But I couldn't leave her. Not anymore. I grabbed the strap of her dress and yanked, tearing the satin strap down her shoulders, spilling her breast free.

That resounding thud in my chest grew louder. The back of my finger crested her small, firm breast. Her nipples hardened instantly. Puckering under my gaze. My mouth watered and balls grew tight. I lifted my focus to hers. Her eyes are wide open; panic, desire and hate swirled inside them like a hurricane. Hate for me...hate for what I'd done...*and what I was.*

"You do this and I'll never forgive you."

"I know," I repeated. Because it's all I have left now.

I know...

I know I don't deserve you...

I know I'm dead after this...so please...give me this moment...just give me...you...once more.

That sickening dread inside me howled and raged, screaming at me to stop. To crawl from this bed like the piece of shit I was. Vile...lowest of the low. I wished I was stronger. I wished I could let her leave, even though she's now ruined...*ruined by me.*

I should wipe myself from her existence. Hand myself over to the Commission and fall on my knees, taking whatever punishment they delivered.

Death.

That's what would come for me. I knew that. There was no way they could let me live. Not once they knew the truth. That need to do the right thing raged in the back of my mind. Still, I gagged that scream, my hand pressed over the bastard's mouth. Muffling his pleas. Hunger is what drives me now, and it has nothing to do with using her anymore. Because I don't want to use her...*I wanted to own her. To consume her...to have her again and again and again.*

The back of my finger circled that tight little rose-colored nub before falling lower. She shivered under my touch. I caught the ripples along her belly before I found my way to the slit of her dress.

She stiffened as I widened the part.

"No, Alexi...*no.*" Her words were a whisper. Still, they howled like a hurricane in my head.

"I'm a weak man, Leila. Weak and pathetic." I lifted my gaze to hers, reaching down to pull her thighs apart. "But weak men are dangerous. They'll do whatever they want...and they won't care about the consequences. You are my consequence. Your hate, your anger. That cold look in your eyes that tells me you're leaving me. I can't let that happen...not now...*not ever.*" I found my way to her panties, pressing my finger against the seam. Feeling her stiffen under me as I moved higher, circling her clit. "I'm so fucking weak when it comes to you."

I slipped my finger under the edge of her panties, slipping along her slick slit, she was practically dripping. "You're so wet. So goddamn wet."

She let out a whimper, thrashing her head. Fighting it. Her hips bucked from the bed, trying to dislodge my touch. But all it did was drive my fingers deeper, all the way inside...where I ached to be. My cock was rock hard, turned on by the way she fought this.

"Fuck, you feel good." I dropped my head beside hers, sliding my fingers in and out, working her body like I knew it needed.

She unleashed a moan. A tortured savage sound as she yanked her hands from my hold.

But she wasn't going anywhere. She was staying right here...in my bed...in my life.

That cold edge of desperation roared inside me. Making me grasp her panties. With a brutal tug they yanked her hips from the bed before the thin black lace ripped. Lingerie she wore for me...*even if she hated me.*

And she did hate me, there was no question about that. She hated and seethed and burned with rage. I shoved my zipper low and unbuttoned my jeans.

"*No!*" She bucked and thrashed with the sound.

Still, I couldn't stop. I released her wrists only to grasp her throat. "I'm going to fuck you, Leila, and you're going to come for me...whether you want to or not."

"*Fuck you!*" Her Russian accent thicker, the more desperate she became.

And she was desperate. Desperate to hit and hurt and kiss and *fuck.*

She howled and kicked, trying her best to get away from me, but at the same time her nails clawed my back, desperate for more. I climbed between her and looked down. The remnant of her panties still hung around her hips. The strands ripped, the lace ruined...all because of me. Tears welled in her eyes. Thick, glistening tears. The sight of them a gunshot to my chest as I shoved her legs wider with mine. I was captured by the shine of her pain. My hands around her throat, my body pinning her underneath me as they slipped free.

"I love you, Leila. Like I've never loved anything else before."

She jerked that seething glare to me. *"And I hate you Alexi! I hate you with my entire being!"*

I plunged inside her, watching that agony turn into something else.

Something sick and depraved...something akin to the hunger inside me. She let out a moan and I drove mercilessly inside her, then eased out.

Hard, brutal thrusts worked her pussy. But it was the rage in her eyes that made her body come alive. I slid inside once more; this time slower, harder. Fucking her anyway I could. I was a beast when it came to her. I clenched my jaw. Clenched until my expelled breath was a hiss between my teeth. A ravenous, unholy beast. "Come for me Leila...but know this, there's no leaving me...*not ever again...*"

6 MONTHS *before*

"WHAT THE FUCK did you just say?" I looked down at the woman spread eagle in the middle of my bed.

A woman I'd been sleeping with for the last three months. A woman I'd let into my life.

And who was now stabbing me in the fucking back.

Cold slipped into my world.

It ran through my veins.

Welling deep in my belly.

The white sheet slid from her long, tanned thigh as she pushed onto her elbow. "I told you, Alexi. I warned you I was trouble."

She reached over the side of her bed, grabbed something from the pocket of her jeans and pulled backwards. "I just didn't tell you how much."

One flick of the leather wallet and she dropped it open beside her. Gold glinted in the murky light of my bedroom. I trailed the outline of the eagle, then the words underneath. *CIA*.

I jerked my gaze to hers.

She's never carried that wallet before.

Never mentioned the Feds. Not in all the time we'd been together. *You mean all the times you fucked? Didn't really leave a lot of time for conversation now, did it?* I thought she was just another female in a crowded bar with money in her sights. But Hannah hadn't been. She'd never once asked me for a damn thing...

Now I knew why.

Everything around me seemed to stop...*everything but her*. "All we want is the file, Alexi. You give us that and we're gone. No one ever needs to know."

I flinched with the words. *The file*...the file. The one with images of a hit...one that could never see the light of day. I understood now, all the fucking questions, all the information I murmured in the aftermath of sweat and sex. Information that could get me killed. "You bitch."

The glint in her eyes dulled. A coldness came over her, a ruthless, stony-hearted stare. "That I might be. But right now, I'm the only thing standing between you and the District Attorney of New York who has a massive hard on for the Salvatores, and he doesn't care who he takes down in the process. So right now, Kilpatrick, I'm doing you a favor."

She was doing me a favor? *She was doing me a favor?* A second ago I was eating her pussy and now...now she was handing me over to the goddamn Feds? I glanced to the sweat-stained sheets.

"We want the Salvatores, Alexi. We want the Rossis." She swung her legs over the side of the bed. "Hell, we want them all, including the Commander."

Jesus...

I jerked my focus to hers. "How the fuck do you know about him?"

She smiled. "We know more than you think."

She fucking smiled.

Rage lashed deep inside. I strode toward her. Steel glinted in the corner of my eye as she rose. The muzzle of my gun peeked out from under the pile of our clothes. *Kill her...kill the bitch. Blow her brains out all over the bed drenched in her cum.* I pushed the thought away, grabbing her around the throat. *"You think this is a game?"*

She stilled, searching my gaze. The muscles of her throat flaring against my palm as she swallowed. "Not a game, Alexi. Just... atonement for all the shit you've done."

The apartment swirled around me...the floor seemed to tilt. I tried to keep my shit together, tried to focus on the feel of her neck in my grasp. *No one needs to know.* I clenched my grip, driving my fingers into her throat until I felt the hard ridges of her windpipe.

She tried to clench. Tried to force her throat to open. The same throat I'd fucked earlier tonight. "I could kill you."

"You could," she wheezed. "But you won't."

Do it...do it...do it. The words resounded. "All this time you were building a case on me?"

"I don't have much to go on. Not really enough to put you behind bars. But enough to expose you, so yeah."

Fear coursed through me with the words.

Expose me...expose me as a snitch.

It didn't matter how many people I'd killed or how many deals went south. All that mattered was I kept my mouth shut about the five families who wouldn't think twice about taking me out to save themselves...*people like the Salvatores.*

"I can keep you out of this." She softened her tone and held my stare. It was the same tactic we used...right before we put a bullet in their brains. Jesus, how much did she have on me? My mind raced, trying put the pieces together. All the damn conversations on the phone to Jager as he took care of every dirty job for our father.

I closed my eyes, as it suddenly hit me.

"You can kill me if you want," she said. "But it won't make any difference. They know, Alexi, they know who and what you are, most importantly, what you've done. Make it easy on yourself. Give me what we need and all this can go away."

I opened my eyes. Make it go away. *Make it all go away.* "What do you want to know?"

That smile came back with a vengeance. Perfect white teeth shone in the dark. "See that's the thing about you, Alexi. You only ever look out for yourself."

"You're a real fucking cunt, you know that, right?"

"Takes one to know one," she whispered.

She was right.

TWO

Alexi

5 MONTHS BEFORE

HEADLIGHTS GLARED into the rear-view mirror from behind me. The same car had been following me from the moment I left my house. I forced my attention back to the freeway, signaled and turned, merging onto the off-ramp that'd take me into the city.

Panicked.

That's how I felt. My cell phone lit up beside me on the passenger's seat. But I didn't need to grab the damn thing to know who it was...*it was her. The CIA cunt who set me up.* The one who wanted nothing more than for me to hand over every filthy goddamn secret on the Salvatores, the Rossis, the damn Valachis and the Commander.

Did she want to goddamn die?

Anyone who lived this life knew you didn't mess with the Commander. Not if you wanted to live. A bead of sweat ran down the back of my neck at the thought. It wasn't just him you had to worry about. It was his brother. The goddamn contract killer, the one they called *'The Albanian'*.

I'm going to fucking die...

The knowledge hit me; that's exactly how I'd end. A gunshot from a sniper's rifle. A knife under my ribs as I knocked into someone turning a crowded city street corner. I'd never even see it coming. Never even know when the moment of my end hurtled toward me.

It could even be tonight.

I lifted my gaze to the headlights in the rear-view mirror. *It could even be him.* A tortured sound ripped from my lips as my phone rang, the sound filing through the speakers in the car. I flinched, glanced at the name on the stereo, hit the button on the steering wheel and snapped, *"What is it?"*

"Jesus...what the fuck is up your ass?" Jager's deep snarl echoed through the speaker.

I sucked in a hard breath and tried to quell the thunderous roar inside my head. "Nothing. Just some asshole in the car behind me."

I punched the accelerator harder, diverting my gaze from the sparkle of the city lights up ahead and the blinding glare from behind me.

"Dad wants to meet."

"What the fuck for this time?"

My phone lit up; a caller ID flashed across the stereo. I winced at the sight of the familiar number. My pulse sped as I tried to swallow that thick wad in the back of my throat.

"He has something he needs me to handle."

I flinched, and jerked my gaze to the flashing number of the waiting call. "Another goddamn hit?" I strangled the wheel. "You know we have men for that, right? Why the hell does he feel the need to drag us into this shit every goddamn time?"

Silence echoed through the speakers of the car long enough to make me glance at the stereo. Did the call drop?

"I don't know if you notice, but I seem to be the one sacrificing a piece of my soul here every time he demands it to be done. It's always me, Alexi. Never you."

The blare of a car's engine came from the sedan tail-gaiting my ass. Headlights swerved across the lanes of traffic as the vehicle surged forward, gaining momentum as I headed toward the heart of the city.

"Did you hear what I just said?"

The sedan pulled up alongside me, windows on the passenger's side rolled down.

"Alexi?"

The asshole in the cheap fucking suit just stared at me, his face consumed by shadows. He lifted his cell phone...and tapped the screen. My heart lunged, slamming against my chest. "I heard you," I murmured; my voice raspy. "I've got my own problems going on here, Jager. Just text me the address of the meet."

But I was talking to a ghost. The line was dead. My brother was long gone. A *beep* sounded a second later and the address of one of Dad's many clubs he frequented came through. Still the asshole in the goddamn Feds' car matched my speed.

*Answer your phone...*the asshole in the passenger's seat mouthed the words.

I punched the brake; my hands worked the gear lever as I down shifted and jerked the wheel. *Get away from them... get the fuck away...*

I tore through the back streets of the city as I headed for the nightclub called *Harbinger*. My headlights bounced against the gatehouse window. I pulled up hard, hitting the button for the window as the guard headed toward the car.

"Mr. Kilpatrick, sir."

I glanced into the rear-view mirror as that sedan slowly rolled past. "Open the motherfucking gate."

Inch by painful inch the sedan rolled past. I stared into the rear-view mirror until my eyes burned as the boom gate rose. I punched the accelerator, tearing through the underground carpark, and headed to the back where my father's Bentley sat parked, and Jager's steel gray Porsche sat hidden in the shadows behind it.

I pulled the Audi up hard, hit the button and killed the engine. My skin crawled as I climbed out, making me scan the shadows as I hit the button, locking the car, and made for the elevator.

I need to find a way out of this...before anyone finds out.

Figure out a way, Alexi. I pressed the button for the elevator and stepped inside when the door opened. *Find a way.*

The heavy thud of music pressed against the steel walls. I unleashed a pent-up breath. My thoughts panicked, scrambling to keep one step ahead...even though I was failing.

The slow, heavy thud of music grew louder until it thrummed through the walls, and then grew fainter as the elevator climbed and finally pulled to a stop. I still felt the vibration of the music through my boots as I stepped out into a hallway. High-class hookers stepped out from a cracked-open door. Two of them wearing nothing more than a skimpy thong strode past, giggling and muttering to each other as they met my gaze.

I glanced over my shoulder, heading for a door at the far end of the hallway as one of the barely-clothed women gave me a wink. Hookers, all of them. No one took their girlfriends up here, not unless they were looking for an addition in the bedroom.

I knocked once, then pushed open the door. Dad lifted his gaze from the sofa as Jager just glared from the other side of the room.

"Took you long enough." Dad grabbed his glass from the table and downed its contents. "Now that you're here, there's a job I need handled, Jager."

"No."

One brow rose as Dad slowly turned his head. "No?" He rose from the sofa and stepped. "No?"

Jager met his stare. "That's right."

There was a cruel bite in my father's tone. "You seem to have made a mistake. I wasn't asking."

Jager shoved off the wall, taking a step toward him. "I think it's *you* who's made the mistake. No more hits. I'm tired of all the blood on my goddamn hands."

"You're...*tired of the blood.*" He held my brother's stare and stepped close. "You're a goddamn heir. There's no getting *tired of the blood*. You *are the fucking blood.*"

The door opened behind me; the faint throb of music spilled in.

"Hey," the slur of a female followed. "Get the fuck off me."

A bouncer shoved the young woman inside the room, glancing from me to my father sitting on the couch. "Will she do?"

Revulsion gripped me as I looked at her. She was young, barely legal. What the hell was she doing on the streets at all?

Dad crossed the room slowly, circling her. She was no hooker, just some female off the street dressed in a short denim skirt and combat boots. She licked her lips, her pupils blown. She was just a kid. A strung-out goddamn kid. I looked away. *Jesus.*

"She's perfect," my father muttered, his eyes glinting as he stared down at her.

"Fuck this. I'm out of here." Jager made for the door.

"*Stay!*"

I flinched with the roar, staring at this predatory piece of shit in front of me. "You, *out.*" He commanded, then glanced to the bodyguard. "I'll call when we're done."

When he's done...that's what he meant.

When the poor bitch in front of me was weeping and used. When her tears stopped flowing and a certain emptiness lingered in her stare. When my father had fucked his way to exhaustion, and only then, would he call the bodyguard to dispose of her like a used condom.

Rage burned inside me. This was a game to him. It was all a game. He liked us to see the trashy women he used. He liked us knowing what he did behind our mother's back.

Or maybe she didn't care.

Maybe she felt relief when he walked out of the house and stepped into his car.

Maybe she prayed one day he'd fuck his whores a little too hard and fall on top of them, dead.

Maybe we all wished for that...everyone but Jager.

"Hey." She licked her lips, shifting from one foot to the next. Her gaze darted around the room as she suddenly saw us clearly. "You guys got any blow?"

The door closed carefully, and we were alone.

"Of course, sweetheart." Dad slid his arm around her shoulders, pulling her toward the sofa. "I've got all the blow you want."

Jager's lips curled as he looked away.

The sound of a zipper, the groan of leather seat. "Right after you take care of your uncle."

"But you're not my uncle," she murmured.

The sick bastard just smiled down at her. "I know."

THREE

Leila

---

5 MONTHS BEFORE

"LEILA." My father's icy tone stopped me cold. "Where are you going?"

The echo of my heels faded in the hallway as a tremor tore through me. That tight sound in my father's voice warned me to be careful. He was stressed, strained...and controlling. "Papa," I answered carefully, turning toward him. *"Please."*

His brow creased as he stepped out of his study. "You know the rules."

There were boxes stacked behind him in the study. Boxes splattered with blood.

I never flinched from the sight, only lowered my gaze to his hands and the glistening crimson smear across his palm. He caught my focus, looked down and scowled as he closed the door behind him.

Boxes and blood, is that what we'd come to now?

"I want to see Viktoriya, Papa." I lifted my gaze to his, desperation filling me. "I *need* to see her before we leave."

He reached into his jacket, grabbed a handkerchief and worked the smear. "I know this is hard. You want to see your friends. But we have no time, *moya lyubov'*."

The door to the study opened once more and Theon strode out. "I'll take her." He adjusted his tie, not once looking at my father. No, his focus was all on me. In that cold, steely stare of a killer was the flicker of warmth. "You want to say goodbye, Mia?" He gave me a sad smile. "Just you and me, okay?"

Hope rose inside me. "Okay, Papa?"

He gave a slow shake of his head. "There's no time."

My heart sank.

"We'll be quick." Theon held my gaze. "Won't we, Mia?"

I gave a nod, my heart thundering in my ears. "You won't even know we were gone."

"You have less than an hour." my father answered, the hardness in his eyes growing cold. "Then we're leaving."

I swallowed and stepped backwards, before turning and racing for the door. It was as good as I was going to get.

Boxes and blood, right?

We were leaving this place, leaving the only place I called home. We were *leaving Russia* and traveling halfway across the world to find a new one. I didn't want to leave, not this house, all my friends. But it didn't matter what I wanted. Still, I wasn't giving up on saying one last goodbye to the only person who knew what my life was like...because hers was exactly the same.

"Theon." Olga rushed forward, my thick white winter coat in her hand. She shoved it at him as he strode past. "See she stays warm."

Theon's footsteps mirrored the heavy thud in my chest as I stopped at the front door and grabbed the handle.

"*Mia,*" Theon snapped, then softened as he slid his hand over mine. Steel-gray eyes bored onto mine. "Me first. Always me first, okay?"

I should know this.

One nod and I slid my hand away and slipped them both the sleeves of my jacket instead. To be Russian was to be cold. I shivered as Theon gently pulled the coat tighter around me. To be Russian was to be savagely secretive, and Theon was...to everyone but me.

I worked the buttons as panic rose. Theon waited for me to finish before he opened the door. I felt like a child around him, around *all of them*. Scolded, controlled. Protected by guns and gates and the whisper of who we were...*Bratva*.

He stepped into the doorway, scanned the grounds, motioning to one of the guards, before he opened the door wider. "Okay, Mia." Theon motioned me forward.

I hurried down the stairs as the black Mercedes pulled up. White plumes of exhaust fumes mingled with the white mist of our breaths. My heels clattered as I hurried down the stairs and climbed inside as Theon opened the door.

We were leaving...I lifted my gaze to the stony mansion as the door closed. We were really leaving our home. I clenched my jaw as the crunch of gravel came around the car and Theon climbed in behind the wheel. One glance in the rear-view mirror and I turned my head to hide my pain.

But he knew...

They all knew.

I didn't want to go.

My heart ached with the thought; I swallowed down on that hard lump in the back of my throat as the car pulled out into the wide circular driveway and headed toward the wrought iron gates at the entrance to the property.

It was white as far as I could see. I glanced down to my white, thick winter coat. White was my world, but would it be in the *United States of America?* I didn't think so. I swallowed the flare of agony as it coursed through my chest.

The gates slowly rolled open, leaving us to pass the guard standing at the entrance. He gave a nod, careful eyes met mine, one hand on the two-way and the other on his assault rifle. This was our life, even if it wasn't one I'd hoped for. Still, I was safe here. The memory of the splattered blood on the box in my father's study and the smear on his hand came back to me.

I was safe here...

But also controlled.

We headed down the long stretch of road that wound up along the side of a mountain before we turned off. The wheels on the Mercedes skidded before catching their grip. Towering houses lingered in the distance. White stone set against the snowy backdrop. Towering steel gates and armed guards. Houses of monsters and men. Was it men who were monsters? The blood on the back of my father's hand whispered the truth.

Theon glanced into the rear-view mirror, meeting my gaze. "You know what to say, Mia?"

"Yes." I knew what to say...what we were telling everyone who asked why the sudden move halfway across the world. Lies. That's what we were telling them.

But that wasn't what I'd tell Viktoriya.

Even if I did, she'd see right through it.

Theon swung the Mercedes into a driveway with a towering gate. But this wasn't any wrought iron. No, this was bricks and stone topped with razor wire. If my world was white, then Viktoriya's was black. Black stone. Black uniforms of the guards as they stepped up to the driver's window.

"Turn around," the guard demanded with a shake of his head. "No visitors today."

What? I tore a panicked glance to Theon. But I didn't need to.

"Check again, Ms. Leila Ivanov has an appointment."

The mere mention of my name had the guard glancing to the back seat of the car. I kept my gaze stony, never once allowing the distress I felt to show on my face.

"We're not leaving. Make the call, *now.*"

The guard stepped away, reaching for his two-way, and turned. Muffled words slipped through the open driver's side window. I couldn't catch the words, but I saw the terror on the guard's face. Something was happening.

Something they didn't want anyone knowing about.

Theon...my protector's name rose inside me as he carefully adjusted his hand on the wheel. The movement covering the true response as he lowered his hand toward his gun. The guard's bark was louder. I caught snatches of his conversation. *Won't leave...Ivanov. Yes...that's who I said.* But then he lowered his hand, glanced toward the car and motioned us through.

The gates rolled backwards, revealing the dark, brooding landscape. Dark wood trees laden with snow crowded the driveway. I'd never been concerned coming here, not in all the years I'd been friends with Viktoriya, until today.

We'd been encouraged to be close. Still there was always a barrier between us. An unspoken one dictated by family. The Korolev family was even older than ours. Steeped in brutality and guarded by a cruel, controlling fist. They called them oligarchs. But they didn't just have money. It was power they controlled. Power, position...more than anyone else, including us.

The stable house rose in the distance, tall, expansive, sitting on one side of the driveway in front of the stables that seemed to stretch forever, leading all the way to the main house. I fixed my gaze on the sight as it rose in the distance. Twice the size and three times as imposing as ours. Black, hulking, cut into the rise of the mountain. Theon slowed the car, pulling along the wide circular driveway, before pulling to a stop. But he didn't turn off the ignition, not yet. Instead, he sat there, scanning the grounds, trusting that instinct honed from all the years he'd protected us.

"Theon?" I scowled. "What's going on?'

The place was quiet...eerily quiet. No guards patrolled the grounds. No trainers walked the horses. There was no one here...like a ghost town.

"I think we should leave." He reached forward and shoved the car into drive once more as the front door opened and a powerfully-built male stepped out.

He strode down the stairs toward us, ignoring the fact we were already pulling away.

"Theon *please*. It's my last chance to see her."

His gray eyes found mine in the mirror. The car coasted, and then braked to a stop at the edge of the driveway.

Still the male strode toward us, opening the rear door for me. "Ms. Ivanov," Mikhail murmured, holding out his hand. "I apologize for the confusion. It seems we were unaware of your visit today."

I scowled at Viktoriya's protector, searching his gaze before I found the speck of blood on the collar of his shirt. Blood red...it seems like it was the color of the day. Still, I grasped his outstretched hand and rose as Theon switched off the engine. "The apology is all mine; I didn't realize I needed permission to see my best friend before I left her and my home behind."

"Leila," Theon warned.

When he used my proper name I knew I was in trouble. I glanced toward the front door of the house, my loyalties and heart ripped to shreds. I was past caring what my father wanted and well past obeying Theon's command. "I want to see her, Mikhail. I *need* to see her."

Her bodyguard gave a ghost of a smile, then looked to Theon before muttering. "Well, you're here now, aren't you? I suppose you'd make a damn fuss if I sent you packing."

"You have no idea," Theon grumbled under his breath.

I made for the stairs, climbing before Mikhail spoke. "Not that way, Ms. Ivanov, if you don't mind." He motioned toward the pathway. One that'd take us along the side entrance of the house and far away from the front of the house.

I followed Mikhail, catching Theon glancing over his shoulder. He was cautious, nervous even. But apart from the lack of security and the overcautious gatehouse guard and the tiny speck of blood on Mikhail's shirt there wasn't a thing that'd keep me from seeing my best friend one last time.

The icy wind picked up, blasting my face as we rounded the corner of the house and made our way along the stony path. Footsteps turned quieter, empty almost. I slowed, turned my head, finding Theon fallen behind. "Theon?"

Mikhail's steps still thudded, the sound mingling with the roar of the wind.

"Stay by my side, Mia." The way Theon spoke sent a chill along my spine. It was more than the sharp winter wind, more than the desperation howling inside me. It was him...this...*everything*.

"Okay," I whispered.

Theon strode ahead, leaving me to follow. The side door was up ahead, black wrought iron gates barring the entrance. Mikhail dragged a key from his pocket, glanced over his shoulder, waiting for us before opening the door and motioning us inside.

But if I thought stepping inside would ease the cold, then I was mistaken. There wasn't warmth waiting for us within the walls of the Korolev mansion. There was just that same emptiness, that same chill in my bones. One that made me hug my middle and wish for the warmth of a fire.

I knew this house, knew most of the wings at least. I turned toward the one that'd take me to Viktoriya's rooms and waited for Theon.

"Leila." Theon motioned me close.

Still the empty hallways gave us nothing but silence. Mikhail left us behind as he headed along the hallway lined with charcoal depictions of Dante's Inferno. Black and gray. That's what this house was. There was nothing warm in here, nothing light. Just an emptiness I'd never felt before, until now. "Theon, I don't like this."

His response was a hand at my elbow guiding me forward as though he knew I needed this more than I needed to run. Mikhail stopped at the towering double doors at the end of the hallway, knocked twice, loudly, and waited.

The door was yanked open. *"What now?"* Viktoriya glared at her protector, her eyes red-rimmed from crying.

Then her gaze shifted. Her eyes widened; breath caught. There was a flicker of surprise, until it was swallowed by fear. "Leila?"

I glanced toward Mikhail who gave nothing away, just stepped aside, leaving me to cautiously step closer. "You didn't think I'd leave without saying goodbye to my best friend, did you?" She stood in the doorway, not moving, not speaking. Something was wrong here, something really...*really* wrong. "You going to let me in?"

She flinched, tore her gaze toward Mikhail as she swiped her eyes with the back of her hand and stepped to the side. I followed her in, leaving the two bodyguards to stand outside in awkward silence. The moment I closed the door I turned on her. "You've been crying." I crossed the room, brushing the back of my hand against her cheek. "What's happened?"

"Nothing," she answered, instantly.

"Doesn't look like nothing." I stepped closer, drawing her into my arms. "Looks a whole lot like a lot of something."

She trembled, leaned into me but didn't wrap her arms around me, just took my warmth, my love and my friendship and finally lowered her head to my shoulder. "Can we talk about you...*please?*"

It was the last thing I wanted to discuss.

The pain. The hurt. The growing emptiness in my heart. "Of course." I pulled away, smiling at her.

"Are you packed then?" She sniffed and turned away, crossing her bedroom to grab a handkerchief from her dresser, and dabbed her cheeks. Her English was always thick when she was upset.

"Yes." That ache burned with the words. "All packed. We leave within the hour."

She jerked her gaze to mine, terror driving to the surface as she opened her mouth to speak. Silence. That's all that came from her.

"I wish you could come with me." I looked at my feet. Black leather boots peeked out from underneath the thick winter jacket.

"To America?" It was the first flicker of happiness as her eyes glittered. "To the lights and the people? *To New York.*"

"Yes, New York."

She gave me a smile, soft and sad as she crossed the room. When her arms wrapped around me she pulled me against her, tight. "Yes, two sisters in New York. Because you are like a sister to me, Leila."

"Not like." I gripped her harder, wrapping my arms around her once more. "You *are.*"

FOUR

Alexi

4 MONTHS BEFORE...

I SLIPPED into my father's study and closed the door behind me. But I didn't reach for the light switch. Not this time. Instead, I made my way through the dark as a shiver ripped through me. Cold made my fingers numb. I clenched my fists, trying to work feeling back into my damn hands. I'd been standing outside for the best part of two goddamn hours, freezing my ass off as I waited for the guards' shift to change.

Until finally they headed to the rear of my father's compound, leaving a fifteen-minute window to get in and out. Then I made my move.

What fucking move was that exactly? One where you betray your own blood?

No. I swallowed hard and grabbed my cell phone from my pocket. Not betray, just use this to get the Feds to back the hell off. I hit the light on my cell phone as I rounded my father's desk and knelt. I could make them think we weren't what they wanted. *I could make them see I wasn't who they wanted.*

Finley Salvatore rose in my mind. They could go after him instead, making him turn on his father. It wasn't as though they were close. Hell, they could make anyone else turn on Dominic. *Anyone but me.*

The safe was hidden in a trap door underneath the desk. I felt underneath for a latch, yanking it before pushing the heavy timber desk backwards. One press of my hand and the trapdoor popped up from the floor, revealing a neon red timer that was counting down. I had sixty seconds to enter the correct code. Sixty seconds before it sent an alarm to my father.

My damn fingers shook as I punched in the digits. Ones given to Jager years before, that wouldn't be traced back to me. The lights changed from red to green, and the lock clicked open. I shone the light inside, casting the glow over the stacks of files. Ones I prayed would get me out of this mess. I lifted the top folder free and opened the cover.

A dark photo sat on top and as I cast the light over the surface it brightened. A man knelt on the ground; his hands bound behind his back. Jager was the one who stood over him, the muzzle of his gun pressed to his head. It was a proof of death photo. Just one more hit my brother took care of. There were others there, men the Salvatores handled, and the Valachis. This was a bloody, messy business.

No more hits. I'm tired of all the blood on my goddamn hands. My brother's words came back to me as I stared at the image. *No more hits.*

He was right, my father never called on me to do this. It was only Jager...only ever Jager.

He used him as a hitman.

Nothing more than a beast who did my father's bidding. I glanced at the other images; they were just more of the same. Men. Women. Bound. Stabbed. *Jesus...*

But underneath those...buried at the bottom was the one image that could never see the light of day. My hand shook as I slipped it out. I'd only seen it once, but once was enough to send chills along my spine.

Carter Benfold...head of the Executive Branch of the White House. Advisor to the President himself. I didn't know the full details of the hit...all I knew was this beyond anything even the Commission sanctioned and yet there they were, my brother, Jager and Dominic Salvatore himself.

The body on the ground could've been anyone. Hands bound, a black mask over his face. But the Fed's knew...*well they did now, didn't they?*

I should've kept my mouth shut when the shit went down. Should've kept it all under control. But I hadn't...I lost it, and Hannah was right there to see.

I looked away, shoving the photos back into the folder. Revulsion burned inside me as I closed the safe door and pulled the desk back into place. But my knees shook when I rose and stared down at the folder in my hands.

What the hell are you doing?

I closed my eyes. For a second fear took me under, sending me spiralling down a black hole. Once I did this, there was no getting out. Once I did this, I wasn't just handing over the Salvatores and the Valachis, I'd be handing over us as well. *Just run, run so far they couldn't find you. Force them to give up chasing you.* I needed money for that. Money I had, but it was tied up in a trust fund.

I could find money. Take out someone on my own. Steal what they had.

But could I do it? Could I take a life? I swallowed hard and glanced at the files in my hand. It seemed to come so damn easy for Jager. But the moment I envisioned myself as the one holding the gun, I started to panic. If I could just get them to back away somehow.

Figure it out, Alexi...figure it out.

A *thud* came from a door somewhere inside the house, tearing me away from the icy grip of fear. I flicked off the light to my phone, plunging the room back into darkness, and slid the file under my shirt, tucking it hard against my back before I made my way to the door.

Heavy footsteps sounded out in the hallway as I stopped at the study door. I gripped the handle, listening the sound fade. I cracked open the door, searched the hallway before opening the door wider, and slipped out. Ten minutes of panic later I'd crossed the driveway, stepping back into the icy winds once more as I hurried to my car.

My heart was hammering by the time I climbed inside. I leaned forward, ripped the file from under my shirt free and tossed it onto the passenger's seat before I started the car and pulled out. *Jesus*...I gripped the steering wheel trying to stop the shudders. *Jesus*...

My phone illuminated with a call, the ringer turned on silent. But I didn't need to look at the caller ID to know who it was. *It was always the same.*

The bitch was relentless. I drove through the streets ignoring call after call while I searched the rear-view mirror. But I hadn't left my house with a damn tail this time. *Run.* The words pulsed inside my head.

My phone illuminated. I reached out with a snarl, grabbed the thing and hit the button switching it off.

Hide the file.

Then yourself.

Fuck the CIA. They could all go to Hell. I drove along the streets, pulling up at a park overlooking the river. But I couldn't stop myself from looking once more. I grabbed the file and scanned through the photos. Hidden underneath was an envelope. One that'd been sealed. I scowled and lifted it to the faint moonlight. What the hell was in this? It was sealed with more than the sticky adhesive. It was signed along the back and by more than just my father.

I reached up and hit the overhead lights. The harsh glare made me wince and check my rear-view mirror. I didn't want to be out here, but going home wasn't an option, not while I had this in my possession. Something told me whatever was in this envelope was worth a lot more. I stared at the scribble, finding my father's signature...then caught the name Valachi...and Salvatore...and Rossi...and finally *Baldeon*.

A chill swept through me.

This was what they wanted...right here in my hand. I knew it...

FIVE

Leila

I caught my breath as we descended. My heart hammered and that weightless feeling swept through me before the wheels of the jet touched down, squealing as they hit the asphalt.

Only then could I finally breathe.

It wasn't my first trip to the United States from Russia, but I was almost positive it would be my last. There'd be no more going back to my winter wonderland. No more seeing the sprawling grounds of my own home. No more riding my horse along the river as it started to freeze. No more being wild and reckless; as reckless as someone hidden behind towering fences and armed guards could be.

There was no more anything.

Everything we own had been boxed up and shipped. Our presence had been the last tie left.

"Mia?" Theon called, drawing my focus from the pain. "Everything okay?"

I met the steely gaze of my bodyguard. I was the one who should be asking that question. I was the one who should be demanding answers. Answers like why were we leaving?

A month ago, everything was fine.

A month ago, my life was normal.

Now, *nothing* was normal.

I fixed my gaze on the blue sky outside my window without answering. Tears welled in my eyes, but I refused to let them fall. I refused to let them see how hurt I was. Still that pain got the better of me and I caught myself glancing across the jet to where he sat toward the front...alone.

I lifted my chin and swallowed the pain and the hurt. Because to show it was weak. To show it wasn't the Ivanov way, was it?

Our way was stony silence and suffering. Our way was to hide our true feelings and be nothing more than the cold, callous Russians the world expected us to be. The jet's engine roared as we turned at the end of the tarmac and headed for the private hangar.

I was tired of being an Ivanov. I was tired of being alone.

The one person I had left in the world who knew what that felt like had been left behind.

My vision blurred, that one tear which threatened to undo all my determination welled in the corner of my eye. I quickly swiped it, covering the movement as I brushed my fingers through my hair and reached for my purse.

In the small mirror of my compact I looked hideous. My eyes shining and shellshocked, because that's how I felt. I dabbed my cheeks with foundation as the jet's engine died down and we slowed, finally pulling to a stop.

My father tucked his iPad under his arm and rose from his seat, adjusted his jacket and left without a glance my way. I flinched, staring as the jet doors opened and he left me behind.

This was how it was always going to be. Me, left behind. I turned away, pressed my seatbelt release and grabbed my bag. Theon rose, opened the compartment doors above and grabbed my thick winter jacket free. One I wouldn't be needing. "I don't want to be here." I met Theon's gaze. "I want to go home."

He was the only one I spoke to. The only one who'd listen, and normally the one who'd tell me what was going on, as much as he could at least. But he'd been strangely silent since we left. And I felt that quiet like a divide between us.

His steel, gray eyes searched mine. Still there were no words of comfort. Just empty silence. So, I stepped around him and headed toward the open door at the front of the airplane, and stepped out into that warm spring air.

The sleek, black limousine sat waiting. The driver already loading our luggage into the car. I scanned the hangar, seeing the rear of a midnight blue sedan already leaving. My father was nowhere in sight. Gone, just like that. He couldn't even wait until we were at least settled before leaving me behind.

I climbed into the rear of the limousine, leaving Theon to sit up front on the passenger's seat. The driver made little conversation as we pulled out of the hangar parking lot and headed toward the towering skyline of the city. What attempt he made was met with silence. I kept my focus on the horizon, watching as the sparkle of the towering buildings grew brighter until they took my breath away. Everything was bigger here. Bigger and bolder and frantic. We drove through the city and headed out the other side, making our way to the houses on sprawling green grounds before the car turned into a driveway, pulling up in front of commanding black wrought-iron gates.

There were no men with guns here. Nothing but the CCTV cameras that followed us as the gates opened and we drove through. The grounds were glaringly bright. Green grass and towering trees that shaded the driveway. The car pulled up in front of a towering brown brick house. I hated it on sight. Hated the white painted windows. I hated the trees, and the bright red roses that wrapped around the front veranda and plunged down the side. I shoved open the door, not waiting for Theon, and climbed out. He scowled and shook his head.

"Not now, Theon," I muttered and headed for the stairs that would take me inside.

The thud of my boots resounded as I climbed. The air was musty and heavy as I pushed through the doors.

"Mia," Theon called.

I spun, letting my pain unleash. *"What do you want from me?"*

He dug into his pocket, pulling out a pamphlet as he crossed the distance between us, those solemn eyes meeting mine. "This is no longer Russia. There, you had little opportunity. But here... here you have more. Here, you're called an heir. So don't you think you should be treated like one?"

I lowered my gaze to the printed paper in his hand. Blue skies and even bluer water. Cosa Nostra, the emblem said on the front. I scowled. "What is this place?"

"A place for people like you. Where you can make friends, and learn how to defeat your enemies."

My enemies...the word echoed inside me.

My breath caught and that same heady, lightness swept through me once more, the same feeling I had just before the tires hit the tarmac. The only enemy I had was the one who called me daughter. "He'll never let me go."

"He will if you demand it. Are you willing to do that, Mia? Are you willing to become the daughter of a Czar?"

SIX

Alexi

1 MONTH BEFORE

"EXCUSE ME." The familiar voice made me stiffen. "You don't happen to know where I can find the main building in this place?"

My blood ran cold. Stomach tightened. I became aware of every movement around me. There were suits everywhere. Dark, drab, black on black as somber music played out from the speakers outside the chapel. I spun, finding the one person I didn't want to see standing right in front of me. The *only* person who shouldn't be here at Cian Salvatore's funeral.

Yet here she was...an undercover CIA agent standing right in front of me.

Hannah smiled carefully, hiding the glint in her eye behind big dark sunglasses. "I just can't seem to find it on the map."

I jerked a panicked glare to my right, catching Dominic Salvatore making his way toward the final resting place of his wife. Grief consumed him as he walked, barely aware of anyone else's presence, let alone mine.

Jager shot me a glare before following the others, leaving me standing at the bottom of the stony steps. I lunged, grabbing her arm. My fingers dug deep as rage found me. "What are you doing here?"

She didn't care if anyone was listening. Instead, she held my gaze, keeping her voice steady. "This is what happens when you stop answering my calls, Alexi. You think you can just walk away, is that it?"

The faint echo of a voice reached me. The call of the pastor as he started the sermon. A sermon I was missing. I glanced toward the crowd in the distance as panic fueled me. "You're a real fucking bitch, you know that?"

"One who's relentless, Alexi."

Rage ripped through me. I clenched my fist and pulled her close. The need to hurt her roared inside my head.

"Careful." She searched my gaze. "People are staring."

Hard breaths consumed me as I glanced toward the funeral service once more, catching the shit-eating grin of Lazarus Rossi as he watched me. A shiver tore along my spine. I forced my grip to ease and took a step away from her. "Get the hell away from me."

"The information, Alexi." She never moved, just pinned me to the spot. "Give us what we want."

I couldn't do it.

Couldn't hand over the file.

Couldn't even open the damn envelope with every one of the Commission's signatures on it. I couldn't do the one thing that'd save myself. Because if I did that, then there was no turning back.

"We'll leave you alone...you and your family."

I turned at the words and made for the service.

They were nothing more than lies anyway. Lies that'd get us killed. I lifted my hand and pointed. "The main building is that way."

Dominic Salvatore lifted his gaze to mine as I neared. Helene glanced my way, giving me a soft sad smile as I slipped in next to my brother, drawing a glare. "What were you doing?"

The hiss was quiet and seething. "She asked for directions, what the fuck did you want me to do?"

Heads turned toward me at the remark. I swallowed and forced myself to focus on the pastor and the gleaming casket in front of me. Dominic Salvatore was imposing at the front of the crowd. Black suit, gray shirt. You'd think a man who claimed to love a woman would at least shed a damn tear. But he didn't. He was stony-faced, his eyes fixed on that black gleaming casket as it sat above the hole.

I didn't want to think about what was inside.

What was left of her.

They said the assassin had been brutal...and Finley was the one who found her. I shifted my gaze to the kid. He was just a kid, they all were. Wannabe gangsters. They didn't understand what it took to live this life. Didn't understand the pressures of being the son of someone who sits on the Commission. Not really...but they would.

The envelope slipped inside my mind, moving in quietly as the pastor gave sermon after sermon and, in the end, waited as a woman sung some damn hymn and the casket was lowered into the ground. Dominic turned then and strode away, leaving his son and the rest of us behind as he made for the house on the edge of the grounds. Benjamin Rossi turned his head, watching Dominic stride away, then caught my stare as the hymn ended, leaving the whirr of the motor as the casket was slowly lowered to fill the void. We all stood there, shifting from one foot to the other while the bright red roses sitting on top of the casket slowly lowered, each one of us waiting for someone to make the first move.

In the end it was a goddamn Stidda asshole who broke ranks. Lazarus strode forward, casting the white rose he had in his hand into the void until it hit the wood with a soft *thud*. Others followed as Lazarus turned and strode away. Some of the Salvatore goons watched him with a look of savagery. The air was charged and violent. One spark and we'd all go up in flames. I waited for Jager to move, following as he cast his rose into Cian's grave and turned.

I lifted my gaze to the carpark as we headed for the wake. But there was no dark sedan waiting for me and no CIA agents waiting to pounce. A shiver tore through me as I walked beside Jager. But time was running out...and it was running out fast.

I stayed at the wake for longer than I wanted, finally slipping out when some commotion came at the back of the building. Fists were thrown. Some fight between the Salvatores and the Rossis had broken out. I headed out of the front door as shouts of rage and retribution filled the air.

Fuck them...

Fuck them all.

I climbed into my car and started the engine. But then I stopped. For the first time in my life I didn't know where to go. My gaze drifted along the immaculate ground of the cemetery, then slowly shifted to the men who worked around Cian

Salvatore's grave. One slowly rolled up the fake grass covering that had been over the six-foot hole in the ground. They didn't want them to see where she was going...didn't want to leave that as the last memory...I swallowed hard, knowing I was looking at my own fate.

I started the engine and backed out, making the long drive to the towering front gates of the compound. The moment I was through, two navy blue sedans closed in. Heat rushed into my cheeks as Hannah pulled up alongside me and motioned me to follow.

I had no choice...I couldn't outrun them and sure as hell couldn't ram them with my car. It'd draw attention. The wrong kind of attention. I ground my jaw and followed while the other Fed closed in behind.

We left the cemetery behind, driving back along the country road and headed back to the city once more. I scanned every car in my rear-view mirror, waiting for someone I knew to pull in alongside me. I pushed the Mercedes harder at the thought, tail-gaiting the bitch in a desperate attempt to get as far away from my father and the rest of the damn Commission as I could.

I knew what she wanted.

She wanted the file.

The one hidden in my apartment.

The car lunged, engine growling as the headlights of the sedan following flashed. I lifted my hand and flipped him the bird. We skirted the heart of the city, heading for the warehouse district in the east. Trucks flew past by one after another, driving blasts of wind against the car. I gripped the wheel as my rage grew colder. By the time we turned into a closed down refrigeration trucking company and drove through the open gates and pulled around the rear of the compound my pissed off anger turned into cold, hard rage.

"What the hell is this?"

A gunmetal gray Lexus sat outside a set of offices. Hannah pulled her car up alongside, parking before she climbed out. I braked, watching the asshole pull in hard behind me, boxing me in. I had no choice but to switch off the engine and climb out.

There was no way in hell I was letting them see me rattled.

I shoved the door closed and swiped my clammy palms against my thighs before lifting my gaze to the open door to the warehouse.

Hannah just waited, motioning me forward with the wave of her hand.

I wanted to take that hand and shove it far up her ass.

But I followed, glancing over my shoulder and not to the muscle who sat behind the wheel watching me either. I looked for a tail, anyone who could be watching for the Commission. Because that was one meeting I wouldn't be leaving...alive, that was.

Trucks turned into the street, leaving little room for a spy. So I turned my attention back to the forced goddamn meeting in front of me, scanning the interior of the Lexus as I strode past. Leather gleamed through the tinted windows. Whoever it was had money. I left the cars behind, following Hannah as she strode ahead.

Darkness swallowed me as I stepped through the open doors of the warehouse, catching sight of two men and a woman standing beside a stack of wooden pallets in the middle of the floor.

The woman and one of the men I didn't know. But the other... the other I did and I didn't like it.

I stopped midway, then turned. But Hannah had fallen behind me as though she knew this would happen. "Uh-uh." She shook her head, then motioned me forward.

I clenched my fists, my top lip curling as I turned back to the asshole who smirked watching me stride toward him. *Sonovabitch.*

"Mr. Kilpatrick," District Attorney Kendall McIntyre muttered as I strode closer.

"McIntyre."

"Ah, good." The smirk faltered. "You know who I am."

"I do."

I focused on the two others. The woman had my attention. Smart. Sexy in a straight-laced kind of way with a navy blue knee-length pencil skirt and a white high-collared blouse. She looked like a nun...but damn, a body like that. I bet I could—

"This is Natalie Goodchild. She'll be assisting me with my case." McIntyre broke my thought.

"Assisting you?" I strode toward the smug bastard, until the other male stepped forward.

"And this is Nick...my bodyguard," McIntyre added, holding my gaze. "In case things get out of hand."

A twitch came at the corner of my eye. I tore my gaze from the asshole. One scan of his jacket and I caught the bulge. He was obviously carrying. "Want to tell me what this is about?" I met the Assistant DA's stare.

"We've been waiting for you to provide us with the information we asked for, so we assumed you needed a little convincing."

McIntyre took a step closer, pulling a handkerchief from his pocket to wipe his hands. "So this is us being convincing." He gave a nod behind me.

I turned, catching Hannah with her damn phone pointed at us. *What the...*

"You're recording this?" I swung back to him.

"Like I said...convincing you to do the right thing," McIntyre added.

I glanced at the woman who shifted from one heel to the other, looking goddamn uncomfortable. "Blackmailing not sitting right with you, Ms. Goodchild?"

"Mrs.," she corrected. "And no, not particularly."

"But sometimes you need to get a little dirty, right McIntyre?" I jerked my gaze back to him, glancing at the handkerchief in his hand. "You prepared to get dirty, Mr. District Attorney?"

The asshole just grinned. "As dirty as I can get."

SEVEN

Alexi

2 *DAYS BEFORE THE ISLAND*

THE HEAVY BEAT of Ghostemane echoed through the nightclub. I sat at the table across from Creedence, Hartford and three new girls they decided to bring tonight. The private area was closed off from the rest of the club. Drinks flowed; our guests laughed. The short-haired blonde even winked at me and brushed her hand across my thigh. Her intentions obvious. But I just looked away, unable to think about anything other than the chaos on my head.

"You okay?" Creedence's brow rose as he pushed the bottle of Grey Goose my way. "You've been jumpy for a while now, brother. Want to tell me what's going on?"

I grabbed the bottle, poured myself another glass and shook my head. "It's nothing."

But it wasn't nothing. It was a whole lot more than nothing.

The music pushed in, thumping in the center of my chest, but tonight it didn't feel comforting. Tonight it felt like I shouldn't be here...not amongst my friends, not out in public. I grabbed my glass, downed the contents and started to rise. "I think I should—"

"Hey, what the hell?" The shout came from the bar, drawing my focus.

The crowd surged forward, pushed in from the front entrance of the club. I caught suits...and not designer. The glint of a badge caught my attention. *They were Feds.*

"Shut it down!" one of them roared, pushing aside a male to scan the rest of the dance floor. "Now!"

The music died halfway through Fed Up, and an uncomfortable silence settled.

They were looking for me.

I knew it without thinking. My stomach dropped. Heat rushed to my cheeks as a sickening feeling swept through me. Screams erupted from somewhere deep inside. The crowd rose up, surging forward like a tide. One that slammed into the wall of police and Feds.

"*Close it down,*" the Fed roared. "Everyone out!"

He scanned the crowd, searching the tables of the VIP until he stopped at me. My heart hammered, the booming sound a roar in my head. *No, no fucking way. This can't be happening.*

I took a step backwards. "What the hell is going on?" Creedence stared at the cops. "They can't just come in here...*can they?*" He looked my way and scowled. "Alexi, you okay?"

I pushed the short-haired blonde out from the edge of the table and stepped around her. "I'm good. Look. I gotta—"

"*Kilpatrick!*"

My name cracked out like a gunshot. I froze. Stared at the big bouncer in front of me as my mind raced. *Don't turn around... don't go back there.* Desperation stole ragged breaths. I swallowed hard and then moved, forcing myself forward as I side-stepped the bouncer and pushed into the crowd.

"Move!" I shoved through. *"Get out of the way."*

The harder the crowd pushed against me, the louder the Feds barked. Cops moved in from each side, their gaze fixed on me as they cut through the partygoers. I moved faster, side-stepping and elbowing my way toward the rear of the dance floor.

I had to get out of here. Had to get as far as I could. One panicked glance over my shoulder and I saw the asshole with a badge headed toward me. Movement at his side caught my eye... and there she was.

The bitch with a badge.

Hannah rushed forward, shoving men and women aside in a desperate need to get to me. *Get out...get out now!* I swung my gaze back to the wall of the club and battled the sea of idiots in front of me, reaching the rear wall of the club. A door waited in the corner of the dance floor, hidden by the heavy black drapes.

"Someone hit the lights!" Hannah screamed.

I knew her voice anywhere. Guttural cries of *Oh fuck, Alexi* resounded in my head. Memories of all the times I made the cunt scream my name. Now she screamed for a whole other reason. I shoved the curtain aside, searching for the damn door I'd used once and smacked my hand against the handle.

I bore down, pushing the door inwards, and stumbled into a darkened hallway. Faint floodlight illuminated the space. I blinked, and stumbled forward, leaving the door to close behind me with a *bang.* The muffled roar of the crowd sounded dull and far away inside my head.

Still I pushed on, steps thudded, growing faster as I hurried along the hall toward the door at the back. I yanked my phone free, swiping my thumb across the screen, and hit the light. The glare was instant, bouncing off the metal lock on the rear door.

The door opened behind me. *"Alexi!"* Hannah's voice resounded as I punched in my code.

Please work...please fucking w—

Click.

The locks disengaged.

I was through in an instant, yanking the handle as the sound of boots filled the hallway, and pulled the door closed.

Thud! The sound of fists came from the other side of the door. But I was outside...cold air wrapped around me tight. A pang ripped through my chest as calls came for the manager. I spun and lunged, driving my boots into the asphalt as I lunged for the alley that'd take me to the street.

Voices grew louder the closer I came. I risked a glance over my shoulder and surged forward. By the time I hit the corner my breaths were savage and had ignited a burn in my lungs. The crowd was already spilling out onto the sidewalk, pissed off from being thrown out. But amongst the raging sea was the slick weather jacket of the Feds.

I charged forward. There was no way I could go back for my car, so I leapt into the street and tore out from between two parked cars.

Horns blared; headlights blinded me. I scanned those oncoming, catching the yellow glare of a taxi, lifted my hand and stepped out.

Tires howled; the driver behind the wheel threw himself toward the window, jerking the wheel as he went. Air buffeted my face as the taxi skidded, narrowly missing me. Headlights from oncoming cars blinded me. Shouts pushed in around me, that dull echo in my head started to sharpen.

"*Kilpatrick!*" My name was screamed in the night.

I lunged forward, jerking open the rear door of the taxi, and barrelled in, slamming the door closed behind me. "*Drive!*"

"*Hey, get the hell out!*" an asshole in the rear seat snapped.

I glanced over my shoulder, finding the Feds rushing out onto the street behind me, and wrenched my gaze back to the driver. "Drive, now!"

His gaze was fixed on the rear-view mirror. I knew the moment he saw the cops. His eyes widened and his scowl deepened.

"Please..." I'd never begged in my damn life. But I was begging now.

"This is my cab, asshole!"

I jerked my gaze to the idiot next to me and, in an instant, the cab lurched forward making me throw my hand out to brace against the rear seat. The rear end of the taxi skidded before tires caught and we corrected. My heart was hammering, punching against the confines of my chest.

"I'll pay." The words were a rasp. I glanced at the idiot. "Okay? I'll pay for your damn ride."

There was a second where the curl in his lip trembled, then settled. "Fine. Share the damn ride."

"Now, was that so goddamn hard?" I fell back against the seat, trying like hell to catch my breath, and slowly lifted my gaze.

Knowing eyes reflected in the rear-view mirror. I just sat there for a second, thankful, stunned. My thoughts reduced to one single need...*to get as far away from the Feds as possible.*

"Where to?" the cabbie asked.

"Madison and Fifth."

He just gave a nod, not asking for anything. Hell, he wasn't even swearing when he hit the indicator and took the street that'd take us deeper into the city. He never said a word, just drove. I knew he saw them knew he saw the badges and the guns.

It hit me.

There was no getting out of this. My life as I knew it was over. If they could walk into a Salvatore-owned nightclub like that and shut it down in an instant, then they could come after me anywhere. Dread filled me, cold and hard. Welling in the center of my chest as the cab swerved, moving with the steady thrum of the traffic until the familiar sights of my apartment building rose up ahead.

The cab driver signaled and slipped from the thrum of the traffic, pulling up outside the building. I reached into my pocket, grabbed my wallet and pulled a hundred dollar note free. "This is for his ride." Then I pulled out four more. "This is for saving my ass."

His eyes widened at the bills, still he took it because everything in this city was currency. A favor for me earned you money. A threat earned you a fucking bullet. I yanked open the door and climbed out, slamming it closed behind me as I strode for the codepad beside the automatic doors.

A second later and I was sliding through. The tinted glass blocked out the sound of the traffic as I strode into navy blue hues. The carpet was soft under my boots, the air cleaner, leaving me to breathe deeply for the first time since escaping the club.

"Mr. Kilpatrick?" The guard rose from behind the counter. "Is everything okay?"

I never stopped to answer, just punched the button for the elevator and waited for the doors to open. By the time I reached my floor I was in full-blown panic mode. My hands were shaking, that ache in my chest cinched tight. I yanked the top buttons of my shirt as my phone rang and then reached down, drawing it from my pocket.

The caller ID was Hannah.

Hannah...

"*You bitch!*" I screamed.

The sound echoed along the hall. But I was beyond caring right now. Beyond these walls and this city. The desperate need to escape only grew more urgent as I swiped my card against the lock and punched in the code to my apartment.

City lights glinted through the floor-to-ceiling glass walls. The sprawling view reached out as far as I could see. Six months ago I would've enjoyed the view...with the woman who betrayed me. But not tonight. Tonight I paced the floor as the phone in my hand went silent.

What do I do?

What do I do?

I had to get out of here. I had to run...

I was inside in an instant, striding through my apartment in the dark, heading toward my bedroom. By morning, the nightclub raid would be all over the news. It was only a matter of time before my name was mentioned. My name connected to the Feds and questions would be asked. I dragged my suitcase from the walk-in closet, dumped it onto the bed, throwing in as much as I could.

I had no idea where I was going. It had to be somewhere they couldn't reach me. That was just it...*where they couldn't reach me.*

Until I stopped.

My breath caught. Panic gave way to a blinding moment of clarity.

I lifted my phone once more, opening up my messages, finding the one from Finley Salvatore.

Something's come up, heading to the island. We'll catch up when I get back.

The island, Cosa Nostra Institute.

One that was off the coast of Mauritius, guarded by not just the Commander but the wrath of the Commission as well. The Feds wouldn't dare come for me there...not unless they wanted a war.

The idea of the Institute grew claws inside my head.

I'd hated the idea of going there before. Hated to be surrounded by young assholes like Lazarus Rossi whose sole purpose was to piss everyone off. But the idea of the amount of armed guards and bodyguards patrolling the island? The District Attorney and his attack bitch, Hannah, wouldn't dare step one foot on there.

I glanced at the mess in my suitcase as I lifted my phone, scrolled through the contacts and made the call.

It was answered in an instant. "Alexi?"

"Matteo." I called the Commander. "Make one more room up for me, I'm coming to the Institute."

EIGHT

Alexi

A SCREAM RIPPED THROUGH THE NIGHT AIR. SHOUTS OF desperation followed, stopping me at the double doors of my building on the island. For a second, I thought some of the heirs had taken their party down to the water, until the shrieks turned into howls of retribution and rage.

"*Get the fuck off me!*" The scream came from the docking boat.

I stepped away from the entry gardens and slowly made my way across the grounds. The feds...*the fucking feds had followed me.* Panic ripped through me. My heart hammered as I moved across the open grounds between the buildings and headed for the dock. One of the island's guards tore past me in a full run, the thud of his boots mingling with the roar of my pulse.

"What the hell is going on?" I barked.

"*Someone's been shot,*" he cast over his shoulder.

"Are we under attack?"

But the guard didn't answer, just kept thundering down the rise of the island, and left me behind.

"*I don't need a fucking infirmary!*" The roar carried on the wind. "*Just find the bastard who shot me!*"

The large luxury cruiser was docked, the engine still running, as two men carried Marcus Baldeon toward the infirmary, the front of his white shirt neon red under the glaring portside lights.

"I'm going to fucking kill him," Baldeon moaned in agony as they carried him off the boat. "*Then I'm going to kill his entire fucking family!*"

The youngest Baldeon raged as he was half-dragged, half-walked to the only person who could help him, the island's in house doctor. Lucky he was used to bullet wounds.

Movement came from the darkness, drawing my gaze. Finley Salvatore strode down the grassy slope and headed toward the boat. His gaze was fixed on the passengers as they disembarked with hushed murmurs, their shell-shocked expressions centered on Baldeon as they rushed him away.

But Finley wasn't interested in the son of the Commission as they hurried Baldeon past him. No, his attention was fixed on someone else, a female who tripped as she walked along the dock, then fell flat on her face with a hard *thud*.

Laughter cracked out as Finley strode forward, his fists clenched at his sides, long, commanding strides rapidly closing the distance between him and her.

"You think that's funny?" Finley turned on the asshole who'd laughed, unleashing that turbulent, dangerous Salvatore rage. "What kind of piece of shit are you?"

Christ, all I could see was his father in that moment. Memories of Finley standing beside the cold bastard at his mother's grave came rushing back. The guy looked like he was about to crack.

"Finley...dude, I didn't know she was with you," the idiot muttered. *Just shut-up,* I growled inside my head. *Just shut the fuck up. You have no idea who you're dealing with.*

"Didn't know she was with me," Finley repeated slowly, and turned toward the guy.

"It's okay—" the little brunette started as she swiped her hands against her thighs.

But her quiet desperation only made things worse. Didn't she know that was who the Salvatores were? If she didn't...then she was about to find out.

"What's your fucking name?" Finley demanded.

The asshole's eyes widened, those who stood next to him took three steps away in any direction they could.

"Your fucking *name.*"

"D-Dominic..." the guy stuttered.

"Dominic *who?*"

"C-Cavalaro."

Idiot. I glared at Finley. He should be finding out who'd killed his goddamn mother, not trying to be the good guy. Murder... and betrayal. It was all I could see, all I could feel. Someone out there was coming after those who sat on the Commission, and deep down, I knew it had to do with the CIA coming after me.

There had to be a connection. One I had to figure out. But as I stood there watching Finley make a fucking fool of himself over some goddamn woman, I realized he just didn't seem to care the tide was turning.

The Commission weren't the predators anymore...*we were the fucking prey.*

I scanned the boat once more, making sure there were no last-minute unwelcome guests coming for me, then left them to their pathetic games. The ache in my chest lingered as I headed back to my building once more, swiped my card through the reader, and strode through the doors.

My thoughts were fixed on the pile of shit I'd left behind. Right now, Hannah and her District Attorney buddies would be fucking furious. But out here, in the middle of the goddamn ocean surrounded by the power of the Commission, there wasn't a damn thing they could do to get to me.

The file and the information they wanted to use was locked away. The images of my brother, the damn hitman, safe and secure. All I needed was time to make a plan. Time and money. I'd make them see using me to get to the Commission was a bad idea. *I had to. There was no other way out of this...none that didn't require a fucking body bag.*

My things were upstairs and unpacked. The apartment was stocked with food and alcohol, exactly the way I liked it. The class schedule was on an attachment on my phone sent from the Commander. Not that I'd be attending any of the classes. I wasn't here to play fucking nice. I was here to find a way out of this goddamn mess and crawl out from under the DA's focus anyway I could.

Beep.

My cell illuminated with a message.

Jager: Want to tell me what the hell is going on?

I swallowed hard, that ache in my chest now coming back with a damn vengeance. I hit the button, killing the screen, and shoved my phone back into my pocket. No. I didn't want to tell him a damn thing. Because to tell him what had happened...to reveal the truth, made us all vulnerable.

That thrum of desperation pounded at the base of my head. I reached up, massaging the knotted muscle. Because I wasn't the only one the Commission would come after...the idea weighed heavy as I made my way into the kitchen, grabbed a glass from the cupboard, and cracked open the bottle of Scotch. Liquid splashed the bottom of the glass, and my hand shook as I pressed the rim to my lips.

I wasn't the only one in the firing line. Unless...

Unless they made me the target.

Unless they forced my family to close ranks, leaving me out in the cold.

I winced at the thought. I knew better than most what happened to those who spoke about the Commission. Whispers of a senator rose in my mind. The Bernardis and the Valachis had both silenced men before, and they would again. Would they make Jager do it?

Those images I'd found in the file weren't far from my thoughts, my brother standing there in the dark, pressing a gun to a bound man's head. Would they make my own brother put a bullet in mine? I swallowed the burn of the Scotch and poured again. They'd give my family no choice.

My father wouldn't care.

I wasn't an heir.

No big loss, right?

By Jager...

Jager wouldn't do it. I knew that in my heart. He might not love me, he might even detest me sometimes. He might be the one pushed to breaking point. But there was no way he'd kill me. *No goddamn way...*

I drained my glass and poured once more, drinking until the tremble in my hand eased and my panicked thoughts settled. The musty scent hit me as I lifted my glass once more. I needed a shower and a decent night's sleep. Then I needed a plan, one that didn't involve anyone other than me knowing the bitch I'd been fucking for the last six months was an undercover operative.

I carried the glass into the bedroom and flicked on the light to the closet. This apartment was the same one I'd been in last time. I knew it as well as my own back home.

Beep.

"What now?" I yanked my phone free.

Jager: I know something is going on, Alexi. Either you talk to me, or I'll find out from someone else.

I swallowed hard as the pounding at the base of my skull grew teeth. I hit the button once more and cast my phone onto the bed. As it hit, the backlit screen flashed off something white on the bedside dresser.

Alexi Kilpatrick.

I froze, my pulse speeding, and slowly took a step forward, reached down, and picked it up. The scrawl was handwritten and neat. I opened it carefully, my eyes focusing on the words illuminated by the light from the closet.

There's nowhere you can hide. Nowhere we can't get to you.

We're watching...

Hannah.

There's no way you can hide, Alexi. Nowhere we can't get to you.

Agony stabbed deep through my skull as my phone went *beep* again.

I cried out, and tore my gaze over my shoulder, searching the empty apartment behind me, finding no one there, before I forced myself to move.

I strode toward the bed...catching the name before the screen of my cell went dark.

It was Vad...Vad Kardinov.

I snatched my phone from the bed and hit the button.

Vad: I know why you're here, Alexi. If you want my silence, then it'll cost you.

NINE

Leila

I scanned the boat, trying to catch snippets of conversation from the others, smiling when someone glanced my way. But I didn't know these people, and I couldn't understand them.

Their rushed, frantic words were hard to translate. I caught the word *Commission* and the names *Valachi* and *Salvatore* and the name *Alexi Kilpatrick*.

The last name met with the glint of excitement, and more than one woman bit her lower lip. They wanted to see him, desperate words of *they're saying he's dangerous*. Dangerous. I glanced away, pulling away from the conversation I wasn't included in. Other than the names I didn't recognize, I remained clueless. So I sat on the seat, tucked away in the corner of the luxury cruiser, a glass of untouched champagne in my hand, and watched as the glinting lights of an island grew closer.

Buildings seemed to rise out of nowhere. We'd left Mauritius far behind, heading into the darkness of the unknown, driving for what seemed like hours. My breath caught as we came closer.

But it wasn't an unknown anymore. We were here...*Cosa Nostra Institute.*

It'd taken a screaming match with my father to get here and more than one idle threat of returning back home. In the end, my father had barked *"FINE!"* And with some foul words muttered under his breath, he stormed off, leaving me alone.

Theon said nothing as he stood silently in the corner of the study. He knew better than to take sides. That only incensed my father and left me out in the cold. For the first time in my life, I'd said enough for the both of us, standing my ground and shocking my father. Now I was here, halfway across the world. I'd rather be home in Russia, but this was the next best thing...

An heir.

That's what Theon had called me. *The daughter of an Ivanov.*

I lifted my gaze as the ship's engine roared, sounding louder as we turned and headed for the bright lights of a dock. Green grass, towering glass buildings, and men waited for us to disembark.

"Get the fuck off me!"

I flinched at the scream, swallowed, and glanced at the bullet holes in the cabin directly in front of me. My pulse still tripped and raced, filling my head with the sound as the bleeding man was carried across the deck of the boat as we neared the dock.

Gunshots had cracked through the air when we were well beyond reach of the mainland. I ducked, pressing my spine against the cabin wall, as the first shot rang out. The boat was swarming with security in a second, and the night was filled with the sharp stench of gunpowder, but not before someone was shot.

Baldeon, they called him.

"*I don't need a fucking infirmary!*" he screamed as the boat slowed, hitting the dock sideways. "*Just find the bastard who shot me!*"

I glanced around the cabin at the shell-shocked faces and rose from my seat, brushed shards of glass from my slacks, and followed the others as they disembarked, stepping up the stairs of the luxury boat and across a small ramp.

"I'm going to fucking kill him," came the moan as they carried Baldeon toward the buildings on the rise. "*Then I'm going to kill his entire fucking family!*"

I swallowed and stepped closer to a group of women as they walked in front of me, driven by the desperate need to make friends. "There's blood...on your dress," I said quietly.

But she didn't hear me and my words were swallowed by a cry as one of them tripped, falling hard as she hit the dock with a thud.

"Shit, you okay?" I stepped backwards as a beautiful redhead rushed forward, grabbed her by the arm and helped her to stand.

The fallen woman gave a nod, brushing her knees as she shoved from the ground and froze. I followed her gaze to a man who strode toward us from high up on the hill. Buildings towered behind him, glinting with glass and steel.

"Finley?" the brunette murmured.

I left them, slipping behind the group of others as they waited for their bags to be carted from the boat, and glanced at my cell.

There were no messages from my father, not that I expected any. But I'd hoped...hoped for *please come home,* at least. But there was none. No doubt he'd even forgotten I was gone already. I thought about sending Viktoriya a text, letting her know I was here and safe, but then I tucked my phone away, waiting.

"*You think this is funny?*" the guy barked.

I took a step backwards, slipping behind the others.

Beep.

Excitement charged through me as I grabbed my cell, lifting it... only to find a message from the Institute advising my belongings had been taken from the boat and were currently being organized in my apartment.

I left them behind as the male turned on those who'd laughed at the woman who'd fallen. I heard her name, *Anna*, before glancing at the map on my cell, then movement from the corner of my eye caught my focus.

Two men strode across the Institute's grounds, dressed in suits, their gazes fixed on me. I froze and looked around for anyone else, but finding no one, I took a step backwards.

"Ms. Ivanov?" one of them murmured quietly, glancing at those behind me.

"Yes?"

"My name is Sebastian and this is Nathan. We've been assigned to protect you."

I scowled. "By my father?"

"Yes, ma'am," he answered, glancing to the others and motioned forward. "We've been waiting for you to arrive. We also have your key for your apartment."

He glanced at the others behind me and lifted his hand. "Ma'am, we should get you inside."

He was rushed, panicked almost, wanting to keep me away from the others. I read his expression. My father had sent them, but were they security, or just more prison guards?

He handed over a key card, and a card with their names and cell numbers written on the back. Deep down, I'd known Theon or my father wouldn't allow me to come here without protection.

I guess I should be grateful Theon hadn't demanded to protect me himself.

"Thank you," I murmured, following when they motioned.

"Either myself or one of my men will be stationed in the foyer day or night," Sebastian spoke. But it was always the same. "We're here for *you*, Ms. Ivanov. *Your* safety and well-being are our *only* concern."

I gave a nod and gripped my key card as we left the boat and the shouts of rage behind.

Then I glanced along the pathway to the buildings in the distance. I was here...in the middle of nowhere.

Make friends, Viktoriya had demanded. *Stop being so shy and be a damn Ivanov. Make them like you. Hell, make them love you.*

"Make them love me," I muttered under my breath, stepping up to the double doors of the apartment building, and pressing the card against the reader.

The light turned from red to green, and the doors opened. The heavy thud of footsteps came from behind me as I stepped into the glaring lights of the foyer and headed for the elevator.

Glass and steel, it filled my view as the doors closed, leaving me to travel with one of the bodyguards. I stepped out as the doors opened and made my way into the empty apartment. The midnight view was spectacular. Floor-to-ceiling windows drew me instantly. I was betting that when the sun rose, all I'd see was the ocean.

I pressed my palm against the glass.

What was I even doing here?

This was stupid. No, more than stupid. It was reckless and dangerous and *not me*.

Beep.

My cell vibrated in my hand, and I glanced down.

Viktoriya: Are you there yet?

I smiled and typed out a reply: *just arrived.*

I should've known she'd wait up. Should've known she'd be counting down the minutes until I messaged her to tell her I was safe.

V: How was it?

Lonely. I answered. *Missing you.*

V: It won't be, soon. Just make friends, okay?

I looked at the last message. Making friends wasn't my strong point. I only had one, and now I'd left her behind. My fingers shook as I typed up the message. *I want to come home, I miss you.*

It took a while for her to respond.

V: I miss you too. I can't really talk about it but something is going down here. Papa is acting weird, and I don't like it. I wish I was there with you. I wish I was on some beautiful island. I want you to try for me, L, okay? I want you to really try, make friends, do it for me. I love you, message me when you can.

I stared at the message, then turned to the dark and quiet apartment. "Try to make friends...so just how do I do that?"

MY ALARM WOKE me with a buzz. I rolled over and reached for my cell, peering at the time. It was still early, leaving me plenty of time to stress and fidget and try to talk myself out of being in this place.

I dropped my cell back against the nightstand, closed my eyes, and let out a moan. "You're such an idiot. Why didn't you stay at home, at least there, you didn't have to try."

A heavy sense of dread bloomed in the pit of my stomach. *What if they didn't like me? What if they laughed...*

But you're an Ivanov, aren't you?

I could almost hear Theon's growl. *Was I an Ivanov?* I wasn't like my father. I wasn't cold, cruel, or even dangerous, for that matter. I was just a bundle of nerves.

With a groan, I shoved the covers aside and made my way into the bathroom. The shower was hot and filled the room with steam as I stepped under the spray.

I took my time washing my hair and shaving my legs. I already knew exactly what I was going to wear for my first day in this Mafia boot camp, picking out my clothes carefully. I dried myself, then marched into the bedroom and pulled on white lace panties and a matching bra before walking back into the bathroom once more.

"Make friends." I met my gaze in the mirror and reached for my concealer.

That was easier said than done. But I'd come this far. I wasn't about to give up now.

I applied my makeup carefully, not too much, I didn't want to stand out, just enough to accentuate my cheekbones and blue eyes. I put on black slacks, a sapphire blue satin blouse, and black pumps. When I was dressed, I checked myself in the full-length mirror inside the closet. "Passable. Let's just hope you make a better impression than you did last night."

When the elevator doors opened at the foyer, my bodyguards were waiting for me.

"Ms. Ivanov," one greeted as he stepped closer me.

Panic filled me. I'd wanted this to be different somehow. I wanted to be...free, not the woman surrounded by men carrying guns. *How can you make friends when they can't even get past the bodyguards?* "Can I ask you to stay here?"

The guard just shook his head. "Sorry, Ms. Ivanov."

"Well, then, can you at least stop throwing my name around everywhere we go?"

He just scowled, confused.

I should've known better than to ask. I headed for the doors, trying my best to pretend men carrying guns didn't haunt my every step. The sun was new and fresh, rising over the water. Choppy waves glinted like diamonds against the caress of the sun. The sight of it stopped me as I stepped out of the building and headed for the path. I'd only seen the ocean three times before, but this was...breathtaking.

Just perfect. I moved closer, forgetting about the men behind me, and stepped off the concrete path to the small patch of grass that ended abruptly with sand.

"It's beautiful, isn't it?"

I flinched at the throaty, feminine purr and glanced over my shoulder. A woman stood behind me, her wide, dark eyes heavily lined with kohl and framed by wild, black hair. My pulse stuttered and panic moved through me in a heated rush. I hadn't even heard her approach. She cocked her head, staring at me intently. "I know you, you're Ivanov, aren't you?"

"You know me?"

She just dropped her head back and gave a chuckle. "I know all of you. In this place, that's all you need. I'm Xael. Nice to meet you, Ivanov," she said turning, only to throw over her shoulder. "Welcome to the Institute."

She was the first person who'd spoken to me. The first person who actually *saw me,* apart from the bodyguards.

I glanced toward them, waiting for me on the path to the other buildings. For some reason, hope filled me. Maybe this place was different...maybe I really would make alliances. Ones my father didn't tear me away from.

I watched Xael head toward the bank of buildings further along the path. One glance at the map on my phone told me that's where I was supposed to head. By the time I reached the buildings, I was out of breath. The roar of voices filled the space as I pushed through the double doors.

My security hung back as I entered, leaving me to head toward the crowd gathering outside the classroom. Xael caught my eye. She gave me a wink and a smirk before running her hand along some guy's muscled bicep as she turned away. "Salvatore," she called him.

He just scowled, his expression dark and brooding, and I remembered him from last night. He was the same guy who'd helped the woman who'd tripped and fallen. The same one who threatened violence against those who'd laughed at her. But he wasn't a player. He didn't smile at Xael, or give her any indication that he was interested in the latest. Instead, it was as though he was used to her flirtatious ways.

The doors opened and the instructor motioned us inside. I waited for the others, following and taking a seat toward the side of the classroom, waiting and watching and hoping someone would look my way.

TEN

Alexi

I BARELY SLEPT, JUST TOSSING AND TURNING, ONLY TO WAKE later than I'd wanted to. My thoughts were slow and lazy, sharpening as the memory of that note slipped in. I jerked open my eyes, finding it in front of me on the dresser.

There's nowhere you can hide. Nowhere we can't get to you.

We're watching...

My stomach clenched as a sickening wave of desperation swept through me. I shoved the tangled sheets aside and rose. Someone was here...on the island in the middle of nowhere guarded by the Commander and his men. I wasn't safe here...*I wasn't safe anywhere.*

I tore my gaze from the note and strode into the bathroom, yanking my shirt over my head. I had to find out who it was, who'd found their way into my room...and I had to silence them. *For good.*

I stepped under the spray and dropped my head back, letting the water run down my face. I needed a way to get out from under this, but evasion wasn't working. I grabbed the soap and washed. Threats and intimidation were all that was left...*unless I could throw someone else under the damn bus.*

Finley pushed into my mind. His little show last night had pissed me off. Cracking like that in front of everyone. I'd never seen him like that, never seen him so fucking violent. Then again, he had just buried his mother. I hit the faucets, ending the spray, and stepped out.

If Hannah and the DA wanted the Salvatores, then why the fuck were they using me to get to them? Why not go for Finley, make him turn on his old man...unless Finley was somehow involved? My mind raced, trying to piece it all together.

If not Finley...then who?

The fucking Rossis. I clenched my jaw and lifted my gaze to the mirror as I dragged the towel over my shoulders. Lazarus...that smug, cocky bastard. I didn't like him. No one did. If I could get dirt on him, I could make the feds see that he was the better option here.

Then they'd leave me out of it.

The more I thought about it, the more concrete the idea became. I dropped the towel and strode through the door, to find a woman standing in the middle of my bedroom.

Her eyes drifted over my body, then widened at my cock, and quickly looked away as her face flushed. "Mr. Kilpatrick."

I glanced at the clean, folded sheets in her hand and the bucket of cleaning supplies on the floor behind her. "I'll be out in a second."

She gave a nod and turned, scurrying from the room. Goddamn staff...they could fucking knock. I dressed quickly, yanking on my shirt and charcoal gray slacks before heading out, catching her quick glance my way, her focus straight at my cock, as I grabbed an apple, strode past her, and headed for the elevator.

Finley Salvatore...I needed to find him, to use him and the games they played on the island for my own advantage. If I made Lazarus Rossi vulnerable, then it'd be an easy deal. I'd hand him over to the feds, then Hannah and District Attorney Kendall McIntyre could go after them however they wanted, as long as they left me the hell alone.

I headed out of the building and checked my phone, found the classroom where Salvatore would be, and turned toward the building. Voices crowded in, but they hushed as soon as I neared. I didn't give a shit what they said, didn't even answer when someone called my name. I caught sight of Finley striding toward the open door of a lecture hall and followed him inside, taking a seat behind him. "Salvatore."

Finley cast a glare over his shoulder. "Kilpatrick."

"I have some information about a certain someone. You know, for the initiation."

"He's all yours," Finley answered, glancing at the brunette at the front. "I have a new target now."

I licked my lips as desperation lashed inside me. *Fuck.* What the hell was I going to do now? I glanced her way once more. She was no one...nothing. Just some nobody. "You want to share? You know the Commission thrives on getting dirt on the other families."

"No," Finley's tone was icy. "I don't want to share."

I sat back in the seat, my mind racing. "So, you really don't want in on Rossi?"

"Fuck off, Kilpatrick," Finley snapped.

Fuck off?

FUCK OFF?

I shoved upwards and strode out of the classroom, pushing some asshole aside as I headed back along the hall and outside. The note still lingered in my mind. I shifted my rage from Finley and directed it to the task at hand, pulled out my phone, and typed out a message...*I need access to the CCTV footage in my room,* before I hit send.

Mateo: Whatever you need, Alexi. You know where to go.

I headed for the main building, cutting across the Institute's grounds. Movement came from the corner of my eye. A gorgeous blonde in a dark blue blouse fidgeted, fixing her hair, looking nervous. I searched my memory, glancing over my shoulder as I left her behind. *Who the fuck was that?*

But then she was gone, slipping through the doors of the building I'd just left.

I stepped through the automatic doors, and strode along the hallway, past the conference rooms where Jager and I had sat next to our father when we'd attended some bullshit meeting about who controlled what in the city of New York.

The door to the secure area was up ahead. I grabbed my card, swept it across the lock, and shoved inwards. My footsteps were hushed against the soft carpet as I strode along the darkened hall and stepped into the command center of the island. One of the guards sat hunched in front of a bank of monitors, staring intently at a file on the screen in front of him.

He hadn't heard me, muttering under his breath until I cleared my throat. "I require information."

He flinched, jerked his gaze toward me, and minimized the file with a click. That alone drew my attention. I glanced at the monitor and the file.

"Yes, Mr. Kilpatrick," he responded carefully.

There was a flicker of annoyance, no...more than annoyance. He was pissed. His dark eyes grew darker, until he looked dangerous. Who the fuck was this guy? I searched for a name tag, but found none. "Haven't seen you before."

"I'm new, sir." The words were forced through clenched teeth.

"What's your name?"

His smile was instant, calculated, and careful. "Damien Blake, sir."

I pulled out the letter left beside my bed. "Someone left this for me in my room and I want to know who did it."

One nod and he turned to the monitors, pulled up the details of my building, and accessed the CCTV cameras. He worked quietly, watching me from the corner of his eye as I casually stepped around the desk and moved closer behind him.

The numbers on the screen raced as they scrolled backwards, I saw myself standing in the middle of my room, pacing the floor from earlier this morning, then in bed, tossing and turning in the dark. He sped up the footage to the time I entered my apartment for the first time, then scrolled the footage backwards.

"There," I growled, pointing to the monitor. "Slow that down."

He adjusted the rewind as a cleaner moved throughout my apartment, making my bed and folding down the sheets before she turned, stilled, then left.

"That's it." I gripped the back of his chair. "Play that again."

He did, rewinding her movements, before pressing play again.

The cleaner was young and pretty, one I hadn't seen before. The staff of the Institute were kept out of sight, and paid well to keep their mouths shut and their eyes down. But as I watched the cleaner, she straightened the pillow, then slipped the note discreetly onto the dresser. A cold shiver raced along my spine. "I want her name."

The guard glanced at the note in my hand. "I'll get that right away, Mr. Kilpatrick." The intrigue in his eyes grew. "If you'd like me to report this to the Commander, I can take that—"

"No," I answered.

He turned his attention back to the screen. But as he worked on another monitor, I grabbed the mouse he'd set aside and moved it across the screen, opening up the document he'd been studying as I walked in.

The names of the Commission were in front of me. Every son... and daughter. I caught my name, as well as Jager's and Helene's. "A little homework?" I glanced his way, catching that glint harden to a scrutinizing stare.

There was something about this guard I didn't like. Something that tugged at me. Maybe I was the one who was jumpy? Searching for betrayal in every action. It was just a list of names...

It could've easily been sent by the Commander.

"Your phone number, Mr. Kilpatrick?" he said cautiously.

"I assumed you had that, you seem to have everything else."

But he didn't answer, just held my stare until finally I gave in, rattling my cell number off. I made my way around the desk, heading for the hallway. Barely a second after I'd left the secure room, my cell beeped with a message.

It was the information I'd asked for. The name, phone number, and room number of the cleaner who'd left this note for me. I headed out of the building, determined to hunt her down, but first there was someone else I needed to talk to. Someone as dangerous as the feds who hunted me, and just as skilled a liar...

Vad Kardinov.

I left the main building behind and cut across the grounds, heading toward the more isolated part of the island. The building sat apart from the others in the distance. Next to it was a hangar the island used for transport. It seemed fitting that Vad Kardinov would be within escaping distance should all hell break loose.

My thoughts were occupied by the cleaner and the Commander. No doubt the guard had relayed the information to Mateo the moment I'd walked out. I only hoped he was a little too preoccupied with Baldeon and his screams of retribution to concern himself with a cryptic message one of his staff left for me.

The less he knew, the better.

I swept my card across the sensor and stepped through the doors when they opened. CCTV cameras tracked my movement as I approached the elevator, pressed the button, and stepped in.

Vad Kardinov wasn't like the others. His father didn't sit on the Commission, or cared to, for that matter. He didn't need to. Money was his power, and dangerous deals were struck with my father and others. Vad was no different, making himself valuable on the island as he smuggled drugs, women, and anything else you wanted from the mainland to the island.

I stepped out of the elevator and caught the heady scent of Cuban cigars. The smell this early in the morning made my stomach clench. But as I got closer, the faint scent of perfume cut through the pungent odor. The place reeked of sex. Faint white lines still clung to the glass counter in front of him, a remnant of whatever party he'd had last night.

I winced and clenched my jaw. The bastard hadn't changed.

"Kilpatrick." The sound of my name came from the sofa in the living room.

Kardinov still wore last night's clothes. His white shirt was open and wrinkled, and a midnight blue satin vest lay next to him. Even his belt was unbuckled. At least he'd had the decency to zip up his damn fly. "Kardinov." I glanced around the apartment, looking toward the bedroom.

"Don't worry, we're alone." He leaned forward, grabbed his glass from the table, and drained what was left of his drink. "So, here you are. Last I heard, you weren't playing these pathetic little games, Kilpatrick. What did you call them again? *Childish*, that's right." He rested his arms along the back of the sofa. "Please, let me in on your sudden change of heart. I'm dying to know."

"Fuck you, Kardinov."

The bastard had the gall to smirk. "A little bird told me one of the Salvatore clubs was shut down by the feds the other night."

My heart stuttered.

"Also mentioned you were there," he continued, holding my gaze. "Said you ran like the devil himself was chasing you. So, let me ask you again, Kilpatrick. What are you doing at the Institute?"

"That's none of your damn business," I snarled, clenching my fists.

"It is if you want my silence."

Fucking asshole.

"Stay the fuck out of this, Vad. I'm warning you." Sweat beaded along the nape of my neck.

His gaze was piercing. "You and I know that's never been one of my strong points."

"What's it going to take?" I forced the words through clenched teeth. "Money? *Is that it?*"

He just laughed, dropping his head back and unleashing a deep, abrasive chuckle. "You couldn't afford me."

I took a step forward, rounding the end of the sofa to stand over him. "Then *what...what the fuck do you want?*"

There was a sparkle in his eyes as the laughter died, not that it was really there to start with. I doubted a bastard like Kardinov knew what real laughter was. "Helene is looking lovely," he stated, his chest rising with a hard breath.

My stomach sank. No...no *fucking* way. "You're not having my goddamn sister, Kardinov."

"If you want my silence, I will."

I grabbed the bastard by his creased fucking shirt and hauled him up from the sofa. "*You stay the fuck away from her, you hear me?*"

He didn't flinch, didn't raise his fists. Just bored his gaze into my fucking soul. "I wanted her before, Alexi, and I want her even more now. Make it happen. Make it happen, or people are going to start to ask questions."

My sister and Kardinov had been a thing...*briefly*. But something had happened between the two of them. Something she refused to talk about. Something that still affected her now. Because every time his name was brought up in conversation, she shut down, like *all the way down*. Now, as I stared into his eyes, I saw that consuming fire.

"I want her, Kilpatrick. Make it happen, *or else.*"

Hate and desperation collided inside me. "I'm trying to do the right fucking thing here."

"So am I," he answered. "And your sister is the right thing for me."

ELEVEN

Leila

I sat in the classroom, listening to how to get out of every interrogation the FBI threw at you. But I wasn't really taking notes, not like some of the others. I wasn't interested in the classes anymore. *I was interested in the attendees.*

From the corner of my eye, I watched as some whispered and laughed. Others were studying each word the instructor spoke, more interested in psychological warfare than getting to know those they sat with. I glanced toward Finley Salvatore, but he didn't even notice me.

His gaze was fixed on Anna, the one who'd tripped coming off the boat last night. She seemed intent on avoiding his gaze.

People watching consumed me. I wanted to know who they were. I wanted to know if their lives sucked as much as mine, if their worlds were motivated by control. Because I couldn't be the only one, could I?

So I spent the next two hours sneaking glances around the room, hoping for somebody to notice me, until the instructor finally gave a nod and crossed his arms over his chest. "Well, I think I've bored you enough for today. We can pick up the rest tomorrow."

Then they moved, sliding out from the rows of seats, and stood. Others pushed away, jostling and laughing, oblivious to everybody else, including me. I waited, standing next to the door, waiting for a chance to leave.

"You don't automatically get respect here, Ivanov." Xael strode closer, stopping in front of me. "No one cares about our last names, even if it is yours. You gotta learn to take that respect for yourself, learn to make *them* wait for *you*. Stop waiting for others to be the white knight. Those rarely come along, and when they do...they usually break your fucking heart."

I swallowed, and forced myself to speak. "Is that what happened to you? Did a white knight break your heart?"

She gave the ghost of a smile, but it was a sad smile. "Shattered it, and ground it down to dust. That's why I'm the one who does the leaving now. No one's gonna break this heart again."

She pushed one of the guys aside and strode through the door.

I wanted to be like her, to make others stand aside for *me*. I surged forward, desperate to follow, until a growl came from behind me. "Move, *blondie*. Get out of the damn way."

I stepped aside, and the guy strode past, glaring at me as he left.

Great, so much for demanding respect.

I waited until they all left before slipping out of the classroom into the hall. Most had already gone, leaving me to find my own way back along the path toward my apartment building. My bodyguards hovered in the near distance.

It took all my strength to not kick off my heels and run, leaving them behind. I lifted my phone and checked the time as I pressed my key card against the sensor and strode inside. It'd be early in Russia, too early to wake her. Still, I was betting Viktoriya would be waiting for my message.

I stepped into the elevator as my fingers moved across the screen. *Today was hard, I miss you. But I think I made at least one friend, at least I think Xael is a friend.*

Then I pressed send, stepped out of the elevator as it opened, and kicked off my heels. I snatched them from the floor and made my way through the kitchen and into the bedroom. The bed was neatly made and fresh pink roses sat beside the bed with a note. I grabbed it, opened the envelope and read the message inside.

I'm proud of you, your father is proud of you, too.

Theon.

I gave a smile, but it didn't last as I turned my attention back to my phone. Usually, Viktoriya would've messaged me back by now, normally her cell was glued to her hand. Maybe she was still sleeping?

So, I waited. Making my way back into the kitchen, I opened the refrigerator and found fruit and cheese and a chilled bottle of champagne. I popped a grape into my mouth and opened the bottle with a *pop*. Bubbles rushed to the surface as I poured.

I walked through the living room, taking the glass with me, and opened the sliding door to the balcony that overlooked the ocean. I stepped out, breathing in the salty air, and lifted my gaze to the perfect blue sky.

But I couldn't enjoy the view, not when I kept glancing at my phone's screen. Worried, I sent another message. *Hey, you there?*

I pressed send and waited, draining my glass and pouring another. I waited as the sky darkened. I waited as the night drew close and music came from somewhere in the distance. I waited while the roar of voices and shrill sounds of laughter came from the others. Others who'd made allies and cemented friendships.

But my alliance was with another.

I drank my champagne, watching as the other people on the island headed toward the building that pulsed with music.

And as I waited for my best friend to reply, a seed of worry grew inside me.

This wasn't like her. I grabbed my phone and pressed the number, listening to it ringing halfway around the world. But there was no answer, and worry slowly turned into dread.

TWELVE

Alexi

HE WANTED MY SISTER...

And I wanted to kill him for it.

There was no way I was saying his name to her. Hell, Helene didn't even know I was here.

No one did.

I strode from Vad's apartment, my stomach clenched tight. I wanted to kill someone. But the person I really wanted to hurt, I couldn't. Hannah's face filled my head. She haunted me like the black dog in my nightmares. Fuck, the sex had been good, but the entire time she'd been riding me, she was milking me for every treacherous thing we'd ever done.

I was trying to do the right thing here. Trying to keep the file and my fucking name out of the DA's mouth. Couldn't anyone see that? Maybe they didn't care...

Maybe that was the Commission's way? Look out for fucking number one. I mean, the whole agreement between the five families was built on lies, wasn't it? Lies and blood...and the entire annihilation of a founding family.

I ground my teeth as the elevator came to a stop. Bodyguards stood at the far end of the foyer, watching me as I left the manipulative piece of shit behind. "My fucking sister?" I groaned under my breath.

I grabbed my cell, found the information about the cleaner, and cut across the grounds. Movement came from the corner of my eye as the guard from the command center headed toward the other buildings. A warning in my gut told me to follow. I didn't like the list he'd been reading, didn't like Jager's or Helene's names rattling around behind those calculating eyes. I glanced toward the staff building, then in the direction where he was heading.

But the moment I took a step, my phone vibrated. I winced and answered. "Yeah?"

"*You want to tell me what the hell is going on?*" Jager barked in my ear.

My pulse sped as I scanned for anyone within earshot. "I decided to come to the Institute, so what?"

"*So what?*" I could hear the anger in his voice. "You pack your bags in the middle of the night and fly halfway around the world without telling me? Dad treats me like a goddamn animal, and you pretend I don't exist. What are you doing there, Alexi? And don't fucking lie, 'cause I'll know it."

Don't say anything.

My mind raced, trying to come up with something to say. I couldn't tell him about the file. Couldn't tell him about the fucking District Attorney and the bitch who hunted me. I couldn't tell him about anything, because Jager wasn't just my brother, he was *an heir.*

An heir to the Kilpatrick legacy and to all the bad deeds done in our name. If I told him about file, if I told him the real reason I was here, he'd be forced to go to my father, and then to the Commission.

"That's just it, isn't it?" I let that panic turn stone cold, and used it like a weapon to punch my words home. "There's a place for you in this family. There's a role for you to play. But not me, I'm just the fuckup, aren't I? The useless idiot who always seems to be in the way. So, this is me *not* being in the fucking way, Jager. This is me trying to get out from under your shadow."

Silence echoed between us.

"So that's how you really feel? That you're a *problem to me?* Because if that's it, Alexi, then you don't know me at all."

I could hear the pain in his voice. But there wasn't a damn thing I could do about it. I had to hurt him. I had to hurt anyone I knew...God help me, I had to hurt my sister, as well. "Helene, is she okay?"

"Why?" he barked. "You going to tell her how you're such a failure, too?"

I closed my eyes as desperation ripped through me. *Your sister,* Vad's words resounded. *I want your damn sister...*

"No," pain tore through my chest. "Jager, I'm sorry."

"Save it, Alexi," his blunt words were etched with pain. "For someone who gives a shit."

The call went silent. I pulled my cell away, finding it disconnected, and tried to gather my thoughts. Desperation turned into the hard edge of anger. I lifted my gaze, focused on the building in the distance, and headed toward the staff quarters.

The sun had lost its bite as I crossed the grounds. Maybe it was just the icy rage inside me, one that kept the warmth away. I slapped my card against the reader, waited for the automatic doors to open, and headed for the elevator.

The cleaner's room was on the second floor, so I pressed the elevator button and waited. Doors opened, leaving me to step in. As the doors closed, my focus was fixed on finding the bitch who thought she could threaten me. But before the elevator could rise, a heavy *thud* came from the foyer. I ignored it, shifting my attention to the lights above the door as they blinked and the elevator rose.

I glanced along the hall when I stepped out, finding the door at the end open. A glance over my shoulder, and I stepped toward the cracked open door, knowing instinctively that was the room I was after.

The apartment was silent when I stepped in. I scanned the space, then headed for the bedroom. Two rooms were on the right-hand side of the hallway, with one further down on the left. Upturned glasses drained by the sink. The kitchen was cluttered, with boxes of cookies, jars of instant coffee, and stacks of ramen noodles reminding me of a dorm room back home. I made my way along the hallway, glancing into the messy bathroom littered with sodden towels and an overflowing basket of dirty laundry. But I wasn't here to critique their damn hygiene. I wanted to find the woman responsible for leaving that damn note in my apartment.

A woman who worked for the feds.

I strode past the two rooms, stepping inside each doorway to peer quickly inside. The beds were unmade, clothes strewn around the room, each of them almost identical. Except for the third room.

I stepped inside and found the room clean and empty. The sheets were in a tangled mess in the middle of the bed. The sight of that unnerved me. I went straight to the closet and flipped on the light, only to find it bare.

What the hell...

I swung my gaze back to the bed, seeing small specks of blood on the sheets. A hard tug on the corner and the end fell open, revealing more. It was fresh, too...bright, the mess still seeping into the fabric. But it could be anything. Certainly not enough to end someone's life. Still—I glanced around the room once more—she was gone. I went back to the other rooms and rifled through their things until I found the name. None were the one I wanted, which left the empty room. And the bleeding woman who'd fled.

But she couldn't have gone far, could she?

I dashed back out of the apartment, consumed by the panic growing inside me, and made my way out of her building and across the grounds, heading for the command center once more.

By the time I scanned my card across the reader and pushed open the door again, I was almost convinced something had happened to her. The bright flecks of blood told me everything I needed to know. She was gone...

I lifted my gaze as I strode up to the bank of monitors and rolling CCTV footage of the island. But the man who sat in front of the screens wasn't the same one as before. I glanced around the room before settling on the nerdy guy with glasses as he lifted his gaze to mine. "Damien?"

"Finished his shift, Mr. Kilpatrick," he answered, shifting nervously in his seat. "Is there anything I can help you with?"

My gut was screaming in warning, still I opened up the message, finding the cleaner's information. "I'm after a woman."

"A woman, sir?"

"*Yes, a woman,*" I snapped. Lies and manipulation. That's what it always came down to. That's what this *entire* island was built on. "This woman," I said as I strode closer, "is a cleaner, one who's now missing. I want her found, and don't bother checking her room, it's empty. Find her and text me the information. I want to know if she left the island, and when. Do I make myself clear?"

"Yes...Mr. Kilpatrick." He scowled and glanced at the details on my phone before punching them into the computer. "I'm on it."

"Good." I inhaled hard. "*Good...*"

I stepped away, feeling like a frantic idiot. But those blood splatters lingered in my mind even as I strode out of the command center and into the hall.

A male's voice came through the double doors up ahead. I lifted my gaze and saw the steel medical cart stocked with vials of drugs left out there.

"Just give me a second..." the doctor growled, his voice echoing along the hall.

But I couldn't stop myself, and drawn by that aching desperation inside me, I headed for the open cart, glancing at the drugs stacked on top of it. Some I knew from dating a doctor years before...*Sodium thiopental*. The words leaped out at me. Anesthesia drug, right? I licked my lips, remembering what she'd said.

Truth serum.

That's right. A dose of that and you spilled all your dark, foul secrets. I swallowed hard as Lazarus Rossi's smirk burned in my mind. I'd find out if he was behind the attack on Finley's mother, and with it, throw him under the damn bus. Without a second thought, I reached out and grabbed a bottle, stowing it in my pocket as I walked away, heading to the doors.

By the time I'd cut back across the grounds, the panic in my head was roaring. Gray clouds were gathering at the horizon, seeping into my world. I clenched my fist around the vial and headed to my building once more, but as I neared, I caught sight of Xael Davies slipping around the corner of her own building.

Davies?

Nothing she did surprised me. The woman had a reputation for busting balls and getting into trouble. But someone followed her around the corner of the building, to slip out of sight. The guard from the command center.

Now, that did surprise me. Drawn by that nagging warning in my gut, I followed, catching a low, guttural moan of feminine desire as I neared.

"Damien..." Xael moaned.

There was a moment when I wanted to turn around and leave, but the need to know more about that guy was stronger. The list of names filled my mind as I stepped around the corner, coming nearly face to face with both of them. Xael faced the wall, hands high, legs spread, his hand shoved down the front of her jeans, fingers deep in her pussy.

"Well, well, Davies," I muttered, watching as they both flinched and glared my way. "It seems no one is off limits to you, are they?"

THIRTEEN

Leila

Days passed and still there was no word from Viktoriya. I left message after panicked message, sitting in the classrooms staring blankly at the screen, unable to hear a word the instructors said.

But the nights were worse, lying there in my bed in turmoil, wondering why she was no longer answering my messages.

Was it something I'd said?

Had she felt betrayed and decided a clean break was better? Better for her...not me. I sighed, closed my eyes, and tried to sleep, then waking only to feel worse than I had before.

I left messages for Theon, but, like Viktoriya, there was no response, until I couldn't stand the isolation anymore. Even Xael's cheeky smile did nothing to ease the desperation inside me, so when I walked back into my empty apartment on the third day, I grabbed my cell phone and finally called.

"Mia?" Theon sounded dangerous.

My voice shook as I whispered. "I can't get hold of Viktoriya. I've been trying, but there's no answer."

"I'll look into it."

"Is everything okay, Theon? You haven't responded to any of my messages."

"Everything's fine. Don't worry, just enjoy yourself, okay?"

But his voice was hard and stony. Giving me nothing, but I knew better than to ask questions, because questions got me silence, even more than I had now. I stood in the middle of the living room and hung up. Music played from one of the other buildings. It seemed all they did here was drink and party.

The longer I listened, the harder the loneliness became. I closed the sliding doors, dulling the noise, and switched on the TV, turning it up to drown out their excitement. I kept myself busy, making a sandwich and a hot chocolate before I curled up on the sofa, tucking my feet underneath me, and watched some reality TV show I didn't really understand.

Until, with a filled belly, I found myself drifting off. I dragged the blanket over my body and fell asleep.

When I woke...*I woke to screams.* Thunder boomed through the apartment.

"*Ms. Ivanov!*" My name was a roar in the darkness. I jolted, shoving upwards. My mind froze for a moment, trying to remember where I was, as security rushed into the apartment. "I'm here! *What is it?*"

My security detail invaded, moving through the rooms and flicking on the lights.

"There's been an attack," one of them answered.

"What kind of attack?" My pulse hammered, the sound booming in my ears.

He searched my gaze. "Someone's been killed."

"Killed?" The word was a mere whisper. *"Here?"*

My phone vibrated on the coffee table, the *buzz...buzz...buzz* insistent. I stepped backwards, my thoughts sharpening as I grabbed my cell. But it wasn't Viktoriya who called me, it was Theon.

"Leila." Theon barked as I answered, sounding desperate and savage. "Thank God you're okay."

"What's going on?" He never called me by my real name.

"Nothing." His heavy breath was a rush in my ear. "Just stay with the security tonight, you understand me, Mia? *Do not go out.* Do not invite anyone over. The entire island is on lockdown."

Fear crept in, stinging as it came. I tried to swallow a shiver, my mind racing, and yet all I could think about was my best friend. "Have you heard from Viktoriya?"

"No," he answered carefully. "But I'm trying, okay? I'm trying."

I hung up the call, staring at the three men in front of me. Three strangers that I was supposed to just trust. Three strangers I didn't know...but Theon knew them. Theon trusted them. Once again, my life was at their mercy.

I stepped backwards, holding their gazes, until I turned and headed for the bedroom. Once inside, I closed the door, shutting them out. I shut everything out, the drone of the TV I'd left on and the icy whisper of fear. A whisper that told me the truth. This was how it was always going to be...me locked away like a prisoner.

I climbed into bed, pulling my knees up to my chest. But there would be no more sleep for me, not tonight. I grabbed my cell and punched out a message to the Commander...*who was killed?* Before I stopped. If someone really was dead, then he wouldn't want to hear from me.

So, I deleted the message and sat there in the dark.

In the morning when the sun rose, I pushed up, staring blankly as the gray skies grew even darker over the ocean, then called Theon again.

I swallowed hard. I wanted to pretend that everything was okay, that my life wasn't just a prison cell equipped with guards and rules and a damn warden.

"Mia, are you okay?" Theon's voice was deep and gravelly, like he'd spent all night screaming.

"What has he done, Theon?" The words slipped out.

I was beyond caring now. Beyond saving myself. Something was wrong with my best friend. There was no way she'd go days without talking to me. *No way* she'd blame me for leaving. No matter what I tried to tell myself. We'd left too fast, packed all our stuff to head to the US. That wasn't right...*none of this was right.*

"Mia," he spoke carefully. "You know you don't ask questions about your father's business."

I closed my eyes. All I could see was Viktoriya's tear-stained gaze, the last memory I had of her before we'd left. "If he's hurt her..." I whispered, and pushed up from the bed. "If he so much as touched a hair on her head, I'll kill him myself."

The snarl was instant and desperate. "And if he hears you talk like that again, he might just do it out of spite. You don't know your father, Mia. You don't know the things he's done. Stay on your pretty island, make your goddamn friends. Stay with your security. They'll keep you safe, I'll make sure of that. And when you come back, we won't speak of these things again, do you understand me?"

He waited for me to answer. Waited... And waited... And finally, I hung up.

My fingers shook as I hit the button. I understood now... understood all too well.

This had all been Theon's idea.

The pamphlet pressed into my hand the minute we'd stepped into our new home.

The island. The guards...

Me, far from my father's reach.

The only thing I didn't understand was...*why?*

FOURTEEN

Alexi

I stared down at the blood soaked concrete and tried to block out the image of Baldeon's wide, unblinking eyes in my head. "Have you found who did this?"

The Commander didn't answer.

"Do you know who they were?" I pressed, my mind racing. *Was this the feds?*

"Do you?" Those steely eyes met mine. "You seem to be spending a lot of time in the command center, Alexi. Want to tell me what the fuck is going on?"

I shook my head. "Noth—"

But the Commander took a step toward me, closing the distance in a heartbeat. "First you come here after telling me how much you dislike the place, then you harass my staff. Don't give me *nothing*, Alexi."

"Harass the staff?" I repeated. I hadn't even found the damn cleaner.

"The next time you wish to interrogate one of my command center operatives, you speak to me first, *got it?*" His dark, unflinching eyes bored into mine before he turned away, glaring down at the concrete. "Fuck, I don't need this shit. Marcus Baldeon was murdered here tonight, *do you* get *that?*"

"Yeah. I got it." I answered.

I got it only too well. The Commander's phone gave a *beep*. "Fuck. See yourself out, Alexi. Next time, come to me when you have a problem, don't attack my damn guards."

I winced at the words, watching him strode away toward the elevator. So, the fucking guard lied and told the Commander I'd harassed him. *Damien Blake.* The asshole's name burned in my mind. He hadn't liked the fact I'd seen him and Xael Davies together, no, he hadn't liked that at all. First came the lies, then the threats.

It seemed the threats just kept on coming.

He had no idea who the fuck he was messing with.

Davies had tried to make excuses, pushing the asshole away until he'd turned and stormed off.

"Don't tell anyone, Alexi," she pleaded. "It could mean his job."

"Then don't fuck the staff, Davies," I shot over my shoulder as I left. "Keep your goddamn pants closed."

But now the idiot had gone to the Commander spewing lies.

He should've kept his mouth shut.

My phone rang as I rode the elevator to the foyer and strode out. I glanced at the caller ID, finding the familiar number of my apartment building supervisor. I answered the call. "Liam?"

"Mr. Kilpatrick, *thank God I got you.*" He sounded breathless, *and terrified.*

"What is it?"

"There's a fire somewhere on your floor. The fire department are here, and they're about to gain entrance."

I stopped walking, standing still in the wash of the foyer lights. "Gain entrance...*gain entrance to what?*"

That sinking feeling swallowed me.

"To your apartment, Mr. Kilpatrick. That's why I called."

My voice was hollow and strange. "Have you seen this fire? With your own eyes, Liam?"

There was a second before he answered, and in that second, my world spun. "No, sir, I haven't."

"Then *do not,* under any circumstances, allow them to enter my apartment, do you understand?" I barked, clenching the phone.

"Yes, sir," he answered.

My mind was racing, filled with panic. I was halfway across the world. No way could I get back to New York in time to stop this from happening. There was only one person who could. Only one person they'd listen to. *My brother.*

I tried to swallow the pounding in the back of my throat, pressed Jager's number, and headed for my apartment, listening to it ring three times on the other end before it was answered by a blunt and caustic tone. "Just the person I was about to call."

Those words made my stomach clench. "I have a problem."

"Yeah...you do."

My pulse was racing, my collar was too tight. "Look, I know you're probably pissed at me. But I need your help. The fire department is about to enter my apartment, and I need them not to be allowed to do that. This is important, Jager."

"Alexi..."

"Jager, *I can't let them enter my home*, do you understand me? I can't let them get inside."

Hard breaths tore from my chest. Fuck, they felt like a damn heart attack. But there was just silence on the other end of the line. I pulled the phone away, expecting the call to have ended. But the second on the call count ticked by and finally I heard him speak.

"Why is the fire department trying to access your apartment, Alexi?"

"Because..." Agony tore across my chest. I had to tell him something, but the truth? The truth would destroy him. "Someone in my building is playing fucking games with me, calling the damn fire department, trying to damage my shit. Get to the building, Jager. Make sure they don't go inside...*please*."

The thud of a car door came through the phone. "I'm on my way...and Alexi, don't bother sleeping tonight. When I'm done here, you and I need to talk."

Relief swept through me. "Sure, whatever you need." I stepped through the doors of my foyer. "And Jager..."

"We're not there, Alexi," my brother warned. "Not by a long shot." Then he ended the call.

I closed my eyes as I stepped into the elevator and it rose. The quiet darkness of my apartment was a sweet relief.

Get there, Jager...

Just get there as fast as you can.

I called Liam, letting him know my brother was on his way. Giving him the instruction to stop the fire department from gaining access until my brother got there.

Jager wouldn't let them inside. He wouldn't let anyone get inside. One look into his eyes and everyone I knew backed down. Everyone but my father, that was. He didn't care that he stared into the eyes of the fucking reaper. Images from inside that file rose in my mind. Because that's exactly what my brother was.

I paced the floor, taking shot after shot of Scotch, and waited. Minutes became hours. Hours where I drank and stared at my cell phone, waiting for the call to tell me it was done...and the file was safe...*for now*.

The words boomed inside my head. How long was *'for now'*? A second. A minute. *A fucking day?*

Until *they* came again.

The elevator doors opened and my security stepped out. "Mr. Kilpatrick?"

"What is it?"

"The Commander is here, sir."

I swallowed hard, and rose from the sofa. I knew this day was coming. Knew it the moment that bitch betrayed me. I'd spoken out of turn, I'd revealed things about us I shouldn't have. I'd let her in, and this was the price I had to pay.

"Whatever you have to say, I can explain," I started.

Mateo just scowled. "You can explain, huh?" He turned his head and gave a nod to his security, who spread out, searching the apartment.

"*All clear,*" the guard barked.

Mateo never once shifted his gaze from mine. "You good, Alexi?"

My mouth was dry, my senses screaming, as the Commander's men left.

"Yeah," I answered, that ache in my chest driving deeper. "I'm good."

The heavy thud of their boots faded as they left. Two of them taking the stairs, leaving Mateo to take the elevator. *The stairs*...the stairwell door gave a *boom* as it closed, dredging up the memory of when I'd stepped into the staff's elevator as I tracked down the cleaner. That sound...

It was the same.

My cell rang, drawing my focus away. "Brother," I answered.

"It's done."

My cell gave a *beep* with a message. One from Jager. I scowled, opened up the attachment, and watched the video of me standing in the middle of my father's study, tucking the file under my shirt.

The file I'd stolen. The file the feds wanted.

"Want to try again, Alexi? Want to tell me how you needed to get out from my fucking shadow? That's just too damn cold even for you. Because what I'm seeing right now looks a lot more like a betrayal."

I couldn't speak, couldn't think. "Does he know?"

"Not yet," Jager answered, his tone filled with sadness. "Are you setting us up, Alexi? Is that why you've run?"

Rage swallowed me, searing the back of my throat. The words I never wanted to say spilled out. "I didn't know who she was, Jager. You gotta believe me. I *swear* to you, I had no idea the bitch was a fucking fed."

FIFTEEN

Leila

My jaw ached from clenching so hard. As much as I wanted to forget Theon's words, they still rang inside my head.

Stay on your pretty island, make your goddamn friends. Stay with your security. They'll keep you safe, I'll make sure of that. And when you come back, we won't speak of these things again, do you understand me?

Fire burned inside me. The kind of fire I'd never felt before, and underneath it...was pain. Theon had been my closest confidant, more like a father than even my own blood. He'd been the one to protect me, the one I trusted more than anyone else.

Now he treated me like my own blood.

"Out of sight and out of mind," I whispered, and lifted my gaze to the mirror. "Right, Theon?"

Right.

He expected me to do exactly that. In fact, I'd bet he was banking on it, stay quiet, say nothing against my father, and put up with anything he threw my way. But I was done with that, I was tired of saying nothing while my whole life was ripped apart.

I grabbed my phone and pressed Viktoriya's number, listening to it ring and ring and *ring*. Until I gave up. I turned away from the mirror. I looked like hell, anyway. I strode out of the bathroom, grabbed my bag, and made sure I had my cell phone before opening the bedroom door and stepping out.

"Ms. Ivanov."

I flinched at the murmur and jerked my head toward the sofa, to find the bodyguard from last night. He rose, straightening his jacket, but not before I caught sight of his gun. "Is there something you need?"

"Classes," I murmured, meeting his gaze.

"Cancelled, I'm afraid." He took a step closer, toward me.

I scowled, heat rushing to my cheeks.

"Until the island is secure, you'll need to stay indoors." *With me...*that's what he meant.

I swallowed hard as my pulse grew louder, booming in my ears, and took a step backwards. "Great," I answered, my cheeks burning.

I couldn't turn around fast enough, scurrying back to my room like a scalded cat, only to close the bedroom door behind me. *Leila Ivanov. Mysterious. Dangerous. Surrounded by security.* If only they knew the truth.

I didn't trust them...*any of them.*

I closed my eyes and leaned my head against the door, listening to the heavy thud of his footsteps coming closer.

"Leila," he murmured from the other side of the door, making me flinch. "I'll be right out here if you need me."

I won't...

Just go away.

Maybe this was Theon's plan, as well? I gripped my cell phone as that thought slammed into me. Send me to an island, then when all hell breaks loose, stop answering my calls. Oh, and hey, let's just throw a gorgeous bodyguard at her when she starts asking too many questions. That'll keep her busy.

Would he really do that? My face burned. I wasn't naive. I knew the things men did with women like me. They treated them like idiots, and plied them with booze and sex, hoping like hell they stopped making a fuss. Sounded exactly like me.

I turned, scowled at the door, and stepped backwards, dropping my purse onto the bed. I stepped out of my dark blue slacks and black top and exchanged them for something more casual. Blue jeans and a soft, long sleeve gray sweater, hurrying before my bedroom was invaded.

I should've stayed far away from this island...at least on the mainland, I could've hopped on a damn plane and flown back to Russia. But here...here I was a prisoner in my own room. *Go to the island,* Theon had said. *Learn how to defeat your enemies.*

My breath caught... Defeat my enemies.

That's really what I wanted. Information, and who knew that kind of stuff better than Xael Davies?

Excitement buzzed inside me. One even an apartment filled with bodyguards couldn't take away.

I stayed inside my bedroom for a while, then slipped out, only to find my apartment empty. Voices came from the hallway outside, near the elevator. Relieved, I made myself some food and coffee, only to take it back into the bedroom, along with my laptop. My father would disapprove of my eating in bed, but then again, he disapproved of nearly everything I did.

Meal times, like everything else in my home, were rigid, hostile affairs. But not here, I thought as I climbed back under the sheets, sipped my coffee, and opened up my laptop. If I couldn't watch them in the classroom, then I'd make sure I read through every delicious secret, no matter how scandalous or false it was.

I spent my day reading, gleaning every snippet of information from the Salvatores and the Davies, then I stopped, trying to remember the other names Xael had said. Only one name came back to me, slipping in with the memory of that boat trip to the island...the one with gunshots and blood.

Alexi Kilpatrick...I heard he's here.

God, I hope so. That man is goddamn fine...

"Fine, huh?" I whispered, taking a bite of my sandwich. "Let's see then."

I chewed and punched in his info. The first image was of a brooding male, dark hair, and the most piercing gaze I'd ever seen. One that looked right through you...*Jager Kilpatrick.* "Not Alexi." I kept scrolling... until I stopped.

Dirty blonde hair, and hazel eyes. That same dangerous gaze as the male before and the most perfect lips I'd ever seen. These weren't kissable lips. They were devouring.

My pulse gave a stutter before my world shut down. There was no flush of heat that raced to my cheeks this time, no scurrying away like I had done from the bodyguard before. No, there was only stunned existence. Alexi Kilpatrick wasn't just beautiful, he was drop-dead gorgeous. I pulled the laptop closer, reaching out to touch those lips. *He was here...on this island...with me.* "Where are you hiding?"

He was someone I wanted to know all about.

I spent the rest of my day combing the web for information about him, as well as sneaking out of my room to grab food and drink before coming back. When the careful knock came at my bedroom door, wrenching me out of my fantasy, I cried in alarm.

"It's just us, Ms. Ivanov," another guard spoke from the other side of the door. "The island has been checked, ma'am. We've been assured it's safe."

"Safe?" I repeated.

"Yes, ma'am."

I jerked my gaze to the door. "Does that mean classes are on tomorrow?"

"I believe so...but if you're worried—"

"No," I cut him off. "I want to go."

"Very well, ma'am. I'll let the security detail know to expect you."

I just turned away, fixing my attention back on those perfect hazel eyes of Alexi Kilpatrick once more.

I WAS SEARCHING for Xael the moment I neared the classroom the next day. Voices crowded in, hushed murmurs talking about what had happened. The moment I heard the name *Baldeon,* I knew who they were talking about.

My steps slowed, and I glanced toward them, catching snippets of conversation. *Beaten. Stabbed. Tortured...do you believe that, right under the Commander's nose?*

Xael was already seated toward the top row of seats. I made my way closer, sliding into the seat beside her.

"Ivanov, you finally showed," she murmured, but there was a sadness in her tone.

"Is it true what they're saying?"

She just gave a nod and swiped her thumb across her cheek. "It was a hit, and on Marcus, of all fucking people."

I swallowed hard as an ache ripped through my chest. She turned those red-rimmed eyes my way. "It could've been anyone."

"Do they know who did it?" I searched her gaze.

"No." She gave a hard bark of laughter. "Whoever it was would be long gone by now anyway."

"I'm sorry, Xael." I touched her hand, but she pulled away, giving a shrug of her shoulders. "It's fine, we're all targets, aren't we? Why should here be any different than it is out there?" She gave a sniff, and focused on me. "Anyway, you came in all excited. Tell me..."

"I need allies, "I whispered. "The more powerful, the better."

She just smiled. "Then I guess you're in the right place." She cast a glance around the room, stopping on Finley Salvatore. "Finley is someone you need to make friends with, and that one," she nodded toward the blonde-haired, blue-eyed male who'd followed Finley into the room. "That one's Lazarus Rossi, the Stidda Prince. If you want power, then those are the two you need to make friends with. Word of advice, though. They fucking hate each other's guts, so be careful, and don't let them walk all over you."

She told me more, pointing out others in the room, relaying bits of information about their families. Things that made even mine seem tame...

You don't know your father, Leila. You don't know the things he's done...

Or maybe it was because I was constantly clueless and kept in the dark.

The more she told me, the easier it became to breathe. I should be scared of these people, should be terrified of the things that I knew. But they were exactly like me, and the more I saw them, the clearer they became.

"Will you introduce me?" I asked her, watching Finley nervously.

Xael just gave a chuckle. "Sure, Ivanov. I'll introduce you."

I breathed a sigh of relief as the instructor started talking, but I barely paid attention. Finley glanced my way. Those dangerous eyes carved through me, until he looked away.

But it didn't matter. I saw them now.

Saw the Salvatrores and the Rossis.

I saw the Davieses and the other sons and daughters of the Commission.

I saw heirs...*just like me.*

By the time the lecture was over, I felt stronger than I had in forever.

I'm coming, Viktoriya. Hold on. I'm coming back home.

"Catcha later, Ivanov," Xael muttered, rising from her seat when the class was over.

I followed in a daze, making my way from the building, heading back to my apartment once more. My steps quickened along the path as I headed back, my security trailing along behind.

When I stepped out of the elevator, I headed straight for my bedroom and the laptop sitting on the neatly made bed. I'd always stayed away from the truth of who my father was. I didn't want to know. But as that storm grew bolder and braver inside me, I punched in my name *Ivanov*...

Nothing.

Not a single article.

Not even a photo of me or my father.

What?! I punched in Viktoriya's name and was rewarded with three small headlines of her father from a news article back home in Russia, but our name...there was nothing. No comment, not even a whisper.

Until a thought slipped into my mind. *Maybe they were too scared to speak of us. Maybe...there was no one left to tell the truth?*

Beep.

I glanced at my phone, finding an automated message. *Institute announcement: compulsory class. Building 1: Room 62.*

Compulsory class? I scowled at the message, then slid the computer from my lap and rose. Now, of all times? I swallowed a flare of annoyance and hurried to the bathroom, used the toilet before I flushed and washed my hands, then checked my makeup and hurried from the apartment.

Thunder rumbled overhead as I stepped out of the elevator.

"Ms. Ivanov?" One of my security staff stepped forward. "Everything okay?"

No...no, everything is NOT okay, I wanted to snap.

"I'm going to the beach, right there." I pointed through the large windows to the sandy inlet. *"Alone,"* I demanded, holding his stare. "Do I make myself clear?"

His eyes widened. It was the first time I'd ever made demands. The first time I'd ever allowed myself to feel anything but that emptiness inside me. I wanted more, wanted more freedom, more control. I just wanted to be...*normal.*

"Yes, Ms. Ivanov," he answered carefully. "Your father—"

I took a step closer. "Do you see my father standing in front of you?"

"No, ma'am."

"And do you know who takes control of our family's holdings when he's gone?"

He just scowled, those dark eyes growing even darker.

"I'm the heir to the Ivanov name and if I tell you to give me a little freedom to walk along the goddamn beach on my own, then I suggest you comply with my request."

"Yes, ma'am," he answered quietly.

My heart was thundering by the time I strode through the doors once more. I headed for the inlet, then glanced at the message on my phone again. I just wanted one hour where I wasn't constantly watched. One damn hour where my every move wasn't scrutinized. No doubt the guard was on the phone to Theon right this very second, relaying exactly what had just happened.

I didn't care. Instead, I lengthened my strides, heading along the walkway, and past the little cove where I'd pointed...then kept on going.

My steps were hurried by the time I glanced over my shoulder to the doors of my building opening in the distance, then I kicked off my heels, snatched them from the ground, and ran.

Hard breaths consumed me as I hurried toward Building One. I stole a glance behind me as I hit the edge of Building Two. The guard was striding after me, and his long, hurried strides made the bottom of his jacket flap in the wind. I jerked my gaze in front of me, catching Finley Salvatore heading into the doors of the building ahead of me.

This was my opportunity to speak to him. My chance to make friends. I sucked in a deep breath and charged along the path after him.

SIXTEEN

Alexi

F*IND A WAY OUT OF THIS, ALEXI...FIND A WAY OR WE'RE ALL fucking dead.*

Jager's last words filled me. That's what I had to do now. "You sure this will go off?"

"It'll fire," the guard behind me answered. "When it does, make sure you're masked."

I gave a nod and glanced his way. Leon stood there, muscles bulging as he crossed his arms over his chest. Former military and a weapons expert. He'd said nothing when I told him what I wanted, just gave a nod and went to work, creating the pressurized canisters that'd fill the air with the drug.

This drug.

I lowered my gaze to the vial in my hand...find a way. Any way I could. I lifted my hand and took a photo of the vial, sending the message to Finley. It was my sister's face that had sealed the deal. Helene lingered in my mind as I punched out the message. *You don't want to find out who killed your mother, then sit this one out like a fucking chump. But don't come begging when it's all done. You can run back to daddy instead...*

I lifted my gaze to the plastic covering the doors and windows. I couldn't inject it, not without knowing how much to give and risk screwing it up. But to inhale the shit...that'd work. I licked my lips and followed the guard's instructions, sending the message to Lazarus Rossi and Finley. *Institute announcement: compulsory class. Building 1: Room 62.*

My phone gave a *beep*.

Finley: What the fuck are you doing?

I winced and typed out a reply. *What you should be. Don't get in my way.*

Then I shoved my phone into my pocket, taped up the last of the covering across the door, and waited. I had a plan. It was a weak one, at best. But along with the truth about the hit on Cian Salvatore, I'd add in a few truths of my own.

Truths like the feds his father was working with.

Feds that were seen with him the night they shut down the Salvatore nightclub. I rubbed that aching pulse at the nape of my neck and waited.

I didn't have to wait long.

The door yanked open and in strode Finley. One glance around the room and the bastard paled, yanking at his collar.

"I knew you'd come," I murmured from the corner of the room.

"What the fuck have you done, Alexi?" he barked.

I moved closer. "If you're not interested in finding out if the Rossis ordered the hit, then I'll do it for you."

The asshole moved fast, lunging across the room to fist my shirt in his hands. "The *fuck* you say to me?"

Hard breaths consumed me. This was more about me getting out of this alive than it was about the truth. But I had to play their games. *I had no other fucking option here.*

I grappled with him, roaring as he clenched his fists, punching into my chest. "What are you waiting for?"

Hard breaths tore from him and as I stared into his eyes, I saw the truth. He wasn't sure...*he wasn't fucking sure.*

He wrenched his fist back again as heavy footsteps echoed along the hallway. *Rossi...now we'll know for sure.*

But it wasn't Rossi who entered. Some schmuck stepped in, glanced around the room, and stilled on us. "This the right place?"

Finley jerked his gaze to mine. "What the fuck is this?"

What the hell? "Leon was supposed to send the message to you and Lazarus."

"Well, guess what?" Finley growled, shoving me away. "Leon fucked up."

The plastic flapped as the thud of boots came once more. The door swung open and there he was...Lazarus Rossi. My way out of this entire mess.

"What bullshit class is this, Salvatore?" He glared at Finley, then the other idiot. My pulse raced as I glanced at the canisters.

"Don't ask me," Finley replied as he shot me a glare. "I got the same text as you."

"Fucking compulsory classes, as if I come here to learn this bullshit," Rossi barked.

I could almost hear the hiss...almost smell the rancid stench of the drug as a petite blonde woman stepped inside. The sight of her hit me. It was her...the one I'd seen the other day.

"Am I late?" she questioned, her Russian accent thick.

"Fuck, no, you're not late." Lazarus turned his head and glared at me. "What the hell is wrong with you, Kilpatrick? You look nervous..."

My pulse was booming in my ears. I glanced at the canisters once more. "No, I'm not nervous."

The door opened and closed and the brunette from the other night had stepped in.

*Shit...*I looked from her to the stunning blonde, who just stood there, staring at me. This wasn't supposed to happen...*they weren't supposed to be here.*

"Anna?" Fin took a step toward the brunette.

She glanced around the room. "What's going on?"

"That's what I was asking," Lazarus snapped.

Thud. The door closed and the click of the lock sounded. *No... WAIT!* I glanced at Anna and the blonde, then jerked my gaze to the door. Through the glass section, the stony-faced mercenary just dropped his gaze to the masks on the counter, and gave a nod.

*Hiss...*the venomous sound captured my focus as the canisters released into the air.

The sharp, bitter tang was instant. It was too late now to stop it...too late to undo what I'd done. My eyes burned and watered as I lunged for the counter, and grabbed the masks, and, as I yanked mine over my head, shoved the one in my hand at Finley. *"Put it on!"*

"*Anna.*" He stumbled toward her, holding out the mask like a damn idiot.

"Over your fucking face, Salvatore," I ordered, the sound muffled in my ears. I grabbed the damn thing from him, holding it over his mouth as the stupid fool wobbled. "*Breathe, Fin.*"

Low, brutal groans filled my ears. Lazarus stumbled forward and shoved out a hand. "*What the fuck are you doing?*" he roared, wrenching his gaze to me.

What was I doing? What I had to.

I straightened, leaving Fin to stumble toward Anna.

"*It's truth serum. I rigged it,*" I barked at Fin.

Thud. The little blonde crumpled hard to the floor. I swallowed a stab of agony at the sight. She shouldn't have been here...*she shouldn't have—*

"Anna, come on, honey." Finley pressed the mask to her face.

"It's too late," I muttered, turning my focus to Rossi. "The drug's already in her system."

It was in *all* our systems. Time to make it count. Time to get this over with.

Your father was seen with the DA.

The feds have a file on us with his name all over it.

You need to run, Rossi...and keep running.

Now, confess your father ordered the hit on Cian Salvatore and this can all be over with.

I ran through the words again and glanced over my shoulder. Fin was busy with the brunette. He'd never hear me...never know a thing. My pulse raced as I took a step.

"I'm going to fucking kill you." Lazarus gripped the counter and lifted his gaze to mine. I reached out, grabbed his shirt, and pulled him close. "Your father was seen with the DA."

The bastard scowled, then wrenched those blue eyes to mine. "What the fuck did you say?"

My heart beat louder. "The feds have a file with his name all over it. The DA, the feds, they all know. You need to run—"

"The fuck he does," Rossi slurred.

"Alexi," Fin called my name behind me. I was running out of time. "The DA…" my vision blurred. I blinked, desperate for it to sharpen. "Did the Rossis order the hit on the Salvatores?"

"Anna…come on, *breathe*," Fin roared. Heaving sounds came from her.

"Open that fucking door! NOW!" Fin roared.

But he wouldn't, no matter how many threats were made. Leon wouldn't do a damn thing…not until the job was done. "The truth, Rossi."

"Open that door!" Finley screamed.

I glanced behind me…to the woman in Fin's arms. She blurred in my gaze.

"Fuck!" Finley pressed the mask to his face, then against hers. "You're fucking killing them, you get that, right?"

I just shook my head as the room spun. "No. It'll be out of their systems in five hours."

The DA…the DA has a file…

Lazarus's knees buckled as he clung to the counter. Jager and Helene filled my head as I pushed forward, grabbing Rossi by the shirt again. "The DA has a file with your father's name on it and he ordered the hit...the hit on Cian Salvatore."

"You fucking lie..." he slurred. "There's no way."

But there was a way...there had to be.

"Get the fuck off me," Lazarus cried, lashing out. "No, we didn't order the goddamn hit. You think we'd do that?"

I reached into my pocket, this was the moment. This was what it all came down to. Exposing his father with the DA and ordering the hit on the Salvatores. It'd be enough to earn them a bullet... enough to take the heat off me. *Of all of us...*

I pressed the button on my phone and the timer rolled as it recorded. "Who ordered the hit then?"

"I don't fucking know." Lazarus punched me away, heaving. "You think we'd do something like that? We're not fucking animals."

"Can't trust..." Anna murmured behind me. "Can't trust the Salvatores. Will kill us."

I turned at the words.

"Launder their money and run," she slurred. "They'll kill us... that's what he said. Can't trust...can't trust any of them."

Finley flinched, the mask still in his hand.

"Going to war," she whispered. "They're going to start a war."

I was moving before I knew...lifting the phone to capture her words.

"He's going to find where dad is hiding. He's going to kill us all..."

"Anna." Finley gently laid her back on the floor.

"The Ghost" She whimpered. *"They'll all find out I'm the Ghost."*

What the fuck...

"No..." Finley cried. "Anna, *no.*"

"Jesus fucking Christ," I muttered as the pieces all slid into place.

The way he'd charged after her...the way he watched her, guarding her...I lifted my gaze as Finley turned and stepped toward me. "Alexi...*I told you not to do this.*"

He lunged, snatched the phone from my hand, and smashed it against the counter with a *crunch*. Glass shattered and fell to the floor.

No...no! My thoughts collided as everything unravelled in front of me. But all I could think of was her words...her words that were the goddamn truth. "*She's* the Ghost?"

"One fucking word, Alexi." Fin stabbed his finger into my chest. "One motherfucking word."

I lifted my hands.

Anna heaved and whimpered, pushing up from the floor onto all fours. Finley stumbled toward the door. "Open that door, or I swear to God I'll shove your head through it."

"Leon," I called, lifting my gaze to the ruthless bastard, and gave a nod. *It was over. I'd failed...again.*

Finley ripped the mask off his face as he stumbled past the blonde. "Take care of her. It's the least you can fucking do."

"Salvatore," I called his name as he knelt and lifted Anna in his arms.

"Can't trust," Anna mumbled. "Can't trust a Salvatore."

"Yeah," he snarled. "I heard you the first fucking time."

The bastard was savage as he stumbled through the door with her in his arms, stopping in the doorway long enough to meet Leon's gaze. "If I were you, I wouldn't sleep...not for a very long fucking time. Because when Lazarus rises, you can bet your ass, I'm sending him your way."

Footsteps thundered down the hallway as Mateo charged in. "What the fuck, Alexi!" He glanced around the room, then stopped on the blonde at my feet. "Jesus...*no.*"

His men barely stepped inside before something barreled into the room, all blind fury and rage. I was grabbed, my shirt balled into Lazarus' hitman's fists as he screamed. *"I'm going to fucking kill you!"*

"Logan," Lazarus croaked and tried to push upright.

I glanced at Lazarus, then pulled my mask free. The gas was gone, the job done, even if I'd failed.

"The Code," Mateo declared, glaring from Logan to me, "forbids violence."

But Lazarus' man didn't back down. The end glinted in his eyes...*my end.* Well, he could get in fucking line. With a curl of his lip, he shoved me away, turning instead to Lazarus.

"Easy, buddy." He lunged as Lazarus buckled. The bodyguard caught him, lifted him, and wrapped one of Lazarus' arms around his shoulders as he walked him out of the room. But not before stabbing me with a glare. The bodyguard wasn't done with me...*not by a damn mile.*

"Alexi," Leon muttered carefully as they left.

But I wasn't listening. My thoughts were a roar inside my head as I knelt at her side and brushed my fingers through her long blonde hair. It fanned around her face, like she was some damn angel. But I didn't care about her...*I couldn't*. There was no room inside me to care about anyone else.

"I thought..." I started, but the words were gone.

Mateo lunged, shoving me aside. *"Get the fuck out of the way!"* He pressed his fingers against her neck as the room was filled with security. "Check him!" Mateo jerked his gaze to the other idiot lying in a heap on the floor.

A moan came from the blonde.

"Jesus...thank fucking Christ she's alive." The Commander opened her eyelids, then glanced at the mask in my hand, his words fierce and forceful. "You have no idea the fucking hell you've just unleashed, Alexi." He lifted his gaze to me. "You better pray she comes through this with nothing more than a fucking headache. Otherwise, the blood that'll be spilled will be yours."

"You know who the fuck I am?" I barked, throwing the mask on the floor.

The Commander rose, those dangerous eyes devoid of emotion as he answered. "The question is, Alexi...do *you* know who the fuck *she* is?"

SEVENTEEN

Alexi

D*o you know who she is?*

I lowered my gaze to the woman on the floor in front of me. Pale skin, full plum-colored lips. Her ash blonde hair fanned out against the filthy floor. For some reason I didn't like that. A grunt came from one of the Commander's men as he lifted the other guy from the floor and heaved him over his shoulder.

"The infirmary," the Commander snapped as he stalked out the door.

But his words lingered...*do you know who she is?*

No. I searched her face, trying to find something familiar. I didn't know, and I didn't have the strength to care.

I turned away from her and headed for the door before something inside stopped me. *Don't...don't do that.* I jerked my gaze back to her, then, with a snarl, I strode back, bent, and slid one arm under her knees and the other around her back before I lifted.

My steps were shaky, at best. Still, I followed the guards as they carried the asshole out the door, down the hall, and out of the building. Drops of blood glistened on the pavement in front of me. The guy who was in the wrong place at the wrong time dripped blood from a gash on his head, the shit splattering against the pavement like breadcrumbs.

But I didn't let myself linger. Instead, I fixed my focus on the building in the distance and tried to block out the feel of her in my arms. I didn't want to look at her, didn't want to see how pale she was in the sunlight or feel the brush of her hair along my arm. The strands felt like silk. I swallowed hard and forced my focus on those glinting fucking doors, hating how good the warmth of her body felt pressed against mine...*and then looked down.*

Her brow was smooth, lips parted with a look of serenity. My heart thudded louder in my chest before I jerked my gaze away. Low, guttural moans came from the guy in front as the guard carried him through the double doors and along the hallway, heading for the infirmary.

I did this... I glanced down at the woman in my arms. *I did this to her.* I shoved the thought aside. I couldn't worry about that now, couldn't think about anything other than the fact I'd failed.

Lazarus Rossi was in his room right now. How much he remembered, I didn't know. *I wouldn't know.* Not until I pressed him for the truth. His goddamn bodyguard rose in my mind, all savage and pissed off. Getting to Lazarus was going to be a problem now.

"What the hell..." The doctor stepped out of a room, carrying a file, and glanced toward the damn wrong-place guy dripping blood along his hallway. His eyes widened before he glanced at the woman in my arms, then he motioned to the guard carrying the guy. "Get him on the bed. I'll get my damn suture kit."

The doc left, strode toward a door, and disappeared inside.

The second they moved him toward the door, the idiot opened his eyes. Confusion flared, turning to panic as he thrashed over the guard's shoulder and fell toward the floor. Boots hit the floor as he stumbled backwards, his eyes widening.

"Get off me. Get the hell off me!" he yelled, and swung at the guard.

"Easy," the guard lifted his hands. "Just trying to help you."

"You..." The idiot licked his lips and fixed a shell-shocked gaze on me. "*You* did this."

My heart thundered as an icy trail slipped along my spine.

"You're bleeding." The doc neared, carrying a kit in his hand. "I need to check the wound."

But the asshole just stared at me, then lowered his gaze to the woman in my arms.

"It's okay," the doc reassured as he stepped closer. "I'm going to take good care of you."

"No, you're not," the Commander countered as he came toward us with long, purposeful strides. "Her first."

The doctor scowled, then stepped closer to touch the side of her neck, before he opened her eyes. "She's still out cold. I can have him patched up in the meantime."

"*No,*" the Commander's voice was unflinching as he held the doc's gaze. "She...*is seen first*. I need to know what the hell I'm dealing with."

The doctor's lips pressed tight until they paled as he glared at Mateo Ristani, then he finally gave in. "Fine, get her on the bed."

I carried her into the room and laid her on top of the sheets before stepping away as the Commander followed me in.

"*What the fuck?*" The rich schmuck stumbled in after us, pressing his hand to his head, then looked at the blood on his fingers. "*I'm the one who's bleeding here!*"

But Mateo didn't even flinch as he fixed his gaze on the woman in the bed. "Out, Alexi," he demanded without looking away. "I think you've done enough."

Dismissed...just like that.

Like I was a goddamn kid.

Anger ripped through me as the doc stepped closer, flicked on a penlight, and flashed it into her eyes. "Did she hit her head?" He pressed his fingers to her skull and felt around. Silence filled the room before the doctor glanced my way, scowling. "*Did she hit her head?*"

"I...I don't know. I guess so." I glanced toward the Commander as heat burned inside me.

The bastard just stared at me with those dead eyes that gave nothing away. *Do you know who she is?* The words resounded. *Do you know...*

I didn't...but Mateo sure did, and he didn't like it one bit.

He should have been used to the danger. Maybe he was...but he wasn't used to *her*. He wrenched his gaze toward me. "Get out, Kilpatrick."

"*Someone going to fix this?*" the asshole behind me roared.

I ground my teeth. That's exactly what I was trying to do...*fix this*. I turned and took a step toward the door.

"I want to be assured she is perfectly fine, Grey," Mateo demanded. "She's not to have anything more than a goddamn headache."

"Name," the doctor ordered.

"Leila Ivanov."

Ivanov? I flinched and my steps stuttered, stopping me in the doorway. I glanced back, meeting Mateo's gaze as he muttered, "Her father's going to fucking kill you."

That icy touch spread out inside me...*Ivanov...she's an Ivanov?*

A faint, feminine moan carried as the bleeding asshole muttered. "She's Russian, right?"

But Mateo didn't answer, just spoke carefully. "You and I know the kind of shitstorm her family will unleash over this."

"You're fucked now, aren't you?" the asshole chuckled. "Those bastards don't mess around."

"*Shut the fuck up,*" I snapped, jerking my gaze to his. "Or I'll do more than give you a fucking head wound."

Ivanov...

The name slammed into me like a fist. I thought they were in Russia...

No wonder Mateo was freaking out. The corridor blurred as I stepped outside and headed along the hallway. Gray clouds had moved in as I strode through the double doors and a faint growl of thunder cracked overhead. My thoughts were frantic, clawing this new information closer, trying to figure out a way out of this mess.

I was a dead man now, either way this played out. If the fucking feds didn't get to me...*then her family would.* Scattered memories moved closer. That second where she'd stepped into the damn classroom and lifted her gaze to mine...

My pulse skipped...then raced to catch up.

Something dangerous moved through my mind. Darker clouds gathered on the horizon. A storm was coming. One that'd unleash on the island. But as the wind picked up, howling through the palms as I crossed the grounds and headed for my building, a thought slipped into my mind.

I could use her...

Use her family, use their wrath.

That thunder in my chest boomed louder, driving the panic deeper until it felt almost like lust. The memory of her gaze lingered. The way she'd looked at me...she was attracted.

If I could make her fall for me, then I might be able to survive this.

I might be able to find a way out of this for good.

You and I know the kind of shitstorm her family will unleash over this.

I needed information. Information about her and her damn family. But there was no way I was calling Jager, not with this. I needed someone who knew more than I did. Someone who knew a great deal about those who were here on the island.

One face came to me, and with it, the list of names of all those who sat on the Commission. The lying piece I needed to speak to, the guard from the command center...the one cock deep in Xael Davies.

EIGHTEEN

Alexi

I HEADED FOR THE BUILDING WHERE THE GUARDS LIVED. My guys had spent enough time bunking with the Commander's men for me to know exactly where to go. When I was halfway to the building, my phone rang. I glanced at the caller ID and winced, pressed the button, and sent it straight to voicemail.

But a second later, it rang again. This time, I answered. "What do you want, Vad?"

"You really know how to dig your own grave, don't you, Alexi?"

"You calling to give me a high-five, then save it." I lifted my gaze to the guards' building and for a second, I thought about asking Vad for the information I needed. But I was already in too deep with him and being in bed with a damn shark like Vad was never a good thing.

I want your sister, Alexi...

"Say what you want to say, Vad, and piss off."

"Our deal."

"*We* never made a goddamn deal!"

His voice was low and threatening. "You want me to tell *everyone* what I know, Alexi?"

"And what is that?" I fixed my gaze on the glinting glass windows, now pinning my damn hope on a woman to save me... not just any woman, Leila Ivanov. "What exactly do you know, Vad? As far as I know, just rumors and goddamn lies. So stop wasting my time, and stop pissing me off. Or the only time you'll ever see my sister is when I'm standing next to you with a gun to your head."

He was silent, his breaths loud in my ear. "Whatever it is you're hiding, Alexi, I'll find out, and when I do, you will be the one feeling the cold end of a muzzle."

I yanked my phone down, pressed the button, and ended the call. I couldn't let him rock me, not now. I pressed my card against the reader and headed through the doors, stopping at the elevator. I didn't know which floor the bastard was on, but I was betting I'd find out soon enough.

Desperation burned inside as I stepped into the elevator and rode it all the way to the top floor. Music spilled out from behind one of the apartment doors as I stepped out. I followed the sound, glancing along the hallway before I gave a knock.

The door was yanked open and a guy in a sleeveless black tee and sweats glared at me. "Yeah?" But it took a second for him to realize who I was, then his pissed-off expression turned to surprise. "Kilpatrick?"

"I'm after Damien Blake," I said, glancing behind him.

"He's not here, sir." He gave a shake of his head. "You might want to try four doors down."

I glanced along the hallway to where he motioned. "Thanks."

There was silence behind the door. I didn't even know if he was here at all. The guy behind me didn't disappear right away, just watched as I knocked on the door and waited. The heavy thud of steps came from inside before the door was opened carefully. Damien just peered at me, but there was no look of surprise, just a careful, guarded glance, before he opened the door and stepped back. I stole a glance at the other guard watching before I stepped inside. No doubt word would get back to Mateo soon enough.

"Kilpatrick," Damien muttered, watching me as I crossed the living room. "Want to tell me why you're here?"

I didn't look at him, just glanced outside the windows to the view of the ocean in the distance. "You went to the Commander and lied about me, I want to know why."

He just gave a low chuckle, and movement came from the corner of my eye as he shifted his stance and crossed his arms over his chest. "So, you're pissed about me telling on you, is that it?"

I turned toward him, meeting the sonofabitch's gaze. "It's more than that, and you know it." I didn't like him, didn't like anything about him. There was something dangerous about him, dangerous in a backstabbing, lethal kind of way. It was more than the sneaking around with Davies, too. It was the lying and the manipulation...and the goddamn list. "You have a list on us, then you tried to deny it, I'm not interested in your lies." I took a step closer to him, holding onto his gaze. "What I am interested in, is Leila Ivanov. I want to know everything you know about her, including what was not on your damn list."

His gaze sharpened, glittering and sparkling...like shards of glass. "Why her?"

"That's none of your business, is it?" I took another step closer. "Now, you going to tell me what I want to know, or do I have to go over your head?"

He thought about that, picking the threat apart, unraveling my determination. I knew the moment he gave in, the moment he resigned himself to his own fate. Because I wasn't leaving, not without getting what I wanted. And what I wanted was a way out of this mess.

"You really want to know who she is?" He bit his lip. "Then all we have to do is take a look at Russia."

"What the fuck is happening in Russia?"

He shrugged. "Let's just call it a change of command."

A change of command? "Is that why they're no longer there?"

He didn't answer, just held my gaze. I looked at the counter next to him. That said all I needed to know. There were things going down halfway across the world I didn't know about, and I doubted many people knew about, including her. "She married?"

"No."

"Her family?" I lifted my gaze to his.

"Her father is a ruthless bastard and is responsible for more deaths than the Salvatores, the Rossis... and the Kilpatricks all put together."

"Jesus."

He unfolded his arms, and stepped toward me. We were not friends, we were not even allies. I didn't like the slimy piece of shit, but in that moment, I held onto whatever information he told me, searching for the truth in those unflinching eyes. "They are not the kind of family you want to piss off, Alexi. They're the kind of family you don't walk away from, and you do not, under any circumstances, doublecross."

Then that made them the perfect ally, didn't it?

"You seem to know a hell of a lot about us."

"I make it my job to know who I'm guarding, *sir*."

The way he said sir was condescending, wearing on my nerves. Through clenched teeth, I snarled, "Stay the fuck away from Davies."

"Or what? You being territorial here, Alexi?"

And if I was, what then? I didn't want Davies like that. I wasn't interested in being another notch on her belt, or her on mine. "Yeah, again, say that I am. Stay the hell away from her, and anyone else I know."

I turned to the door, leaving him behind.

"Well... Well... Well... Alexi Kilpatrick, trying to be the good guy. Don't bother, it doesn't suit you. You're not the good guy, Alexi, no matter what you think."

What I thought? I grabbed the handle and yanked open the door. It wasn't about what I thought. It was about what I could control. And seeing Xael used and ridiculed for sleeping with the fucking staff, was something I couldn't live with. I strode out of the building and made my way to the elevator. The moment I stepped out into the foyer, I was grabbed and wrenched to the side.

The fist came out of nowhere, hitting me right on the cheekbone. My head snapped to the side, and stars blinded me. I was hit again, only this time even harder, on the side of my mouth, until my breath caught as I stumbled to the side. "What the fuck!"

"I warned you, asshole." Lazarus' bodyguard came for me again like some vengeful angel.

But this time, I wasn't taking a hit without fighting back. I stepped backwards, caught my stance, and raised my fists. "Want to try that again?"

"I know the kind of man you are, Kilpatrick," Logan sneered. "Heir or not, you touch Lazarus again, and you won't need to worry about whose seat you're taking at the table. There won't be one with your family's name on it at all… You feel me?"

The tang of blood bloomed in my mouth. I licked my lip, finding the sting. "Fuck you, Logan. You're going to stand there and threaten me?"

"Threat?" He glared at me and shook his head "That's no threat, Kilpatrick. That's a goddamn promise. I don't give a fuck who your brother is. The Rossis are off-limits to you and your entire fucking family. You come for them again…and you'll leave in a damn body bag."

The bastard just stood there, his fist smeared with blood…*my blood*.

The elevator opened and the asshole whose door I'd knocked on stepped out. He glanced at Logan, who gave a slow nod.

So it wasn't the Commander who was called.

Their alliance was to each other first…

NINETEEN

Leila

Hazel eyes. I saw them in my dreams. But I didn't see them when I woke. I blinked, my eyelids fluttering as they opened. A heaviness weighed down on my chest. I tried to breathe, but the ache moved deeper until it was all I could feel. I tried to glance around the room and pushed up from the bed, but the movement made my head spin. I let out a moan that tore through the back of my throat. A burn followed, one that made me panic.

What happened? I tried to think, tried to remember where I was. Sparkling blue water came to me... The island. That's right, I was on Cosa Nostra Island.

"There you are, you're finally awake."

I flinched at the voice. Footsteps echoed, filling the room, as the doctor walked around the partially closed curtain, lifted his gaze to mine, and smiled. "You gave me a scare there for a while."

"What happened to me?"

"You inhaled a short-acting barbiturate. Not enough to do any permanent damage, but it seemed to hit you pretty hard." He came closer, switching on a penlight to shine in my eyes before flicking it away. He grabbed his stethoscope, pressing the cool steel against my chest. "Deep breaths for me."

I did as he asked, even as it ached. He seemed concerned about something. "Is there something wrong?"

"With your health? No, not at all." He straightened, smiling down at me. "In fact, you're in perfect health, physically, that is. How much do you remember?"

That was just it, I didn't remember anything. I tried to think, but as soon as I did, the room started to spin once more. I lashed out, grabbing hold of the steel railing on the bed.

"Easy," the doctor cautioned, grabbing my shoulder. "Don't push it, you've had a bit of a scare, so your brain is trying to protect you."

A scare...

My breaths came hard and fast. I glanced down at the bed. "How long have I been here?"

"Not long, a few hours maybe."

Viktoriya? I searched the bed for my cell, but I couldn't see it anywhere. "My phone."

"It's here," came a deep murmur as the most dangerously stunning male I'd ever seen strode around the curtain.

Hazel eyes...

That's what I saw when he looked at me.

And that's all I remembered, but with the memory came panic. My pulse boomed, the sound thrashing in my ears. He cut a glare at the doctor as the poor man stepped in front of me. "Alexi..."

"Save it, doc," he muttered, flanked the doctor in one stride, and held out my phone to me.

I just looked at it. The screen was cracked.

"You dropped it," he explained, shifting his weight from foot to foot nervously.

The doctor just scowled at him. "You shouldn't be here, Kilpatrick."

"Thank you," I murmured, taking the phone from him.

"Well..." the doctor muttered. "I need to do some final checks on Ms. Ivanov."

The heavy thud of boots rang out in the hallway, but I could hardly hear them over the sound of my heart. Alexi gave a nod and took a step backwards. I couldn't help but feel a flare of urgency, of desperation to hold onto him, to have him stay a little longer.

"Alexi," came a deep growl from the doorway. "You need to leave."

I was captured by the bead of blood in the corner of his mouth as the beautiful male winced, then headed out the door. Another man entered, but this was no blonde Adonis. He was dark, haunted, and very much in control.

"Ms. Ivanov, how are you feeling?"

I didn't know this man, not his name, or why he was in my room. "Fine." I glanced toward the doorway Alexi had left through.

"I see Doctor Grey has given you a checkup. And she's free to leave?" He asked, glancing toward the doctor.

"As soon as she feels well enough, by all means."

"Your name," I demanded, sliding my feet over the side of the bed. The room spun, and I gripped the railing, waiting for it to slow, before I settled my gaze on the man standing before me.

"My name is Mateo Ristani, but most call me the Commander." He glanced at my fingers, my white knuckles wrapped around the railing.

So, this was the Commander? I'd expected someone older perhaps, someone not quite as dangerously good looking. As dangerous as he was, he didn't like seeing me tremble as I slid from the bed until my feet hit the floor. Panic flared in his gaze, and he took a step forward, reaching out to grab my arm before I pulled away. "Don't touch me."

I didn't want his comfort or his care, or even his presence. I didn't want anything from this man except for him to leave my room, and Alexi to come back in.

"Your father..." he murmured, meeting my gaze. "Have you had a chance to speak to him about this?"

So that's what this was really about. It had nothing to do with my welfare, and everything to do with his. That's why he was here. He was scared of what my father might do to him once he found out about the attack. My stomach tightened, and annoyance burned inside me, turning into something I could use.

I released the railing and took a step. "No, are you suggesting that I do?"

There was a flare of surprise in those dark, bottomless eyes. Did he expect me to go running to my father? Did he think I was so weak I needed to cry on my father's shoulder at the slightest little thing? But this wasn't a little thing, was it? The room kept spinning as my head felt like it was being crushed in a vise.

"Not unless you want to, of course. I will respect your wishes."

"My wishes?" I glanced toward the doorway. "Then I'll politely ask you to leave and, while you're at it, please send Alexi back inside."

He was surprised at that, one brow rose, as he scowled. "I don't think..."

I took a small step forward, my knees shaking. "I'm not asking you to think, Mateo. I'm asking you to leave."

With a curt nod, he turned away and headed for the door. His footsteps resounded as I swallowed hard and glanced at the doctor. He stared at me, his eyes wide, and a look of utter shock on his face.

"You said I'm free to leave, is that correct?"

"As long as you feel up to it, there's nothing medically holding you here," he answered, then hesitated. "But I want you to call me at the slightest change, will you do that?"

"Yes," I answered as movement came from the corner of my eye.

Alexi stepped back into the room, glanced at the doctor, then at me. "I was told you wanted to see me?"

"The doctor said I'm free to leave. I was wondering if you would walk me back to my apartment?" Hope filled me like sunlight. He was that sunlight, those blinding rays of promise, enough to fill my darkening world.

"Sure, I can do that." He was nervous, taken back by my request.

The doctor just gave a careful nod. "I want to be called if anything changes, Mr. Kilpatrick." He jerked his gaze toward Alexi.

"Yeah, sure," Alexi muttered. "You'll be the first to know."

I took a deep breath as the doctor cut me another glance, then strode from the room...leaving us alone.

Alexi licked his lips, then combed his fingers through his hair, leaving narrow furrows through the dirty blonde strands. He didn't think I saw him. He didn't think I saw that scared man behind the mask, the one he kept carefully controlled.

"I can walk you to your apartment." He came closer, holding out his hand. "Just in case you feel a little dizzy."

The second I pressed my palm against his, electricity tore along my arm, sending shockwaves into my chest. I curled my hand around his, gripping tightly. "Thank you."

There was a flash of a smile, one that made my pulse race, before he nodded to the doctor and guided me toward the door. My steps were slow, my knees trembling, but I held onto him, taking strength in his touch, and we slowly headed along the corridor of the unknown building. "I don't even know where we are."

"This is the main building on the island, with the infirmary and offices." He gave a jerk of his head, motioning behind us. "You will know by now, that down there is the island's command room, and further along is the Commander's office."

"And there?" I glanced at the closed double doors as we passed.

"That's the boardroom, where members of the Commission and their heirs attend meetings."

"And are you an heir?"

He just gave a slow smile and shook his head. "No, second born. My brother Jager is the poor bastard who carries the line."

He didn't like that fact. I got the sense it wasn't jealousy, but more like sadness. I moved closer and gripped his hand tighter, feeling the slow slide of his fingers as they slipped between mine.

But what about Viktoriya? The thought rose. You weren't to be distracted, right? Eyes on the prize and all that. But as Alexi spoke, divulging secret after secret about his brother and his sister Helene, I felt myself holding onto every word he said. He let me in...me, a stranger. He let me in. He wasn't cold or controlled, wasn't holding me at arm's length, or giving me one-word answers before he shut down any questions I asked with a shake of his head.

He wasn't lying to me...but nor was he being entirely truthful. He was...careful, catching himself when he said too much as we headed out the main building's entrance and back along the path.

"*Kilpatrick!*" The roar blasted through the air.

Xael stormed across the grass toward us.

"Oh shit." Alexi slipped his hand from mine and took a step away. "You might need to distance yourself from me for this."

"*You fucking bastard!*" she screamed, then took a massive step and lunged, swinging her fist as she went. "You told him to stay away?"

Alexi caught her fist with one hand and wrapped his arm around her waist, catching her before she fell. "Easy, Davies."

"How fucking *dare* you!" She was savage, shoving him away with a punch to his chest. "*You've got no right!*"

"Believe me, I'm doing you a favor," he answered.

My heart beat louder at the words, trying to piece this all together.

"Are you fucking jealous? Is that it, Alexi?" She glanced my way, swallowing hard before lowering her voice. "Because you can get that idea out of your head. That's *never gonna happen.*"

Jealous...

Alexi was jealous?

Heat raced to my cheeks as a pang of agony tore through my chest.

"Jealous? No, can't say that's ever crossed my mind, Davies," he muttered, holding up his hands in mock surrender as he stepped back. "I'm trying to do you a favor here."

"Do *me* a favor? What, you couldn't save your sister from a psycho like Kardinov, so now you're overprotective, is that it?"

He winced like she'd slapped him. There was a second when that bright sunlight dimmed in his eyes, a second when there were only shadows left behind, and I caught sight again of the real man...the one carefully hidden behind the mask, the one he didn't want me to see. He glanced my way and swallowed hard before turning back to her. "That's a low fucking blow, Davies, even from you."

"Yeah, well..." she sucked in a hard breath, faltering.

I could see the alliance between them, it wasn't quite friendship, nor was it love. It was something else, something that I wasn't entirely unfamiliar with, something I wanted more than anything.

"I don't trust him," Alexi declared. "I think you shouldn't trust him, as well. Something I don't like about him, something about him that rubbed me the wrong way."

"That's not really a concern, now is it, Kilpatrick? Stay away from me, and the guys I fuck, okay?" She looked my way, then took a step backwards, distancing herself. "Ivanov," she muttered. "Stay away from this one, he's trouble."

Then she was gone, stomping away. Her anger was mirrored by the growl of thunder that came from the gray skies overhead.

"Well, that was interesting," he grunted.

"Did you really threaten the man she's in love with?"

He cast a surprised look my way. "Love?" He gave a hard bark of laughter. "Davies doesn't know how to love, anyone but herself, that is."

He held out his hand for me once more. There was a slight tremor in his fingers, a vulnerability he didn't want me to see. I closed the distance between us, taking his hand in mine again, letting him lead me back to the path, and we headed to my building.

My security strode toward us, the guard who'd made me feel heated and uneasy from before leading the others. His top lip curled when he looked at Alexi, then he lowered his focus to our hands, our fingers still entwined. "Great," I muttered under my breath. "Just what I needed."

Alexi missed nothing, giving them a nod as we neared. "You can stay in the foyer. I'll see Ms. Ivanov up to her apartment."

"Yeah?" The jealous guard cocked his eyebrow "I don't think so, buddy."

Alexi stopped, jerking my hand with the sudden movement. My arm was wrenched and I stumbled backwards, bumping him hard. "Buddy?" Alexi repeated slowly, stepping toward the guard with a savage glare. "Do I look like *your buddy?*"

The bodyguard glanced my way as though I'd somehow save him.

"Don't look at her," Alexi snapped. A charge of fear tore through me as Alexi stepped to the side, directly in the guard's view. "I'm giving you a direct order, stay in the foyer, or else." The threat lingered in the air, making the guard flinch. He knew better than to argue and, with one careful step backwards, he was put back into his place. "Leila," Alexi murmured.

I followed him as he pressed his card against the reader and the doors opened.

That charge of excitement stayed with me all the way up to the apartment and as we stepped out into the living room. He dropped my hand, and crossed the space until he stood at the windows. "You have a balcony? Of course you do."

"Yes," I answered. "Would you like to go out?"

He turned, shaking his head, and met my gaze. "No." Desire filled the air between us. It was like nothing I'd ever felt before, making that flare of panic I'd felt before with the bodyguard insignificant.

I became aware of my breaths, became aware of the distance between us and the heat that seared in my veins. "Leila," he started.

"It was you, wasn't it?"

His eyes grew colder, that mask he wore hanging on by its last thread. I was the one who closed the distance, driven by the need to know him...to know his truth. "The drug they said I inhaled, that was you." Panic filled his eyes as he tried to find words. But he didn't need to, I already had them tucked away. "I forgive you." I reached out and touched his arm.

"You forgive me? What, just like that?"

"Yes." I answered. "Just like that."

He flinched at my touch, like he was unworthy, like I was the one who burned him, and dragged his hand through his head. "It's too easy. You gotta at least make me take you for dinner, try to explain."

"We're on an island, Alexi."

He winced as though he just realized. "Your family... They'll kill me." He muttered, lifted his gaze to mine as he handed back his phone.

At his words, my phone vibrated and rang in my hand, I needed to look at the caller ID to know who it was. Instead of answering, I lifted my hand and touched his cheek, my thumb brushing the corner of his mouth with the blood dried. "It looks like you've paid enough," I murmured, then lowered my hand, hit the button, and canceled the call.

TWENTY

Alexi

SHE PRESSED THE BUTTON, AND THE PHONE WENT SILENT.

My heart pounded, I didn't need a fucking map to know what it meant. Nor did I need a guide for the desire in her eyes. *Use her... Use her to get out of this.* With the words ringing in my head, I took a step closer and lowered my head.

All I could see was a way out of this, and I'd use my body to seal the deal. The slow exhale of her breath blew against my cheek before she spoke. "Thank you for walking me back to my apartment, Alexi. But I think you should go."

Go?

I slowly straightened. She wanted me. I saw it in her eyes. *Kiss her. Kiss her anyway.* Panic filled me. She was moving me to make a decision...make this count, or walk away.

This was my opportunity. The only one I was probably going to get. But that quiet voice in my head warned me that if I chose wrong, she'd pull away. I couldn't take that chance, not when I'd already failed today.

I straightened, pulling back from her. The last thing I wanted to do was ruin this. So, with a nod, I stepped away.

"Before you go, Alexi." The way she said my name made me tremble. "May I have your number? In case I feel dizzy."

"Sure." Hope rose inside me.

She gave a smile, unlocked her phone, and handed it over. I took it, glancing at the crack in the screen, a crack that I was sure at any other time a woman like Leila Ivanov would not tolerate. So I punched in my name and number, then saved them to her contacts before handing the cell back.

It wasn't desperation I felt as I left her apartment and headed back to the elevator, it was confusion. I expected her to come running after me. Hell, I expected most women to come running up to me. Maybe I was losing my touch? That thought stayed with me as I stepped into the elevator and traveled down to the foyer. The guard lifted his head as I stepped out, his smirk instant, pushing my buttons.

I wanted to cross the floor and beat the living shit out of him, but I didn't. Instead, I made for my own building, ignoring the thunder that growled overhead. I rode the elevator up, stepped out and made my way to the kitchen, then poured myself a drink and swallowed the burn.

Maybe I *was* losing my touch, maybe this whole goddamn shitshow was bringing me undone.

I drank, crossing the living room to stare out my window. But all I could think about was her. The way she'd talked to me, the way she smiled.

I forgive you...

Those fucking words made my hand shake as I lifted the rim of the glass to my lips once more.

I didn't deserve it, not a goddamn bit. That pit of despair waited for me as I closed my eyes. And yet...all I could hear was my own name as it spilled from her lips.

Alexi...

My heart thudded, the sound heavy and aching. This wasn't about love, nor was it about lust. This was about one thing and one thing only. *Getting myself and my family out of this goddamn mess.* I opened my eyes and turned, then lifting my hand, I pressed the number for my brother.

"Alexi," he mumbled, sounding half asleep. "What happened?"

"Nothing. Sorry, I should've checked the time."

The sound of the bedsheets rustled through the line. "I'm awake now."

"Tell me what's going on in Russia?"

His voice sharpened, sleep slipping away. "Russia, why?"

I closed my eyes. "Nothing, just tell me."

"One of the oligarchs has been murdered, another is sequestered in his home, and there's talk..."

"Talk that Ivanov's behind it?"

"Yes." The way he said it told me the truth. There was more than talk, more than suspicion. Jesus, if he was right, then the woman I'd hurt...the woman I could've killed, was more dangerous than anyone else on this island...including me.

I forgive you...

Christ, did she know? Did she have any idea the kind of brutality it took to take down the bratva? I licked my lips and cast a glance toward the darkening sky outside the window. I was betting she didn't. I was betting that whatever blood sport her father entertained never reached her ears.

My pulse thundered.

"Alexi," my brother snarled, dragging me back to the moment. "What the fuck have you done?"

Beep.

My phone vibrated in my hand. I was too scared to look. Deja vu hit me like a damn tidal wave. The last time I'd spoken to my brother and received his message, I'd seen my own betrayal. "Did you just send me another video, Jager?"

"What? No."

Confusion bordered on fear. I pulled the phone away, catching the caller ID across the screen. *Hannah.*

"I've got to go."

"You going to tell me what the hell is going on here?" Jager barked.

"Later," I answered. "Go back to sleep."

I ended the call, opened the message, and stared at an arrest warrant with my brother's name typed clearly.

Give me the file, Alexi. Give me the image with Carter Benfold, or else.

TWENTY-ONE

Leila

I WATCHED HIM WALK AWAY, LISTENING TO THE SOUND OF the elevator while my heart hammered and my pulse raced. I reached up, touched my lips, and thought of what had almost been real. He'd wanted to kiss me, and I'd wanted to kiss him back. My phone beeped in my hand, drawing my focus back to Theon's message...

Leila, answer me...

My focus shifted from the words to the long crack in the screen. Pain cleaved through my head as memories slipped in. The classroom. Finley Salvatore...and him...*Alexi.*

Alexi Kilpatrick. I glanced toward the elevator as those memories pressed in. I winced at the agony and pressed my fingers against my temple, feeling the driving pulse. There was something he was hiding. Something about his screams in that classroom...something about me. I wasn't stupid. A man like Alexi didn't just suddenly become interested in me, not without a reason.

My phone vibrated in my hand once more. I left the living room behind and headed for the bedroom as the sound of the elevator doors came once more.

"Ms. Ivanov?"

I stopped in the doorway of the bedroom. "Yes?"

"Just checking, ma'am," he murmured.

Agony drove a spike through my head and a blinding flash in my eye followed. "I'm fine."

"Mr. Volkov..." he started.

"*Can wait*," I snapped. I never snapped...not until now. "I have a headache and I'm going to bed."

"Yes, ma'am. We're downstairs should you need—"

"I won't," I cut him off, stepping inside the bedroom and closing the door behind me.

My stomach clenched, forcing me to stumble for the bathroom. I slapped blindly for the light switch as that agony in my head boomed. I wanted to shut them out...I wanted to shut *all* of them out. The bodyguards. Theon. My father...*but not* him.

Not Alexi.

I sank to the cold floor while my stomach clenched and heaved. I clung to the toilet, desperate for the cold and the quiet, and waited for the nausea to pass. Acid burned along the back of my throat as I waited. I closed my eyes as the burn splashed against the water, and with a moan, I sank back down, slowly kicked off my shoes, and pressed the soles of my feet against the tiles. I sat there for ages, waiting as the radiating waves of agony eased until I could open my eyes without seeing neon streaks of lightning.

My phone beeped out in the bedroom. I ignored it, slowly unbuttoning my blouse before I worked my way to my pants and my underwear and crawled into the shower.

Icy water splashed down from above. I shivered, drew my knees together, and sat in the cold as slowly memories of my home slipped in. The first shock of winter snow. The way the river iced at the edges. My horse, Kaleidoscope, galloping along the bank, his long black mane wild and free. That's where I wanted to be...*free.*

Free of this fear.

Free of this not knowing.

My thoughts drifted to Viktoriya, and the last words she'd whispered before I left. *Sisters*...that's what she'd called us, and we were, sisters bonded by violence and control. We only had each other...and now I couldn't reach her. I let out a low, terrified whimper. It was the first frightened sound I'd uttered, the first sound of weakness. The brutal thud in my head eased as the whimper resounded in the bathroom. I let it carry, let it rip from my chest and fracture the silence.

I was sick of being silenced.

I was sick of being controlled.

When the agony had turned to a dull ache, I switched the shower off and slowly rose. I dried hastily, then opened the door to my bedroom, listening for the thud of boots before I stepped out and hurried for my closet, pulling on something soft and warm before I climbed into bed.

Sleep came quickly, pressing against that throb in my temple until it, too, gave way. With a shuddered exhale, I drifted off into the darkness, where all I saw were those perfect hazel eyes.

BEEP.

My phone woke me with a start. For a second, panic filled me, *where was I?* The room slowly came into focus, and with it came the memory of where I was...and who I'd been with. The heavy thud pressed against my temple again. I winced and probed the pulse, fighting the urge to shove upwards and climb out of bed. Instead, I reached for my phone, blinked, and waited for my eyes to adjust. That ache pressed against the back of my eyes, making the screen blur.

Theon: Answer my goddamn calls, Leila, or I'll have my security force the phone to your ear.

I froze, my heart hammering as I blinked and re-read the message. *Force...Theon...threatened me?* I slowly pushed upwards, sliding my feet out of the bed, and sat there. This wasn't like Theon...this was like my father.

I read the message again...and shivered. This wasn't the man I'd known all my life, not the man who called me his Mia, or my protector, who journeyed out in the cold no matter how childish I'd been. A man who put my well-being above even his own. This was a *stranger*.

Something bad had happened. I knew it in my heart. There were too many questions, too many demands. I dropped my phone to the bed and walked into the bathroom to use the toilet and shower once more.

The dull ache in the back of my head didn't ease. Not under the cold spray of the shower, not even after a buttered piece of toast and some painkillers. It lingered as I walked out of my apartment and headed to class, even though I'd already missed a class. I wasn't about to stay in my room and cry. I refused to be weak, refused to give in...refused to submit to Theon's demands, even though, as I walked toward the building, my phone vibrated once more.

"Give it a rest, Theon," I muttered, and pushed through the doors.

The soft drone of voices filled my ears. I lowered my gaze and headed for the classroom. My steps were quiet, my shoulders curled, taking up less space...just like I took up less space.

"It's *her*..." someone muttered.

"*Ivanov*," another chimed in.

I lifted my gaze to the group of women looking my way...and then to the others behind them. They all looked my way... *every...single...one of them.*

But the moment I met their gazes, they looked away. Heat rushed to my cheeks and that low throb in the back of my eyes grew stronger. I didn't like to be seen, didn't like being noticed, didn't like the way they moved away, whispering as they went. Were they whispering about me? I stepped into the classroom behind them and lifted my gaze.

Xael sat in the back row, arms folded across her chest. Those dark eyes met mine the moment I strode toward the seats. But there was no smile of greeting this time, no '*Ivanov*' to call me over. Just a hardness, a carefulness. Like all the others, she was guarded around me and as that heat burned in my cheeks, I slipped into a seat at the front of the class.

"Okay, everyone, we have a lot to get through...welcome to the art of manipulation," the lecturer called out as he stood at the front of the room.

But his words only made that pounding in my head louder... drowning out their whispers.

But it did nothing to hide their sideways glances, or the motion of their heads my way. This was a bad idea...this class...these people. Light flared in my eyes, stabbing as it went.

I had to get out of there...

Now.

I shoved to stand up, not caring that they watched me. They were looking anyway. The lecturer never stopped speaking, even as I yanked open the door and rushed out into the hallway. Hard gasps tore from my chest as I stumbled back along and out into the foyer.

"Ms. Ivanov?" my guard called as he rose from his seat at the end of the space and headed my way. "Everything okay?"

But I didn't answer, just hurried for the doors, desperate to get back to my apartment once more. The wind howled outside, blowing a torn leaf from a palm across the grounds. I stumbled under the force as the gusts rose, whipping strands of my hair into my eyes.

The island blurred as tears came.

"Ms. Ivanov?" The guard was insistent, pushing through the door behind me.

"I'm fine!" I screamed. *"Just leave me alone!"*

I left him behind, hurrying back along the pathway as I returned to my building. The brutal gusts made me stumble, but I caught my fall and hurried forward, head down, glancing at the ground before I stepped around the protection of my building. I sucked in a hard gasp, lifted my gaze, and strode forward, pressing my card against the scanner before rushing into the foyer.

I pressed the button for the elevator and stepped in, taking it all the way to my apartment once more. I didn't want to be in the classroom, didn't want to be under their gazes. I didn't want to be the reason they whispered and stared at me, terrified.

But the moment I stepped back into my apartment, I realized I didn't want to be there, either. I didn't want to be anywhere...

My phone rang in my pocket, the shrill sound making me jump. I grabbed it, and desperation surged inside me as I fought the need to hurl it across the room. Instead, I switched it off, kicked aside my shoes, and padded barefoot into the kitchen before I poured myself a drink.

This was reckless...I picked up the glass and eyed the vodka. I didn't care that it was still morning, didn't care the sun was still rising. I didn't care that, unlike my father, I'd never developed a taste for alcohol.

All I knew was I wanted this desperation inside me to stop.

I took a swallow, wincing at the sudden burn, then I coughed and spluttered. My eyes were still watering as I lifted the glass once more. I stood there, staring out the window at the howling wind and the destructive storm clouds that moved in, and I drank until that out-of-control feeling left me.

The dark gray clouds were mesmerizing. I lost myself in the churning as they rolled overhead, and moved closer to the window, then without thinking, I unlocked the door and stepped out onto the balcony. Movement came from the corner of my eye. A dark blur rushed from the edge of the water and hurried across the grounds. *It was a man...no, not one man...two.* Another followed, only he didn't run. He strode along the sandy inlet just to disappear behind the corner of a building.

But they didn't look like security, not any kind of security I'd seen here before. *Were they sent from Theon?*

With his threat still lingering in my mind from this morning, I stepped back inside and locked the door. I threw a glance over my shoulder toward the elevator, waiting for the sound of opening doors to follow.

But it didn't...I waited, wrapped my arms around my body, and tried to stop from falling apart.

Violence and threats were everywhere.

I was crushed under their control.

I thought I heard the faint sound of a scream, or maybe it was just a trick of the wind.

There she is...

Memories of those in the classroom slipped in.

That's her...*Ivanov*...

I headed back to the kitchen and another drink, trying my best to drown out their whispers. When the dull roar eased, I stumbled to the sofa with my next glassful, and sank down. I tugged the blanket across my lap and closed my eyes. Vodka wasn't so bad, once you got past the bitter taste, it was cool and warm all at the same time, slipping down the back of my throat.

I don't know how long I sat there, taking sips, letting it flow through me. The thunder of boots dragged open my eyes. With the sound, I turned my head, finding my security team lunging out of the elevator and heading straight for me.

"*Leila!*" the bodyguard screamed.

I shoved upwards on the sofa, the blanket spilling to my feet. "I'm here."

"Search the apartment!" he roared.

Terror consumed me, burning through the alcohol in my blood. "What is it?"

But he didn't answer right away, his eyes were wide, hard breaths tearing from his chest. "I thought... I thought it was you."

"You thought *what* was me?" A chill raced along my spine.

He scowled, then answered. "There's been a kidnapping."

TWENTY-TWO

Alexi
___

THERE'S BEEN A KIDNAPPING...

I flinched at the words, rereading the message. A kidnapping, here on the island? I punched back a reply to the Commander. *Who is it?*

Not sure, all I know is that it's a female.

A female? My heart punched against my chest. I tore my gaze toward the elevator, then lunged. The elevator would be too slow, so I yanked open the stairwell door and threw myself down the stairs, taking two and three at a time. *A woman...*

In my head, all I could see was Leila Ivanov being stolen away from me. I couldn't allow that to happen, couldn't let her slip away. The dimly lit stairs blurred in front of me. By the time I hit the foyer, my ankles were screaming with the pain. Still, I barrelled through the doorway and out into the foyer, tore through the automatic doors, and raced toward her building.

I lifted my phone, but then I realized I'd given her my number without getting hers. I thought of calling the Commander, but by the time I got the information I needed, it'd probably be already too late.

I lengthened my stride, driving my boots into the ground, and raced toward the glinting lights in the distance. The seconds felt like hours, my steps too slow, too heavy. By the time I reached her building and slammed my card against the reader, fire consumed my chest. I stumbled inside and scanned the foyer, to find one of her bodyguards standing at the stairwell door. "Is that her?" I screamed. "Answer me! Is it her?"

He gave a shake of his head. "No, she's upstairs. Ms. Ivanov is safe."

She's safe...

I stumbled to the elevator, punched the button, and waited. It wasn't her, it wasn't her...

The elevator door opened, and I stepped inside, still sucking in hard breaths. The pounding of my heart was deafening as I stepped out and made my way along the hallway. "Leila!"

"I'm in here," she answered, her voice muffled and strange.

I barged into her apartment, caught her bodyguard's glare, and found her standing in the middle of the living room, her eyes red from crying. "Do they know who it is?"

"No," I answered, coming around the sofa to grab her shoulders. "It wasn't you, that's all that matters right now."

She shook her head. "You're wrong, it does matter."

The guard's two-way crackled as information was barked through the handset. I caught the name VanHalen and winced.

"What is it?" she asked, staring into my eyes.

All I could see was the bright shine of unshed tears and her pain, but I couldn't stop this, no matter how much I wanted to. "It's Katerina VanHalen."

"VanHalen?" she whispered. "I...I know that name. It's her... she's the one they took?"

I scowled at the way she said it, the way she glanced toward the window. "I thought they were guards."

"What did you say?" The bodyguard behind me intruded.

She glanced back at him. "I thought they were just guards."

"Who, Leila?" I gripped her shoulders more tightly.

"The two men I saw running from the water."

"Jesus," I muttered.

"When was that, Ms. Ivanov?"

Her brow creased as the guard relayed the information into the radio.

"Think, Leila," I pressed. "This is important."

"An hour ago, maybe. I don't know, I..." She glanced toward the kitchen.

I followed her gaze to an open bottle of Grey Goose. She'd been drinking? By the haunted look in her eyes, the answer was a resounding yes. She looked rattled, even more than she had yesterday when I'd left her.

"An hour," she said. "No more than an hour and a half." Her words sharpened with conviction, but it wasn't me she focused on, it was the guard. She took a step away, slipping from my hold. "If they took Katerina, then they can't have gone far. They're still out there."

She changed in an instant. Gone was the red-eyed, vulnerable woman I'd seen a second ago. Her eyes glinted with danger, and her body stilled, until I couldn't even tell if she was breathing. "Find them," she demanded. "Find them all."

Jesus...

"They will," I reassured her.

"Can you tell me exactly what happened, ma'am?" the guard asked.

She told him, rattling off the information in precise detail, how she'd watched two men dressed in black come across the inlet further along the island and disappear behind the building in back of hers. As she spoke, a chill raced along my spine. We were under attack here, sitting goddamn ducks. I didn't like it...I didn't like a whole damn lot here, not the way I'd fucking run from the feds or the sons of the Commission being murdered.

We needed to get off the island...

Find somewhere to hunker down, and make a plan of attack. I lifted my gaze to hers as she turned back to me. The only problem in my plan of attack was her.

"I know her," she whispered, and crossed her arms over her chest, closing in the pain.

"I know..."

She met my gaze. "She was on the boat with me, Alexi...I know her."

"I know, and I don't like it." I dragged my fingers through my hair as the guard strode out of the apartment, speaking into his radio once more.

"You don't like what, exactly?" she asked carefully.

"You, here...alone." There was a second when fear ignited in her eyes, but then her shoulders straightened and she met my gaze.

"I'm not alone, Alexi," she protested. "I have my bodyguards."

"Men who work for your father, if I'm correct." *Careful...I didn't want to scare her.* "Come stay with me." I brushed a strand of her ash blonde hair from her temple.

"But my security..."

"Can you truly trust them?" I murmured, drawing her closer against me.

The answer was no...she couldn't trust them, or anyone...

Not even me...

TWENTY-THREE

Alexi

She just scowled, and glanced toward the hallway. But I knew the question had made an impact on her, the words still ringing in the air.

Can you truly trust them?

"I don't know," she whispered, the words trembling and significant.

My pulse surged. This was the moment I'd been waiting for. The crack in the armor, a way for me to become useful to her, to become safe for her. To become *everything* for her. "My apartment is secure, you'll be safe there."

"With you, you mean?" Excitement and fear danced in her eyes.

"Yes..." I lowered my hands from her shoulders. "You have nothing to fear from me, Leila. I have a vacant bedroom, and you're welcome to it, no strings attached."

She looked around the apartment, then glanced toward the balcony. I knew exactly what raced through her mind, I could see it all playing out on her face. Two men had invaded the island in front of her, two men who'd kidnapped an heiress. Not even her own security could save her. And Leila...had seen it.

"They won't get to you, not while I'm there," I urged.

She flinched, her lips parting with a hard inhale and, in the quiet of her panic, she lifted her gaze to mine. "Will you wait while I get my things?" she asked quietly.

"I'll do one better," I answered. "I'll help you pack."

She licked her lips, swallowed hard, and gave a nod. I let her step away as I moved toward the bedroom. I didn't want to invade her space, not yet. I needed to give her time, to let her come to me. I wanted her to feel safe around me, so everything I did now was aimed at that. "How about we take the bottle of Grey Goose with us? I think we could both use a drink."

She didn't answer, but I could hear the rustling of her suitcase being unzipped. I stepped toward the bedroom, making sure I stood outside the doorway. "Can I help you in there?"

"If you can pass me my clothes?"

I smiled, and stepped inside her bedroom. "Sure."

I was surprised when I entered her closet. There were no bright colors, no glaring shades of any color. There were shades of dark blue, black and gray. This woman fought hard to remain unseen. I grabbed the hangers, pulled the garments free, and handed them to her one by one. We worked in silence. In fact, that's how this woman was. Quiet, careful, controlled.

I doubted that she'd done anything reckless in her entire life. I doubted she'd ever had a chance to. I slid a sheer silver top from a hanger and reached out. My fingers brushed hers, and she stiffened, meeting my gaze.

"I like this." I glanced down at the thin strap across my fingers.

She followed my gaze, her breath catching, before she looked away. Her cheeks reddened, and the sight of that made me smile. She was nervous, too nervous...

It hit me like a blow. She wasn't...experienced. Jesus...*was she a goddamn virgin?*

My cock hardened in an instant as heat rushed through me. She was...she was brand goddamn new. Christ, I couldn't remember that time in my life. I sure as hell hadn't fucked one before. But as she avoided my gaze, took the top from my hand, and hurried to fold it, I realized exactly what I was in for. This was no normal seduction, no exchange of desires. This woman didn't even know what she desired.

"Are you going to hand me more?" She met my gaze again before looking away, her cheeks burning.

"Absolutely," I answered, my mind reeling as I turned and grabbed the last pair of slacks, folding them before handing them over.

She stowed the last of her clothes away and turned to the bathroom. She barely made a sound, the only indication I knew she was in there at all was the sound of a zipper. Then she was stepping out, crossing the bedroom to stow her large makeup bag inside her suitcase. "All set."

I gave her a smile, zipped up her suitcase, and pulled it from the bed. "Is there anything else you want to take with you?"

"No." She glanced around. "Not really."

I held out my hand, unsure if she wanted the connection. Yesterday, her hand in mine had felt so natural, but today things had changed. She had changed. She was scared, erratic and drifting. My hand lingered in the air for a second longer than I wanted it to, but then she surprised me, taking my hand in hers. "I'm ready," she announced.

I grabbed the bottle of vodka on my way out, wheeling her suitcase and leading the way. I motioned her inside the elevator when the doors opened, and when we exited at the foyer, her security was right there waiting for us.

"Is there a problem?" The asshole bodyguard glared at the suitcase in my hand, then met Leila's gaze.

"You mean apart from the kidnapping and the murder?" I answered. "Leila thinks it's safer if we combine security, so she'll be staying with me." I took a step forward, daring the bastard to say a damn word.

He just held her gaze. "Ms. Ivanov? Is that what you want?"

The way he said the words without looking at me made me want to close the distance and drive my fist into his face. But he was insistent, taking a step closer to her, drawing her gaze.

"If it's your safety you're concerned about, I can assure you you're safe here." He lowered his voice. "I'll make sure of it."

I let out a hard bark of laughter. "There's nothing on this island you can be sure about, that's a hard fact. Leila..." I turned toward her.

She just gave him a small nod, her voice quiet. "I think it's best..."

I took a step, tightening my grip on hers, pulling her with me as we headed for the foyer doors. I didn't stop, didn't slow, just turned my face into the howling wind and headed along the path to my building. By the time we stepped inside, my ears were burning from the wind. Her cheeks were red, even redder than before, and her blonde hair was wild and untamed.

I stepped inside the elevator, dragged her suitcase next to me, and brushed her hair down as the doors closed, carrying us upwards. She was nervous when she stepped out. I let her walk on ahead, making her way through my apartment, taking in everything. "You have a view of the rest of the island?" She neared the windows and looked out.

Trees bowed and swayed, lashed by the almost violent winds outside. The view made me feel frantic and scattered. "Not much of one today," I answered as I pulled her suitcase with me, making my way to the second bedroom in the apartment. "Your room's down here."

I gave her space, letting her find her way around, and placed her suitcase on top of the bed, opening the zipper once more. The refrigerator door was opened, then closed, the cupboard doors followed. I was aware of every sound, listening to her as she explored.

"It's nice," she murmured from the doorway.

"Your bathroom's through there." I straightened and turned toward her. "I want you to let me know if there's anything you need."

The air was charged with electricity between us. I closed the distance and reached up to cup her cheek. But unlike before, I didn't brush my fingers through her hair. I captured her chin, tilted her face to mine, and kissed her.

TWENTY-FOUR

Alexi

SEX GOT ME INTO THIS, AND SEX WAS GOING TO GET ME OUT.

I took her mouth carefully and slowly. I kept my fingers on her chin, not wanting to scare her away from me...not yet. She was frozen, her lips unmoving while I took my time. Slowly, she warmed, opening her mouth wider, letting me take more.

I broke away, and straightened. "I want you to know you're safe here. There's nothing I won't do to protect you."

Her lips were parted, her breath panicked and rushed. It was as though she'd never had feelings like this before, or never allowed herself to have them. But then she did something totally unexpected. She stepped closer, then reached up and clamped her hand around the back of my neck, pulling my lips to hers again.

The kiss was hungry, and urgent. Her body trembled, as though it could barely contain her lust. I let her take what she wanted, opening my mouth, taking her signal as she arched her back, pressing her breasts against my chest before she broke away. Her eyes were wide, her chest heaving. I dragged my teeth across my lip, finding the ache. "Well, that was unexpected."

She glanced away, her cheeks flushing.

"Are you embarrassed to kiss me?" I curled my finger under her chin, guiding her focus to mine. "You don't ever have to be embarrassed about kissing me, Leila." My words only made her blush harder. She looked scared now, glancing rapidly around the room. "How about I give you a little space? I'll be in the living room if you need anything, okay?"

She gave a careful nod, leaving me to step away. I released the top buttons of my shirt, and rolled my sleeves upwards, then made my way into the kitchen to pour a drink. She took her time, unpacking her things slowly before stepping out of the bedroom and wandering into the kitchen. She watched me as I pulled the packets of salmon from the fridge. "I thought you might be hungry, is salmon okay?"

She gave a smile. "It's perfect."

The silence was awkward, but I kept busy preparing the fillets before placing them in a searing pan. Light vegetables, a creamy sauce, and I plated up our meal and motioned toward the dining table. We ate in silence as she picked it her food until I was sure that she hated it. But then she placed some on the tip of her fork and into her mouth.

I sat back, watching her eat. Her nervous glances and her pathetically small bites told me she was scared to be here. Hell, she was probably scared to be in her own apartment. I had to find a way to change that. Her phone vibrated, the caller ID that flashed said Theon, but she made no move to answer it. Instead, she hit the button, sending the call to voicemail.

"If you need me to leave to take that, I can make myself scarce," I offered.

She just shook her head, her focus on the table in front of her. "No."

So she didn't want to take Theon's calls, whoever that was. I waited until she was done and placed her fork gently on the plate, before I rose. "You know, you remind me a bit of my sister, Helene."

I made my way into the kitchen, scraping the plates and rinsing them before stacking them in the dishwasher.

"You have a sister?"

I gave a chuckle. "Yeah." I dried my hands on the hand towel and grabbed my phone, pulling up the images of last Christmas, when Helene had made me wear the most hideous green Christmas sweater she could find.

The moment Leila saw the photo, her brows rose. "Oh my."

I just laughed. "And that's not even the worst of it. You should see the one she bought for my brother."

"It was worse than that?"

"It had antlers."

The smile was instant, quickly covered by her hand, but it was there. The mood seemed to lighten a bit as we chatted about my family gathering. I didn't mind, as long as I left my father out of it. But the mood lift and the conversation seemed to help calm her.

"I spent my Christmas with my best friend," she offered quietly.

"Oh, yeah?"

The smile died as she looked away. "But no more. I will be going back there."

"To Russia?" I probed. If I could just get her to open up, find a crack in her armor, and I'd find a way inside. "Judging by your accent."

She met my gaze. "Yes, Russia."

I walked back into the kitchen, grabbed two glasses, and poured more of that Grey Goose, before I made my way back, handing her one. "Sounds like you miss the place."

"Her, as well." Her words were very quiet as she stared at the glass in her hand and took a sip.

"That's easily fixed, call her," I suggested, motioning toward the cell on the table in front of her.

Tears shimmered in her eyes. "I can't, because I think something's happened to her."

My pulse stuttered as Jager's words came roaring back to me. They'd left Russia quickly, and all the suspicion pointed to foul play. "And this friend of yours, did she know who you really were?"

A nod said it all. "Yes, we were the same, she and I."

Here was the test point, the moment when she would either run, or open up to me. "What's her name?"

"Viktoriya Korolev."

Holy shit...the daughter of the head of the Korolev empire? There was more she wasn't telling me, but if I pushed too hard, she'd close down and pull away. "Is there something I can do? Name it, anything. I don't have many connections in Russia, but I can try."

She swept her thumb under her eye and shook her head. "No." The moment she answered, her phone rang once more.

Anger blazed in her eyes as she hit the button again and unleashed a turbulent roar of Russian. I drank, letting the burn slide all the way down as she finally fell silent. "I'm sorry," she apologized. "I forgot myself."

"Sounds like forgetting yourself is exactly what you need. Go ahead, unleash. I do it all the damn time, feels good, right?"

"It feels..." She sucked in hard breaths, then met my gaze. "It feels like I can't breathe."

I took a step, leaned down, and let my fingers slide through her hair before I kissed her hard, until my need became deep and bruising, then I broke away. "Then don't breathe...just act."

Her chest rose, and fell, as she slowly stood, then reached for the buttons of her blouse.

"What are you doing?" I met her gaze.

"Exactly what you said...acting."

TWENTY-FIVE

Alexi

I GRIPPED THE BACK OF HER NECK, PULLING HER CLOSE. I wanted to feel something other than this ache inside me. Something more than this unraveling. I wanted to be the one in control. the one who was the predator and not the prey.

She let out a low moan, pressing her body against mine. Her fingers still worked the buttons of her blouse, her hand crushed between us. I wanted her...her family. Her power...*I wanted her to fall for me.*

I broke the kiss and pulled away. Her eyes were closed and her lips were parted, red and swollen from our kiss. I slid my thumb along her jaw and tilted her head back as I moved in to nuzzle her neck.

"Alexi..." she whispered.

"Mmm?" I nipped the flesh over her pulse, making her jump.

Her chest pressed against mine in hard breaths.

"You like me...*right?*"

I froze, my fingers pressed against the back of her head, my thumb commanding the tilt of her head. Like her? Like...*her*. I didn't even fucking know her, nor did I want to. This was just sex, just fucking currency. I'd take her fucking virginity for her, and she'd make my problems disappear.

Well, her father would...

"Yeah," I answered, bending my head to the task as I cupped her breast. "I like you."

"Okayyy," the word was a moan.

I smiled, kneading her breast. I didn't need to be psychic to know what her question meant...I could read between the goddamn lines, especially with someone like her. I lifted my head and our gazes collided. "I like you, sweet Leila."

Fear. Hope. It all shimmered in her clear blue eyes. I was used to women wanting me, used to that ravenous need to fuck and be fucked. But when I looked at her, she wanted me in another way. Something more than just the physical...and that's exactly where I needed her. Right there, soft and pliable in my hands.

She pulled her blouse free from her waistband. I slowly lowered my gaze, taking in the dusty pink lace bra. Fuck, she was sweet. So goddamn sweet...too sweet for me.

I slid my finger under the strap of her bra and dragged it off her shoulder, meeting her gaze once more. "You sure you want to do this?"

With a tiny nod, she answered, "Yes."

Her body trembled, her flesh shivering under my touch as I lowered my head and kissed her shoulder. Warmth touched my lips as I dragged them over her skin. Slowly, that's how you won someone like her. Slow and seductive, drawing her deeper into me. I was lost on the sensation, captured by the unusually sweet scent of her perfume...*what the fuck was that?*

Until the sound of the elevator fractured my focus. Footsteps followed, heading this way. "Mr. Kilpatrick?"

"Not now."

But the bastard didn't leave, instead he stepped in closer, forcing me to slide her bra strap up to cover her damn modesty and turn, barring his view.

"Ms. Ivanov's men are asking for instructions, sir." He kept his focus on me, never once looking her way...he knew better than to look at what he shouldn't see.

Anger burned inside me. Ms. Ivanov's men, my ass...it was only one man...one fucking thorn in my damn side. Her cocky bodyguard with a goddamn hard-on for her. But the moment I thought of her guard, another slipped into my mind.

The asshole from the command center, the one with a list of the Commission's sons and daughters on the island...including me. "Make double shifts. I want Leila...*Ms. Ivanov,* protected at all times, and I want you to keep an eye out for the Commander's men. I want to know what they're doing."

He gave a nod, his focus slipping for a second to the woman behind me.

"Is that all?" I demanded.

He flinched and jerked his focus back to me, giving nothing away as he answered. "Yes, sir."

"Then leave."

He stepped away, disappearing. I listened to his fading steps before I turned.

"Are we safe here, on the island, I mean?" She searched my eyes for the truth.

I needed to give her that truth, to do everything in my power to make her trust me. "I don't know. But what I do know is we have double the men now. Double the protection. The storm's going to make it difficult to leave. But first chance we get, we're out of here. I'll make sure you're safe, Leila. I'll make sure you stay with me."

I hated the way the words resounded. Hated the rush that came with them.

They were just words. Just fucking words. Still, they meant something to her. I caught her tremble, so I cupped the back of her neck and kissed her again. She reached around and unclasped her bra, holding the lace cups against her, before pulling away. "Then make love to me."

She knew what she wanted, taking a step backwards toward the bedroom. I followed, closed the distance between us, and reached out, then grabbed her around the waist and lifted. She was so light in my arms, and the memory of her from before came rushing back, and with it came the knowledge of what I'd done in that classroom.

The warmth of her body as I carried her toward the infirmary. the silk of her hair as it slid over my arm. Those resounded the loudest. She wrapped her legs around my waist, gripped my neck, and slid her fingers through my hair.

I carried her into the bedroom, and was laying her down on the sheets as out in the living room her phone rang. She flinched and glanced toward the doorway.

"Leave it," I murmured, sliding my hand along her thigh. "They can wait."

This was the first step, the first demand. The first time she gave into me. Drawing her focus to mine, I kissed her again, then rose up, caging her in, until all she knew was me. I bruised her lips, only to pull away and stare down at her. Stars shone in her gaze. Or maybe it was me...*yeah, maybe I was the star she saw.*

My pulse thundered with the thought as I slipped her bra free and lowered my head, kissing the crest of her breast until I took the hard peak into my mouth.

She moaned...and I was captured by the sound.

"Alexi..." she whispered.

I licked the tip of her peak. "Yeah?"

But there was nothing left to say...nothing the shudder that tore through her didn't tell me.

I wasted no time moving to the button of her pants, and slid her zipper low. She held my gaze as I skimmed the elastic of her panties, then slipped my fingers inside.

One slow slide into her slit and she arched her back, moaning as I pushed in, finding her little clit. I'd bet she'd never been touched like this. Bet 'all she'd had was her own fingers. Her own fantasy...she'd been missing out.

"Have you ever...done anything like this?" I danced around that nub, drawing slow careful circles, never once sliding into her pussy, even as she bucked her hips against me.

"Does it matter?" she whispered, staring into my eyes.

It mattered to her, I saw that. "Not in the slightest," I growled, pushing my fingers deeper until I slid all the way inside.

Her eyes fluttered and her breath escaped with a whoosh. I was hooked on that sound. The rush...the *intensity*. I slipped in, only to draw out and circle her clit once more. "Yeah, you're brand fucking new, aren't you, tsarina?"

She bit her lip, dragging her teeth across the swollen fresh, still red from my mouth. "This is what you want, right?"

My smile grew wider. "Let me show you what I want." I pulled my fingers free from her. Slick glistened against the tips as I slid them into my mouth.

Her breath caught. I could almost see the desire rippling through her as I sucked, taking the salty, perfect taste of her deeper before I pulled my fingers free and gripped the waistband of her pants. I eased away, pulled her pants from her body, and cast them aside.

"I want you to see yourself. To figure out what gets you off..." I looked at her, lying there dressed in nothing more than blush pink panties...that I was sure were the color of her pussy.

She swallowed hard. "W-what gets me off?"

"Yeah, tsarina...what makes you wet." I gripped the edges of her panties and pulled them down her thighs.

Her hand slipped between her thighs, covering herself. I dropped her panties to the floor, and met her gaze. Inch by inch, I lowered my head until I kissed the inside of her thigh.

"You're still dressed," she whispered.

I kept going, kissing higher. "This is all about you, tsarina."

"You think I'm a princess?"

I kissed the back of the hand she held over her core. "My Russian princess," I answered, and licked the creases of her fingers. One hard probe of my tongue, and her fingers splayed, revealing perfect pink.

I licked again, drawing a guttural moan from her. She was fucking perfection, widening her fingers for me as I probed deeper. I didn't rush her, let her widen her fingers at her own pace, until she drove her hips into the bed and splayed herself wide. I wound my arms underneath her, tilting her hips to my mouth. "Like I said, princess...what makes you wet."

A shudder rippled through her core at my words before I pushed against the mattress, rising above her. "Want to know what you taste like?"

Hard breaths came as she slowly nodded. I took her mouth, driving my tongue in as I slipped my fingers along her crease. I pulled away, sliding my other hand around her back and pulled her upright. "Watch yourself," I urged.

Her gaze went to my hand between her thighs. I slowly fucked her, sliding my fingers inside. I said nothing, just watched her watching herself. My fingers slipped in easily as she rocked her hips against me. She was so fucking wet. Her core tightened around me as she bit her lip and whimpered.

"That's it." I urged. "Come for me, princess."

With the words, she dropped her head back and thrust upwards, crying out her release. I sucked in hard breaths, watching her. I didn't love her...I barely knew her. I wanted to use her, use her body, use her fucking heart. I'd leave her if I had an option, leave her behind and never look back. But as I watched the flush rise in her cheeks, something else fluttered from that dark hole inside me, like a feather rising on a gust of wind. A feather that rose higher and higher, until without thinking, I leaned in and kissed her.

But this kiss was different...

This kiss was for me.

She opened her mouth. Her hand found mine, pressing against her back. Her long fingers slid between mine, holding me against her. I deepened the kiss, my pulse booming as I grew hard. That hunger burned in me, and for a second, I forgot about the wall I found myself up against and I gave into the moment, letting myself *feel* her.

Her heat.

Her body.

Her mouth.

She rocked her hips once more...but this time it wasn't for her, it was for me. She wanted me, wanted me to see myself between her thighs, wanted me to imagine myself cock deep in her pussy. A groan tore free at the image...until I broke the kiss and pulled away. I slid my hand from under hers and eased back off the bed.

Her eyes opened as a look of confusion swept across her face. "Alexi?"

I tried to force a smile, tried and failed...the room spun as my pulse rocketed out of control. "I'm fine, everything is fine."

But that look of concern on her face only grew darker. I stepped backwards, then turned, headed for the kitchen, and I poured myself a drink. My hands were shaking as I lifted the glass to my lips. I took a long swallow, letting the hate burn all the way into my belly. She was too real in this moment, too warm, too... everything, and I didn't know what to do. I closed my eyes and drank again, until that panic inside me subsided. I listened to the pad of her bare feet on the floor. It took a moment before she walked out, dressed in her panties and her blouse.

"Is everything okay?" She was nervous when she came closer. I hated to see that, hated the fact that I'd done that.

"Yeah, I guess that it just all hit me."

She came around the counter and slid her hand along my arm. "Your friend, Baldeon?"

I met her gaze and nodded. "Him, and everything else."

"You know, you don't need to go through this alone, you have me."

That was just it, wasn't it? I did have her. I had her right where I wanted her, in my bed.

I needed to keep focused on that. I drained my glass and grabbed the bottle in her hand, pulling her toward the bedroom once more. I took her back to bed, and kissed her as the wind howled and raged all around us.

I kissed her until kissing her felt like the most natural thing in the world.

I kissed her until I hated myself, until finally she closed her eyes and slept.

TWENTY-SIX

Alexi

HER PHONE RANG AGAIN FOR THE THIRD TIME. I LOOKED down at her exposed bare leg, the edge of the sheet barely cresting the curve of her ass. She was beautiful, even if she was clueless. I bent down, grabbed her phone, and looked at the caller ID.

Theon...

My jaw clenched as I looked back at her, then switched the phone off. She didn't need Theon, whoever he was. She didn't need anyone but me. I took the phone with me as I left the room, leaving her asleep. It was late, and dark outside. I'd made love to her for hours, taking my time...but not taking my fill, not yet.

I went into the kitchen, placed her phone on the counter, and grabbed a fresh bottle of Scotch as I lifted my gaze to the storm that lashed the island. It was dark outside, just after midnight. She'd been asleep for a few hours. I lay there beside her, still fully clothed, as she curled her body around mine, until I couldn't lie there any longer.

My cell gave a *beep*, so I eased up slowly, went into the living room, and grabbed it from the sofa.

Jager: word is that Haelstrom Hale is on his way there. Stay out of his way, Alexi. We don't need trouble like that in our lives.

Haelstrom Hale...

I reread the name. What the fuck was he doing coming to the island? I lifted my focus to the howling wind outside, especially now. The question haunted me as I raised the glass to my lips and drank. I lost myself as I stared out the window, watching the brutal storm unleashing on the island. The window glass trembled and vibrated. I glanced toward the bedroom, expecting her to awake from the roar. But she didn't. If she woke, she didn't come out of the bedroom. So I drained my glass before pouring another.

Tomorrow the storm would be over. Blue skies would be revealed once more...ushering in a new day...and my way out of this mess. I glanced behind me to her phone on the counter. First things first. I'd need to figure out who her attack dogs were before I rewarded them with her safety...then used them against the feds.

Thud!

The sound snapped my gaze back to the darkness outside. I stared at the heavy palm, uprooted and hurled through the air like it was nothing. It seemed a lot of things were being unleashed tonight...my purpose was only one of them. I drank until the darkness outside blurred and the wind no longer howled. I drank until I found myself sitting on the sofa, staring out the window, nursing what was left of the Scotch...until the darkness outside slipped in...and claimed me.

THE EMPTINESS GREW LIGHTER, and the rush of my own breath in my ears pulled me closer to the surface. I became aware of another sound, another rush of breath, and cracked open my eyes.

She stood there, her hair wet, the long sodden strands soaking my shirt...my shirt she wore. For a second, I panicked, trying to piece it all together, until her name came to me...*Leila Ivanov... that's right.* "Morning," I muttered.

"Good morning," she said carefully, glancing at the sofa beside me.

I slowly lowered my gaze, agony throbbing in my temples with the movement, as I saw the almost empty bottle of Scotch beside me. That explained a lot. *Beep...*

My phone lit up with a message.

Vad: I'll tell them...I'll tell them everything.

Panic punched to the surface. I snatched my cell from the sofa and met her gaze, searching for a flicker of alarm. But she gave nothing away, just turned her head, then met my gaze and murmured, "I was thinking about making omelette for breakfast."

I licked my lips. In the corner of my eye, the storm clouds were even darker than last night. "You cook?"

She cocked her head. "You sound surprised."

I forced a smile, pushing up from the sofa. "Pleasantly."

She chuckled at that, the sound deep and husky, so very different from everything else about her. I tried to gather my thoughts as she walked into the kitchen and the sound of drawers opening came, before the clunk of a frying pan. I waited for her to be busy, before I turned over my cell.

Fucking Vad...

My pulse raced. She'd almost seen...almost realized I wasn't the man she thought I was...she'd almost had an opportunity to run.

I'll fucking kill him.

I winced as I looked at the time. It was after noon. Christ, I'd slept through the morning. *Haelstrom Hale is flying in...*Jager's message rose in my mind as she cracked eggs into a bowl.

"Your cell rang last night." As I watched her from the living room. "I switched it off, I didn't want to wake you." I explained, knowing she'd see the cell sitting there.

The smell of onions, and bacon wafted through the space as she poured eggs into the pan making my belly howl. She cooked and I watched, until she cut one omelette into two and slid them on each plate. "Whoever it was, they seem insistent."

She flinched as she sat, glancing at her cell, and murmured, "It's nothing."

I followed her to the table, sat and picked up my fork, cut the corner and heaped it into my mouth. "Nothing? Didn't seem like nothing to me."

She jerked her gaze to mine, her eyes widening. "Are you jealous?"

I just gave a shrug, trying my best to look unaffected. But it worked. She gave a shake of her head. "I'm not in a relationship if that's what you're implying."

The cell vibrated as it loaded. I leaned over the counter and glanced at the screen. "Ten missed calls, doesn't seem like nothing to me."

She pressed the number then put it on speaker, and across the distance, I heard the phone ring.

"Mia!" The bark was savage, and desperate. "Where the hell have you been? Why haven't you answered my calls?"

"I've been busy, Theon. If you don't already know, there's been some problems on the island," she answered carefully, her eyes never once leaving my gaze.

"Of course I know, why do you think I've been so frantic to get hold of you?"

I could hear the barely restrained savagery in his voice, the desperation for her to obey. This man was dangerous, no, it was more than dangerous. He was exactly what I wanted, the kind of man that would take on the world for her. And I knew it.

I stepped closer, keeping my voice steady. "This is Alexi Kilpatrick. I want you to know that Leila is safe here with me."

Silence came through the phone, one that carved me to the bone.

"Mia? Are you safe with this man?"

I kept my gaze fixed on the cell, never giving her an option to read my mind.

"Alexi has been very hospitable," she answered carefully. There was a shaking her voice, one she didn't like, but one I enjoyed. "I'm staying in his second bedroom, we decided it was best to combine security."

"But does it have to be in his apartment, Mia?"

That was the question wasn't it, that was what this man, whoever he was to her, needed to know about everything else. What exactly was she doing here? What exactly was I doing to her? I could tell him...but then I knew without a doubt, I'd be digging my own grave.

"I can assure you, Mr...."

"Volkov," he supplied.

"Volkov," I continued, "That Ms. Ivanov is perfectly safe here. My brother, Jager, is working to find a way to get us off the island at the first opportunity."

"As soon as the storm clears." It wasn't a question, more of a demand.

"The moment the winds die down, she'll be out of here," I promised.

"Mia, take me off speaker," he said carefully.

She obeyed, pressing the button and ending the growl of the man's voice as she lifted the cell to her ear. She spoke in Russian, rapid words punctured by long silences as the man on the other end of the phone spoke. But his tone had changed when it was just them. I turned away, busying myself with the unmerciful gusts of wind that tore across the island, all the while doing my best to listen to the call.

She loved him, that was easy to tell in the way her tone lowered until she was barely audible, then there was silence.

I let it linger until it was a heavy, hostile thing before I turned. "That went well," I said with a smile.

Tears shone in her eyes. I froze at the sight, the loud thud in my chest growing louder as a murderous, icy rage moved through me. *The fucking bastard...*

I tried to rein it in, tried to keep my voice from shaking as I glanced away. "Who is he to you?"

She gave a soft bark of laughter. "That's a very good question. My security, my replacement father. But right now...he's a stranger."

Emotions were high between then, at breaking point almost. I forced myself to focus, striding around the counter to open my arms to her. "Family fucking sucks."

She didn't hesitate, just wrapped her arms around me and pushed her face against my chest. I held her, sliding my hands over her back, but there was nothing erotic about it, nothing that I needed. In that moment, I wanted to give, wanted it more than that need to survive whispered. I needed it for me.

We stayed like that for a while, until she pulled away, her eyes dry. "Thank you, Alexi. Thank you for everything."

I grazed my thumb against her cheek, then gently tilted her head to mine before I leaned in and kissed her. The kiss was slow, comforting. Everything she needed, and everything I wanted to give. But I didn't let it turn into more this time. I straightened, remembering. "The day's getting away and we still need to find out when this damn storm is going to end."

The words felt like more than words. They felt real, and dangerous.

She gave a nod, leaving me to step away as I headed for the bedroom, then stepped into the bathroom. But this time I didn't close the door behind me. I left it open, undressing slowly, before I hit the tap and stepped into the spray.

I felt her there, felt her presence come closer to the doorway, until she gained enough confidence to step in. I dropped my head under the spray, not wanting to scare her. I was playing the long game here, the kind of game where I'd be the winner, now that I knew who I was using as my attack. I washed, taking my time, drawing her gaze across my chest as I scrubbed, until I lifted my gaze and met hers. I skimmed the cloth along my stomach, muscles tightened...her gaze was electric as I reached down and cupped my cock.

She swallowed hard...

Yeah, I had her...hook, line, and fucking sinker. "That...Theon seems very protective."

She just nodded, and that made me smile. I cupped my balls, then slipped to my cock, sliding the washcloth along the shaft and all the way to the tip. I grew hard under her gaze. Fuck me, I both hated and loved her watching me, all at the same time. Hated that I loved it...loved that I hated it.

I dropped the washcloth and it hit the floor with a *slap*. Then it was all skin, my fingers curled around my length as it thickened. She said nothing, just watched me, her cheeks blazing red, but she was transfixed. And I was *hooked*...

Watching her watch me as I stroked all the way to the base, then back again. I licked my lips, letting the water run over my shoulders and cascade down my chest.

Talk to her...tell her what you want...

I swallowed hard, shoving that voice to the back of my mind. To speak now would shatter the spell...and right now, it was all about the spell.

Crack!

I froze and jerked my gaze to the doorway as the faint sound of a gunshot rang out.

Crack!

Fuck! I hit the taps, ending the spray, my erection dying away in an instant.

"Alexi?" She stepped backwards and turned toward the bedroom. I strode out, still dripping, and grabbed my jeans from the bed, yanking them on. "Stay here...okay?"

She didn't answer, and I didn't wait, leaving her behind as I strode through the apartment and out into the hall. The elevator was still, unmoving. No sound came from behind the doors, which only left one place...*the stairwell.*

I moved to the door and cracked it open, then stepped into the darkness. My fucking heart was thundering as I raced down the four flights of stairs. Halfway down I cursed, realizing I'd left my fucking cell behind.

But I hurried, hitting the foyer floor as my chest burned and reached for the handle, opening the door an inch to stare through the crack.

The foyer was empty...no fucking guards. No fucking anything. I stepped out just as the glass at the end of the foyer exploded with a *boom!*

Glass flew, crashing against the floor. Outside, a battle raged as three of our guards opened fire, their gunshots cleaving through the howling wind *crack...crack...crack!*

What the fuck? I stepped out, catching sight of three men dressed in black taking cover behind the corner of the building opposite.

I didn't freeze...didn't think. Instinct screamed inside me...demanding I do the only thing I could.

Run!

TWENTY-SEVEN

Leila

Alexi left, charging along the hallway to open the stairwell door and disappeared inside. I tried to hear over the pounding of my heart and the howling wind from outside. But I couldn't hear them. There was no crack of a gunshot... No screams. But I knew they were coming, I knew from the cold dread that spread inside me. I glanced toward the kitchen. *Protect yourself... Protect him.*

I hurried into the kitchen, where the dishwasher was still running from the breakfast I'd made earlier. A large kitchen knife glinted, drying beside the sink. I grabbed it, my fingers curling around the hilt as I made my way back to the hallway, stared at the closed stairwell door, and waited.

I waited for what felt like hours, straining to listen, until footsteps thundered before the door to the stairwell was thrown open, slamming against the wall with a *boom!*

Alexi rushed in, glanced at the knife in my hand, and barked. "We're leaving...*now!*"

I jerked my gaze to the open stairwell door behind him. "What's happened?"

"Nothing good." He disappeared into the closet, and tiny electronic beeps came a second later.

I followed him in, staring from the doorway of the closet as he pulled two guns free from a safe, shoving one in the back of his jeans. "Jeans, Leila, and a sweater. Grab your cell and your passport, we're getting the hell off this island."

Panic tore through me as I did as he said, hurrying from his bedroom and into mine. "How?" I called over my shoulder.

"I don't know, but I'll figure it out."

I tossed the knife to the end of the mattress and quickly pulled on jeans, then socks and boots. I yanked Alexi's shirt over my head as my mind raced, conjuring up terrifying scenarios while I yanked on a sweater and grabbed my weatherproof jacket and my bag, stowing my passport inside.

"Ready?" Alexi asked from the doorway. I nodded, grabbed my knife, and hurried after him, snatching my cell phone from the counter as I raced past.

He slipped into the stairwell, turning to hold out his hand for me. I took it, following him down the stairs. Inside the murky gloom, the wind still seemed to scream, the sound terrifying. Still, I followed Alexi, gripping the railing with one hand and the knife with the other. The moment we stepped into the foyer, I froze. There was glass everywhere, wind tearing through the gaping holes in the glass wall. "What happened?"

"Come on, follow me." Alexi pulled me with care, scanning the grounds before we pushed through the automatic doors and stepped out into the violent winds.

Crack!

Gunshots rang out and Alexi was lifting his hand, the muzzle of his weapon aimed beyond our guards as he returned fire. Two men dressed in black took cover around the corner of the building in front of us. Then one stepped out, raised his gun, and opened fire, hitting the guard in front of us with a *smack*.

The guard stumbled backwards, then went down to one knee as blood bloomed from his shoulder. The sight was terrifying.

I froze, jerking my gaze to Alexi as he opened fired again. But he didn't rush to help the guard, instead he glanced over his shoulder, tightened his grip on my hand, and pulled me forward at a run.

We were almost across the grounds when another man dressed in black rushed toward us, his arm raised over his head. The glint of the knife in his hand was barely visible.

"*Alexi!*" I screamed as the attacker veered through the palms outside the building and lunged.

Alexi lifted his gun, but he wasn't fast enough, taking the blow with a grunt as the killer hit him hard. They hit the ground with a thud, Alexi punching to try and get out from under him, but without success. The man was not just a murderer, he was probably an ex-soldier, grappling with a savage, steely grip.

I caught the knife as it sliced through the air before it hit Alexi. He screamed, agony tearing across his face. I couldn't stop myself, charging like a madwoman and raised the knife

I drove the knife down and plunged the blade into the attacker's shoulder. He jerked upwards, flinging his arm around to knock me sideways. Agony roared through my side as I fell, hitting the ground hard, but then I pushed upwards and scrambled toward them again.

My knife was gone, knocked from my hand by the blow. One fast scan of the ground, and I found it lying in front of the asshole as he wrestled with Alexi. But I couldn't use their guns, I didn't dare in case I hit Alexi. So I used what I could...*my nails.*

With a scream, I leaped, landing on the attacker's back. I shoved my fingers into his eyes and dug them in. He thrashed underneath me, but this time he let Alexi go. That was all I could see, all I could feel, as the attacker tried to turn on me. But I fought, I fought for Alexi and I fought for me. I screamed my rage into his ear as I continued to dig my fingers into his eyes as hard as I could, until the squelch made me freeze.

The bastard swung and hit me in the chest, then he was on top of me, his eyes streaming thick bloody tears. I tried to fight as he wrapped his hands around my throat and screamed at me. "Fucking bitch!"

Alexi pushed upwards. *"Get the fuck off her!"* he roared, lifted his gun, pressed it to the man's head, and pulled the trigger.

Boom!

Splatters of warmth hit my cheek as I screamed. But Alexi didn't stop, he just bent down, grabbed my hand, and hauled me upwards. "We have to keep moving."

But he was bleeding, the bright red stain spreading across his shirt, sticking it against his skin. "Alexi, you're hurt."

He glanced down and winced before shaking his head. "We can't worry about that now." He lifted his head, and froze.

I spun, following his gaze as he caught sight of a man running from a building in the distance, heading toward the hangar.

"Sonofabitch," he growled, curling his lips. "Come on."

He pulled me with him as we hurried across the grounds, heading toward the towering steel structure where a man had disappeared. I didn't know who we were following, all I knew was that with every step Alexi turned more savage. He lifted his gun as we neared the closed door at the back of the hangar and dropped my hand. He got to the door first, sweeping the gloom inside before he stepped in.

I followed two steps behind, my heart pounding, and the roar of the wind deafening, until we were inside. But the moment my hearing adjusted, I heard what sounded like a jet's engines starting, the low whines gaining momentum until they snarled.

"*Going somewhere, Kardinov?*" Alexi yelled.

Through the darkness, a man was climbing the stairs into the jet. He froze and lifted his gun as he turned toward us. Cold, calculating eyes met mine before they turned back to Alexi. "You know how it is, Kilpatrick. Every man for himself."

"We're coming, too," Alexi snarled, pulling me toward the stairs.

Until the asshole halfway on the jet lifted his gun and took aim in the middle of Alexi's chest. "I don't think so..."

Panic filled me. I sucked in hard breaths as gunfire erupted outside the hangar once more. Alexi didn't stop, taking a step forward. "I'm not asking, Vad...*I'm telling.*"

"You know what I want," the man roared, his eyes wild as he glared at Alexi. "Give me that and you can come."

Rage flashed across Alexi's face, turning it dark and bestial as the asshole took a step up the stairs.

"*She's my FUCKING SISTER!*"

"I know." The man called Kardinov answered. "Give me what I want, Alexi, and I'll let you on."

The jet's engines grew louder, smothering the cracks of the shots behind us. Terror moved through me as Alexi turned away, glancing behind us, then with a roar, he turned back, yanking me with him as he headed for the stairs.

Kardinov just smiled, then stepped into the jet, leaving us to race after him.

TWENTY-EIGHT

Leila

We climbed onto the jet as it started moving. Alexi closed the door, locked it in place, and stumbled as the jet surged forward. We were already moving, rolling out of the hangar as Kardinov slid into a seat, watching us as we stumbled to the other side and fell into ours.

Blood smeared across the white leather seat. I stared at the mess, then lifted my gaze to Alexi, who ground his teeth, his lips pressed tight.

But there was nothing we could do, only buckle up as the jet tore down the runway.

I'd barely had enough time to buckle my seatbelt before we were rising, lifting higher and higher. I didn't have enough time to be terrified, not like I'd been before. Out the window, all I could see was blue. My stomach clenched as the jet rose, barely missing the water, it seemed. Then we soared upwards into those thunderous gray clouds.

Kardinov stared straight ahead, then slowly turned to meet my gaze.

I didn't like him. His cold, calculated gaze turned back to the front of the jet. "You're bleeding all over the leather, Kilpatrick," he muttered.

"Yeah? Suck my fucking dick, Vad," Alexi spat.

His words conjured the memory of where he was right before the sound of gunfire had exploded. My pulse raced as the image of him filled my mind. My God, he was beautiful, standing under the shower spray, water running in rivulets down his sculpted body. I'd never seen a man so stunning, never seen a man like Alexi before.

He pressed his hand against the wound and winced. I could see he was in pain, his skin paling.

"Let me help," I demanded, dropping my hand to my belt.

He just shook his head. "No. Not until we reach altitude."

So we waited, and I watched him grow even paler, until I could barely take it a second longer. "Now, Alexi," I insisted, staring at the spreading bloodstain.

"The first aid kit's in the bedroom," Kardinov muttered. "Help yourself to both."

I yanked the clasp on my seatbelt and pushed to rise, stumbling until I caught my balance. Alexi just lifted his gaze, looking up at me before he followed, unbuckling his belt and rising. I glanced around the cabin, finding a doorway in the back of the jet, then gripped his waist, guiding him between the seats.

But he never buckled, just lifted his hand and braced against the wall as I opened the door and stepped in. The room was small and gloomy. A large bed took up most of the space, but on the other side was a small bathroom. "Come on, let me get you fixed up."

Alexi closed the door and followed me around the bed, sitting on the edge as I flicked on the overhead light and searched under the sink for the first aid kit. It was hard to miss, big and red. I grabbed it and rose, turning around to find Alexi staring at me.

I worked in silence, setting the kit beside him before I tugged at his shirt.

"You went after him," Alexi commented as he lifted his arms while I pulled his shirt over his head. "Never seen anything like that in my entire life."

He glanced at my fingers. I didn't need to think further to know what he meant. "He was going to hurt you. I couldn't let that happen," I answered and opened the kit.

The wound wasn't as deep as I'd expected, but it still seeped, and I wasn't the one he'd want trying to stitch him, especially not in a jet. I threw out my hand and gripped the edge of the mattress as the jet bounced. Then I opened a vial and grabbed some gauze, cleaning the wound. It gaped, and blood oozed from the edges. "You'll need stitches."

"But I'll live, thanks to you," he answered.

I flinched. He was right...*because of me*. Heat rushed through me as I grabbed some bandage strips, closing the wound together with the slim pieces of adhesive, until he reached up, gripped the back of my neck, and guided my mouth to his.

He kissed me like this was the end. Hard, consuming, pulling me close. After a second, I gave in, letting myself melt against him. His other hand moved between my thighs, gently rubbing me. I was absorbed by the feel of him, his hand around my neck, his fingers pressing against my core. I knew where this was heading, but this time I wanted more.

I didn't want him distant, didn't want him fully clothed while I was naked. I wanted all of him...his panic, his passion...even the things he'd kept from me. Things like the message from Vad Kardinov on his cell this morning. I broke the kiss, pulled the blood-splattered sweater over my head, and pulled down the straps of my bra, staring into his eyes. "I want you."

He stared at my breasts, then slowly lifted his gaze to mine, giving me the ghost of a smile. "Sorry, tsarina. With all the stabbing and the shooting, I didn't come prepared."

"I don't care," I assured him as I shifted my gaze to the wound on his side, then met his focus once more. "I'll be careful."

He froze, that smile fading in an instant, leaving behind something haunted. "You really want me riding you bare for your first time, princess?"

Bare...I licked my lips and dropped my gaze to his pants, to the thick outline of his cock inside his jeans. My core clenched and my pulse stuttered. "Yes," I answered. "That's exactly what I want."

There was a flicker of surprise on his face before it was swallowed by fear. He licked his lips, then his gaze moved down to my breasts as I reached around and unhooked my bra, letting it fall to the bedroom floor. We could die here, with our recent run of luck, it was probably inevitable. There's no way in hell I was going to die a virgin. "Unless you don't want to?"

"Yes." The answer came in a rush as he lifted his gaze to mine. "I want to."

I lowered my hands to the button of my jeans then released it and the zipper before sliding them to the floor. "Good."

His hand went to his jeans and, unlike last time, he didn't hesitate. My chest fluttered with happiness. He'd been holding himself back from me, giving me things he thought I needed. He'd treated me like a conquest...that had hurt me.

But I still put my faith in him, knowing that underneath the lies and the deceit was the man I wanted...and in this moment, the way he looked at me, I saw that man rise to the surface.

He shoved his jeans down and placed his guns on the pillow beside him. My panties hit the floor, that sense of urgency roaring inside me. But that's where I wanted him...right there, teasing and tasting. He kicked his jeans free and reached for me, grabbing me under my arms before pulling me closer.

A wince of agony cut across his face, but he didn't stop...he didn't even slow, sliding my body over his until my legs splayed wide, straddling him.

"You sure about this, princess?"

I reached down, cupping his cock. "Surer than I've ever been in my life."

He closed his eyes with the contact and released a pent up breath. I wanted to look at him forever, that look of serenity...that *rush*.

But I needed to know him, needed to look and taste and feel. I slid my body down, guiding him to my mouth.

"Jesus, Leila," he groaned.

A charge of happiness swept through me with the sound of my name. The thick vein pulsed under his shaft, making him thicken in my hand. This wasn't what I'd dreamed of for my first time. It wasn't anywhere near...*it was better.*

I closed my eyes and opened my mouth, taking him inside. The head of his cock felt smooth against my tongue, gliding as I moved deeper, taking as much as I could.

"Tsarina..."

Princess...his Russian princess...

I gripped his shaft, closed my mouth around him, and sucked.

The guttural moan was like a drug. I took him again, letting the tip of my tongue dance around the ridge before he slid his hand under my jaw and tilted my head upwards. I opened my eyes and our gazes collided. He was everything in that moment. My protector, my lover...the man I knew I wanted.

He pulled me against him, looking down between my legs. I was already buzzing, already charged. One slow slide of his finger along my slit, and I shuddered with desire.

"So wet, tsarina," he murmured.

I lowered my gaze in shame and slowly nodded.

"No shame here, not when it comes to me, okay?" He gripped my chin, forcing my focus to his.

Darkness welled in his gaze. The kind that terrified me, the kind I'd seen in my father...and Theon. Still, I was used to that darkness, used to the deceit. I just wished for different. He slid his finger along my crease, curling it to dance around my nub. I shuddered, gripped his arm, and dropped my head.

Emotions rushed to the surface. They were so close here, so close with him. He gripped my hips, pulling me higher, until his cock slipped against me. I caught my breath, my pulse a panicked thrum in my ears as he rocked me, slowly riding the length of him until, with one slight shift of his hips, he pushed inside me.

He held his finger against my chin, staring into my eyes, and that slow rocking drove him in deeper...until he could go no more.

"Right here, princess," he said, his voice husky. "Don't look away."

He gave a hard thrust, driving against the barrier. An icy burn stole my breath and tore a whimper free. Still, I clutched hold of him, riding out the searing sting. He thrust slowly, then looked down.

I followed his gaze to the bright red smear on his cock.

"Fuck me," he groaned, and thrust again. "You're mine now, tsarina. *All mine*...no one can have that now. That was all mine."

His...

The word moved through me, easing that pain, until there was only the desire behind. Hate turned into flames, until I found myself moving with the slow rock of his hips. A look of concentration filled his gaze as need raged inside him. I clung to his arms, driving my hips up against him until, with an uncontrollable surge, lightning tore through me.

I dropped my head back, unleashing a low moan that came from the back of my throat. He dropped his hands to my hips, his grip taut until his fingers bruised my flesh. He moved, pushing forward until there was nowhere for me to go. Slow, steady thrusts turned brutal until he unleashed his power into me, fucking me until I lost control.

That lightning returned, blazing through me until I saw stars and, with a growl, he stilled, deep inside me...

TWENTY-NINE

Alexi

She curled her body around mine, her hand sliding across my stomach, needing to touch me even as she slept. I didn't like this urgency I felt, or this ache in my chest when I looked at her.

Christ...I didn't want to see the smear of her blood on my cock, and the memory of what I'd done.

I took her for the first time...took that which should've been another man's to take.

A better man...someone other than me.

This was getting too complicated. *She* was getting too complicated. I reached down and gripped her wrist, carefully pulling it from my body. But the moment her warmth left, I stilled. I didn't want her to move, didn't want the bed beside me cold anymore. I didn't want to be looking over my shoulder. For the first time in forever, I wanted more than my lonely existence.

I wanted her...

I winced and turned away, listening to her steady breaths as she slept thirty-thousand feet in the air. I closed my eyes, letting myself drift off, until I felt the stillness. It was more than stillness...the sound of the engines had changed...almost as though we were on the ground. The sound of footsteps outside the bedroom drew my focus. Something wasn't right, something had changed.

I opened my eyes and glanced her way. She still slept, her lips parted, a perfect look of peace on her face. I reached up and brushed the strands of her hair aside, then quietly rose from the bed.

I pulled on my jeans, then my shirt, padding barefoot to the closed door. A clink came from outside the door. I opened it and stepped out, finding a stewardess, who spun and stared at me. "Mr. Kilpatrick, I hope I didn't wake you, sir."

I scowled, scanning the jet and found us on the ground. "Kardinov?"

"He's gone, but he left instructions for you and Ms. Ivanov not to be disturbed. He's also taken the liberty of ordering you fresh clothes and food."

I glanced toward the closed door as the jet started to move. "Where are we?"

"Dubai, sir," she answered.

I gave a nod. So Vad had left us, scurrying back to whatever rock he'd crawled out from under. I glanced at the hanging clothes, the neat suit for me, expensive by the looks of it. I stepped closer, fingering the fabric as I glanced at the caramel-colored slacks and sheer off-white top for Leila. Whatever else the man was, he wasn't cheap.

The smell of food hit me and my stomach growled as the door opened behind me and Leila stepped out. But she didn't smile, she just winced, holding the cell phone to her ear, then met my gaze and murmured, "It's Theon, and he wants to speak to you."

THIRTY

Leila

Put him on the phone, Mia...

The words rang in my ears as I stepped out of the bedroom of the jet, to find Alexi talking to a stewardess. I didn't have time to feel jealousy, all I felt was fear at Theon's cold, dangerous tone. I held out the phone. "It's Theon, and he wants to speak to you."

But Alexi didn't even blink. It was as though he'd been expecting it. He just stepped closer, took my cell, and held it to his ear. "This is Alexi."

I couldn't hear the words that were spoken on the other end, but there was silence from the man in front of me. Silence as he listened to the wrath of my bodyguard. He didn't speak, other than to say. "I understand." once or twice.

But did he understand?

Or would he leave now?

After a few moments, he lowered his hand, the call already disconnected. "Well, that went as well as I'd expected."

"They knew about the attack," I murmured, meeting his gaze.

"Everyone must know by now." He motioned toward a seat as the jet began to move again.

I followed him, taking my seat and clasping the seatbelt closed, then glancing at the clothes hanging from the hangers outside the bedroom door. "Did you do that?"

"No, apparently they're a gift," he forced the words through clenched teeth.

"Vad?" I asked.

A nod was all he gave me. He didn't like the idea of Vad Kardinov buying us clothes, yet here we were, riding in his jet. I scanned the space, searching for him.

"Don't bother," Alexi growled. "He's gone."

So he'd left us to fly to the US on our own? That seemed almost...nice. Silence filled the space between us as the jet surged forward and rose into the air once more. I wanted to ask him what Theon had said, but part of me was too scared to know the truth. Whatever it had been, it wasn't good. So, we passed the time, me lost in my panicked thoughts and Alexi gripping the armrest as he stared straight ahead. When we were high enough, the pilot switched on the no seatbelt light and we could finally move. I looked down at my blood-splattered clothes and winced, suddenly desperate for a shower.

"Do you mind if I use the bathroom?"

Alexi glanced my way. "Use anything you want, tsarina. You don't need to ask me for permission."

I rose from the seat, grabbed the clothes from the hanger, and stepped inside the bedroom once more. The shower was small, but the water was warm. Still, I hurried, not wanting to use it all, and scrubbed my body, working the spots where blood had dried, before stepping out.

I dressed, taking my time, then glanced at the crumpled sheets on the bed as I slid my hand between my legs. The ache was still there, a dull throb. I closed my eyes and bit my lip. I couldn't believe what we'd done, couldn't believe a man like Alexi wanted me. I could still feel him inside me, still taste him on my tongue. I still felt that flying feeling inside me as he'd thrust deep.

I stayed in the bathroom until the hot flush in my cheeks dulled a little, then stepped out. I took my seat next to him, trying to avoid his gaze in case I grew red once more. We spent the rest of the flight in comfortable silence. But the nagging thought in my head continued. I wanted to know what Theon had said to him, I wanted to know what demands he'd made. I could only guess, and guessing felt like torture.

When the plane finally descended and turned, I looked out the window, catching the lights of the city underneath us. "Are we there?"

"We are," Alexi answered.

I gripped the armrest, lost in the sight of the city as we slowly touched down, the jet braking hard to pull up at a private hangar toward the far side of the airport. But when we stepped out of the jet, it wasn't Theon waiting. I scanned the hangar, my heart thundering in my chest. A dark sedan waited for us, the driver standing beside it. But there was another man at his side, one who stood with his arms crossed over his chest. Alexi strode down the stairs and headed for him, opening his arms. They hugged hard, fists thumping against their backs.

The man with brooding dark eyes turned his attention to me. One brow rose. "So, this is..."

My gaze caught his as I neared. "Leila Ivanov."

"Of course it is," he muttered, driving an elbow into Alexi's stomach. "I'm Jager, the better looking brother." He stepped closer and reached for my hand. "I'm glad you two are safe. But don't get too comfortable, Alexi, you and I have things to discuss."

He didn't wait for an answer, but strode toward another car waiting at the edge of the hangar and climbed inside. We were already heading for the waiting driver as he left.

"Is everything okay?" I asked, sliding into the back seat of the sedan as the driver held the door.

"Everything's fine, tsarina," he lied.

I looked out the window as the doors closed and we pulled away. I was captivated by the sights of the city, drawn deep into its clutches as I leaned against the window and looked upwards. Everything in New York was up. We drove to a towering apartment building in the heart of the city. Alexi explained the layout of the city, pointing to the third highest building. "That's it. Not hard to miss, right?"

I couldn't speak...in awe as we pulled into the underground parking garage.

The moment we walked into the foyer, a man rushed around the counter and strode toward Alexi. I was surprised when Alexi shook his hand, murmuring words of thanks. I didn't know what he was thinking. But then Alexi was smiling and turning toward me, but there was a glimmer of fear behind his smile, one I didn't understand.

Alexi motioned me toward the elevator and we rode it all the way up to the penthouse floor. I'd never seen a place like it. It was so far removed from the sprawling grounds where I'd grown up. I was lost in the magic as Alexi strode to the door at the end of the hall, pressed his card against the reader, and opened it for me.

I followed him inside, catching my breath at the sprawling sight in front of me. Mesmerized, I strode forward until I stopped at the floor-to-ceiling window. The city was a blanket of glass shards in front of me, the edges catching the sunlight, glinting into my eyes until I didn't know where to look.

"You like being up this high?" Alexi asked as he opened a refrigerator.

I could only nod. I was more than okay. I didn't ever want to come down. Alexi disappeared into a bedroom, calling out, "I've ordered some food. You probably want to take another shower. God knows, the shower on the jet wasn't the best. I can organize your clothes—"

"When is my father coming?" I asked quietly.

Alexi stepped into the doorway, scowling... Yet, he didn't lie, at least that was something. "Tomorrow," he answered.

Agony carved through my chest with the word. I didn't trust myself to speak, so I gave a nod, strode toward him, and slipped around him as he stood in the doorway.

"Don't you want to go back home, tsarina?"

Tears pricked my eyes as I stepped into the bathroom. It was stupid, I barely knew him... And he doesn't know me, not the real me. Maybe that was best.

"Of course," I answered, working the buttons of my blouse with trembling fingers as I undressed and stepped into the shower.

Warmth cascaded over my head and down my shoulders. I took my time, using his shampoo as I washed my hair, then sank down to the slate tiles and pulled my knees to my chest. The water beat against my back, and under the cover of the shower, I cried. Of course he gave into Theon, because Theon always got his way... just like my father.

They never changed, the thought rippled through me.

But I had... I'd changed, hadn't I?

I lifted my head at the sound of movement in the bedroom, seeing Alexi step into the bathroom. The moment our gazes collided, I knew with certainty what I wanted...and what I wanted was him.

THIRTY-ONE

Alexi

The sight of her sitting on the shower floor, her knees drawn to her chest, brought me undone. With a growl, I yanked my shirt over my head and shoved down my jeans. Anger ripped through me at the sight of her trying to hide her tears under the spray of the water.

She lifted her head and her gaze met mine as I stepped toward her bare form and bent down, lifting her from the floor. My hands cupped her ass, pulling her against me as I pressed her spine against the wall and kissed her. Her hands went around my shoulders as her mouth met mine. She kissed me back this time, her desire ravenous. Still, the sight of her haunted me.

I wanted to fuck the sadness from her, wanted to tear it from her mind and replace it with me.

I eased my hand between us, guiding my cock inside her. She gave a moan with the intrusion and closed her eyes. I braced my hand against the wall and thrust inside her until I lost myself. When I couldn't wait any longer, I hit the taps, held her against me, and walked us from the bathroom, falling onto the bed.

The sheets were soaked, the pillows cast to the floor. I fucked her until I didn't feel like such a bastard. I fucked her until she was all I felt. The bed moved, bouncing hard on every thrust. I closed my eyes, driving deep.

I didn't love her...

The sight of her rising over the bastard who'd stabbed me on the island filled my mind. I lowered my head, kissing the side of her neck. I didn't love her...*because I couldn't love anyone.*

My pulse boomed as her nails stung my back and, with a growl I came...*hard.* Her breaths were harsh in my ear.

"Fuck." I shoved upwards and looked into her eyes. "I'm sorry... you didn't..."

Her arms went around me, pulling me back to her. "I want this...just like this. My body is still...*learning.*"

Learning.

The way she said things made me smile. I looked into her eyes, finding her lips curling.

"I like it when you smile," she murmured.

A quiet knock came at the door. "Yeah?" I pushed from the bed. "I bet you'll love King's pad thai even more."

"Pad thai, what is that?" she asked behind me.

I gave a hard bark of laugher as I yanked on a pair of sweats and strode toward the door. "Don't tell me you've never had Thai food before?"

"No," came the answer behind me as I opened the door and nodded to the security guard, taking the bag of takeout from his hand. "Thanks, Gabe."

"No problem, Mr. Kilpatrick," he answered with a nod. "Good to have you back home."

I closed the door and carried the food into the kitchen. The smell that wafted from the containers made my stomach howl with hunger. I grabbed two plates, then decided to put one back. I piled the mess of silky noodles, sprouts, and peanuts onto the plate, grabbed a fork, and headed for the bedroom. "Then you're in for a treat, aren't you?"

I stepped into the bedroom and sat on the bed as she sat up, the sheets falling around her waist as she looked at the food on the plate. "That looks...unusual."

"Open up, you're going to love this."

She did, parting her lips as I twirled the noodles onto the end of the fork and placed them into her mouth. She was hesitant at first, slowly chewing, savoring, until she swallowed and licked her lips. "That's delicious."

"More?"

She nodded, and elation swept through me. I didn't love her... didn't love the way her eyes sparkled, and the fucking pad thai sauce glistened on her lips. I froze, unable to move as fists beat inside my chest until, with a moan, I set the plate down...and decided to give her that orgasm she'd missed out on...licking the salty sauce from her lips...before I moved between her thighs.

THIRTY-TWO

Alexi

"You okay?" I brushed my fingers along her arm, catching her shiver. We stood in a private hangar of an airport just outside of the city, waiting for her family's jet to arrive.

The wind picked up, tearing across the asphalt, reminding me too much of the howling gusts on the island we'd left behind. I caught the tilt of her head as she lifted her gaze to the sky, and followed the focus. A jet descended, dropping through the clouds, and I knew in my gut this was it. This was the moment I met the Ivanov family and played my hand.

The wheels touched down, and the plane turned, heading toward us. It was expensive, sleek, silver, and fast. The door opened before it barely had a chance to stop moving, and the stairs were lowered. She stiffened the moment a towering male strode out the door, his gaze sweeping the hangar and narrowing in on her.

That had to be Theon.

The way that dangerous gaze moved to me made my gut clench in warning. Another male strode out right behind him, wearing a long, thick gray coat, even as the sun shone above him. I fixed my gaze on Maxim Ivanov as he gripped the railing and made his way down the stairs. He was smaller than I'd imagined, didn't look quite as dangerous as I'd been led to believe. But the towering male in front of him, the one who now strode across the asphalt and headed straight to us, he was dangerous enough for both of them.

"Mia?" He gripped her neck, his thick thumb tilting her jaw as he stared into her eyes. "Are you okay?"

I didn't like the way he touched her, didn't like his hands on her. My jaw clenched as a brutal chill swept through me. I cleared my throat, drawing his focus as her father made his way toward us. But he didn't look at his daughter, just fixed his gaze on me. There was no life in those eyes, nothing but ice.

"Mr. Kilpatrick." His quiet voice was thick with his accent.

I stepped forward, holding out my hand. "Mr. Ivanov, nice to meet you."

He didn't smile, still hadn't even looked at his daughter. This man was all business, all control. I now knew what it felt like to step into a viper's den.

"You hurt? Did they hurt you, Mia?" Theon demanded.

"No," she lied.

She *was* hurt. There were bruises on her sides and scratches on her body. I'd watched as her skin turned purple, and kissed where it was raw. But she wouldn't admit that to this man. Not now, maybe not ever. She wasn't the quiet, timid woman I'd thought she was at first.

She took a step backwards, leaving his hands to linger in the air before they fell.

"When you're on the plane, we'll discuss exactly what happened." Theon held her gaze, never once meeting mine.

"I'm not coming," she announced.

There was a sharp blare of a siren behind me. I spun, finding two silver unmarked sedans racing toward us, lights flashing behind their grills. What the fuck? I knew the moment they pulled up, knew with a sinking feeling what this was. I winced at the glare from the sun glinting off the windshield as the passenger door opened and Hannah climbed out.

One movement of her hand, and two more agents climbed out of the second vehicle and strode toward us.

"Leila Ivanov?" Hannah strode toward her, pulling her badge from her pocket and flashing it at us. "You are under arrest for suspicion of espionage. You have the right to remain silent. Anything you say can be used against you in court. Do you understand?"

My stomach dropped and panic ripped through me as the bitch I knew so intimately pulled a set of handcuffs from her waistband and came toward us.

"What?" Leila gasped, her eyes widening. "I don't understand."

"What the hell do you think you're doing?" Theon stepped in front of her as the agents got closer to us.

Not once did the bitch look my way as she lifted the cuffs in her hand. "Move," Hannah ordered, staring up at the bodyguard. "Unless you'd like me to arrest you too."

"Theon," Maxim called.

There was a second when I thought the bodyguard was about to draw down on the bitch. A second when I imagined the terror we'd fought through on the island had found its way here...and this time, neither of us would make it out alive. The bodyguard seemed to recognize that. His lips curled, teeth bared, until with a slow step, he moved away.

"I'm sure you have questions." Hannah glanced my way as she pulled out a card and handed it to Maxim Ivanov. "I'll be happy to answer any you might have..."

The agents surrounded us as Hannah fastened the handcuffs around Leila's wrists.

"You fucking bitch," I snarled, clenching my fists.

Only then did she turn her head and meet my gaze. "Take her," she ordered before she turned and strode back to the car.

There wasn't a damn thing I could do to stop her, not without risking it all. Panic filled me as I watched one of the agents grip Leila's arm, pulling her until she stumbled sideways.

"I don't understand, what's going on?" Leila's voice was shrill, her eyes wide as she stared at her father. She fought them, like I knew she would, yanking her arm from the agent as he pulled her toward the vehicle. "*Get the fuck off me!*"

Maxim didn't flinch, just watched as they led his daughter toward the open door of the vehicle and shoved her inside. My mind raced, trying to figure a way out of this, a way that got Leila free and kept me alive.

A car's engine roared to life. There wasn't a damn thing I could do as I watched Hannah back her car out onto the runway, and drive away.

"I think it's about time you told me what the hell is happening..." Maxim turned his head toward me. "Don't you?"

THIRTY-THREE

Leila

The driver's door opened as I twisted in my seat, staring back through the rear window at Alexi, Theon, and my father.

Theon was enraged, clenching his fists and striding toward the car. Alexi and my father just stood there, wearing the same cold, steely expression. They could almost be the same man.

The passenger's door closed with a *thud*. The driver's door followed, and the car started, pulling away, leaving my family behind. I didn't say a word, staring at the woman who'd just arrested me. *Espionage.* That's what she'd said, right? They thought I was a spy? I tried to think of any reason they'd think that.

Spy...

My heart raced as memories came flooding back. The gunmen and the attack. Could it have something to do with them? I'd thought we were free of them, thought whatever horror had happened, we were safe holed up in Alexi's apartment.

A sickening feeling washed through me as we left the small airport behind. They said nothing to me, driving in silence as we headed back toward the city. I clenched my fists, trying to hold on to the thin thread of sanity. How could they think that about me, how could they believe I'd come here to spy?

I'd come here because of my father. Because I was a good girl and did as I was told. I'd come, even though I didn't want to, when I'd rather have stayed back home. Viktoriya's face filled my mind. Could this have something to do with her?

They drove me across the city, but this time I didn't look up at the towering buildings as they closed in on the sides. This time, I stared straight ahead, desperate to see where we were heading. I twisted to reach for my pocket, pulling my cell free. There was a message, one I'd received with the ringer turned down.

Theon: Hang tight, we're going to get you out of this.

I swallowed hard, whispering a prayer...*please hurry*. The car slowed, then turned sharply into the driveway of a building and pulled up at the guard hut outside. The woman in front flashed a badge and the boom gate lifted, leaving us to drive through. Tires squealed against the concrete as the car turned in then pulled up in front of a set of doors.

My heart jumped as car doors were opened and slammed shut, before the rear door was opened beside me. They didn't say a word, just waited until I slowly shifted across the seat and climbed out. The woman motioned me forward with a nod of her head, as another agent stepped close and gripped my arm.

I had no choice but to follow as they led me through the set of doors and into a foyer. The letters CIA were embedded in the floor under my feet. I stared at it, until I was pulled toward the elevator. We still moved in silence.

When the elevator doors opened, they escorted me along the hallway and into an empty room. The moment I stepped inside the cameras in the corner of the room shifted toward me. One of the agents stepped closer, releasing the cuffs, leaving me to rub the ache.

"Sit." The woman motioned to a chair.

I looked at her and the man next to her, unable to move for a second, until I finally took a step and sank onto the chair. The door opened, drawing my gaze.

"Do you need an interpreter?" the woman asked.

But I was too busy staring at the man who strode in to hear her.

He seemed almost familiar, with rolled-up sleeves on his white shirt and the top button undone. He glanced toward me, but those dark eyes gave nothing away.

"Well?" the woman snapped.

I flinched at the bark. "Sorry?"

"Do you...need an interpreter?"

I shook my head.

"Good." She folded her arms across her chest and stared down at me.

"What's going on here?" I asked, looking from the man to the woman, desperate to try and make sense of this.

"What's going on, Ms. Ivanov...is there is a suspicion against you."

A suspicion against me? I didn't know what that meant. The woman crossed the floor, carrying the file the man had handed to her. She dropped it on the desk in front of me with a *slap*, making me flinch.

"I want you to tell me about this," she said, opening the file and spreading out photos of me and my father leaving Russia. I knew it was Russia, knew by the thick white coat I wore, the same one I'd had on the last time I saw Viktoriya.

"I don't understand. This is us leaving Russia to come here." I lifted my gaze to hers. There was a spark of cruelty in her eyes, one that blazed hatred. She hated me, hated me for reasons I didn't understand. A knock came at the door and the man leaning against the wall opened it and walked out, closing the door behind him. I was captured by the movement, my heart pounding in my chest.

"What were you doing with Alexi Kilpatrick?" The question was low, barely audible. I flinched and jerked my gaze to hers.

My breath caught, as the door opened once more and the man strode back in, crossed the room, and leaned down to whisper in her ear, forcing her to turn her head.

But I'd seen it...the spark of rage, the venomous stab of jealousy. That was it...she was jealous. Jealous of me being with Alexi. My gaze drifted over her as the man whispered in her ear. She was beautiful, in a hardened way. Hungry and ruthless, she knew what she wanted, and, as the man straightened and she turned back to me once more, I saw that what she wanted was revenge.

"Your passport says Mauritius, Ms. Ivanov. Want to tell us why you were there...and why you left?"

I heard the words, but they didn't make sense. Because I was still trapped by that rage inside her, and the image of her in my head. Images where Alexi had her on a bed, arms braced on either side of her as he fucked her...just like he had me.

This had nothing to do with espionage. It didn't even have anything to do with me, this was all about Alexi...

"Mauritius," she demanded, leaning closer. "Tell me what the fuck happened."

I stared into her ruthless gaze and prepared myself to do the only thing I could...*tell the truth.*

THIRTY-FOUR

Alexi

"I think it's about time you told me what the hell is happening...don't you?"

I swallowed hard as Theon stared after the feds' sedan as it disappeared. "Yeah," I said as the ground seemed to drop out from under me. "It's time."

But the words wouldn't come. No matter how many times I'd rehearsed this, it always sounded the same...

As I opened my mouth, my cell vibrated. One look at the caller ID and I scowled, answering instantly. "Helene?"

A low, gut-wrenching moan filled my ears, followed by sobs. "Alexi...it's Jager, he's been shot."

My heart stuttered in my chest as her words hit home. "What do you mean, *shot?*"

"*They got him!*" she screamed in my ear. "*They shot our brother.*"

They...

"Is he..." *Dead...*I could say the words.

"He's alive." She answered and I rocked with the relief.

"Who?" I was already moving toward my car, my long strides eating the distance. "Who was it?"

"I don't know," she sobbed. "I don't know anything at all. Just get here, Alexi. We're at Princeton."

"I'm on my way, just hold tight, okay, I'm on my fucking way." I didn't stop to explain to Maxim, just strode to the parking lot and hit the button on the remote, unlocking my doors.

I couldn't think, all I could do was drive after I punched the button, started the engine of the Audi, and tore out of the lot, heading for the city.

Panicked thoughts raced through my mind. All I could hear was Jager's warning in my head...*fix this Alexi, or we're all dead.*

This was my fault. This was all my fault...

I raced through the traffic, heading for the hospital. I didn't care about anything else in those moments, nothing but my brother. I pulled into the hospital parking lot, parked the car, and headed for the entrance. A quick scan of the area, and I headed for the registration desk. "Jager Kilpatrick," I demanded as a clerk lifted her head. "He was brought in with a gunshot wound."

"Are you family?" she asked.

"*Yes*," I snapped. "I'm his brother."

She gave me the directions and pointed toward a bank of elevators. I strode toward them, frantic. "*Move*" I barked as a woman stepped in front of me. The moment I was inside the elevator, my thoughts turned to Leila. I lifted my hand, massaging the back of my neck.

The thought of her in the back of that car made me want to tear something apart. She'd looked so damn small...so fucking frightened. *Christ, what a mess.*

I clenched my fist as the elevator doors closed and took me upwards. By the time I stepped out, I felt savage. I hurried to the waiting room at the end of the hall and found Mom and Helene standing near a corner, arms around each other.

Helene lifted her head, her gaze finding mine as I neared. "Have you heard anything more?"

She broke away from Mom and rushed toward me, slamming against me hard, her arms wrapping around me as she sobbed. "He's still in surgery. They say he will be for hours."

"Jesus." I looked over Helene's shoulder to Mom.

She looked devastated, her face almost gray. I stepped closer and opened my arms. "Mom."

She was nervous, taking a step forward, then clenched her face and froze. Helene pulled away from me, her cheeks shining with tears as she turned toward the woman who'd seen more than her fair share of trauma. "Come on."

She came to us, a frightened, shattered woman, a broken seam, unraveling at the edges. She wrapped her arms around us and I pulled her in tight. "He's going to be okay, do you hear me?" I murmured, trying to give her strength when I had none. "Jager is going to be okay."

Helene stiffened, drawing my attention. I turned, and found the two men I most didn't want to see striding into the waiting room. Vad Kardinov and my father.

"Helene." Vad gave a careful nod. "I was in the city when I heard the news."

I clenched my jaw. Like fuck he was. One glance my way, and I knew the truth. I pulled away and strode toward him, grabbed him by the shirt and wrenched him close. "Who the fuck did this?"

He turned his head carefully and met my gaze. "If you think I had anything to do with this, then you don't know me at all. I'd never hurt your family, Alexi. Not like this."

I didn't know what to believe, I didn't know what to think. I lifted my gaze, meeting my father's, and I saw the unspoken words in his eyes. If Jager died, then it'd all fall to me, the second son.

No...no fucking way. That wasn't happening.

I turned away, dragging my fingers through my hair, torn between the desperate desire to stay here and the need to get Leila away from that psycho bitch who'd set me up. We waited, sitting on the hard plastic chairs and staring at the wall. Hours went by while we sat there. Hours of nothing. Hours of thinking. Hours of slow goddamn torture.

Helene couldn't stop crying, and as much as I hated it, Vad comforted her as she grieved. My father stared at me without saying a word. I bet he was almost disgusted, calculating all the wasted years he'd put into my brother, honing him into the fucking murderer he was...

He lifted his gaze and met mine. A killer he'd wanted and a killer he'd get...I knew in that moment who my first bullet would be for.

Movement from the hallway drew my gaze. A surgeon walked in, looking fucking exhausted as he pulled his mask free and glanced around. I took a step forward, preparing myself for the news. "Jager Kilpatrick..."

"Is alive," the surgeon answered with a careful nod, glancing around the room at my family. "For now. But I don't want you to get your hopes up. There's evidence of brain damage, but how much, we won't know until he wakes up. *If* he wakes up."

If he wakes up...

If. He. Wakes. Up.

He had *to*.

My cell gave a *beep*, piercing my numbness. I looked down and saw a message from Theon Volkov.

Leila's being released as we speak. Condolences on your brother.

I stared at the message until the words blurred. She was out... she was out...and my brother was alive...*for now.*

THIRTY-FIVE

Leila

"Tell us what we want to know, Ms. Ivanov," the female agent demanded, leaning over the desk and staring down at me. "And we'll let you leave."

My mind raced as I stared into her eyes. Tell them what they wanted to know?

Tell them about why we'd left Russia, or why I'd left Cosa Nostra Island...*or what I was doing with Alexi Kilpatrick?*

Because that's what she really wanted to know, right? I saw it in her eyes, that blistering rage of jealousy. Did this even have anything to do with my family? Was it all just about him... Alexi Kilpatrick?

The walls seemed to close in as heat raced to my cheeks. *He's mine*...my breaths turned light and rapid, the neckline of my top too tight. "Alexi..." I started as the hard crack of footsteps resounded and the door opened.

"Ms. Ivanov." The sharp Russian tone drew my gaze. A man dressed in an expensive black suit strode in. One look at him, and I knew he was the lawyer, the lawyer my father had sent for me. He didn't even glance at the agent, just held my gaze. "Please, do *not* say a word."

But the female agent kept staring, boring that hateful gaze into me.

Behind my father's lawyer came another man. Only that one was no lawyer...not dressed in a cheap suit with a look of permanent exhaustion on his face, one that seemed to deepen as he shot the female agent a glare.

"Davids," he barked. "Let her go..."

"No," she answered, still glaring at me. "Not until she tells me what I want to know."

My father's lawyer just held out his hand, beckoning me. "Leila."

I rose and followed him, drawing her deadly stare as I left. I felt it burning the back of my head, marking me. I followed my father's defender, and made my way back out the door and into the elevator once more. The moment we were inside, I murmured, "I didn't say..."

He shook his head and lifted his finger to his lips. "Not here."

I knew then, realized that silence in this place was the only thing that could protect me. Silence and the law, that was. I glanced at my phone, but there were no messages, no calls from Alexi. Did he even care at all? Agony carved through my chest with the thought. I hardly expected a howl of revenge, but a message would've been nice.

I glanced toward the lawyer as we rode down the elevator. "Did my father send you?"

"Does it matter?" he answered, staring straight ahead.

I swallowed as we came to a stop. I guessed it didn't. My steps were hurried, but the lawyer beside me took his time, walking with complete confidence, demanding everyone and everything around him match his pace. I couldn't wait to be out of there, couldn't wait to be far away from that building...and her.

The moment we made our way out of the building and were striding toward the waiting car and its driver, I turned to him. "Why did they think I was a spy?"

He motioned for me to enter as the driver opened the rear door. I slipped in, sliding across the seat as he followed me inside. The moment the door was closed, he answered. "This was nothing to do with you, Leila. They wanted a way to get to your father, and they found that way. You're safe now, I won't let them get to you. We'll get you out of the city and back home."

We pulled out of the parking space and into the steady stream of traffic. The moment we were outside, my phone gave a *beep*.

Alexi: My brother has been shot, I'm at the hospital now with my family. He's just come through surgery and as soon as I can get away, I'll be with you. Text me when you can, we need to talk.

We need to talk...

The female agent loomed in my mind. Yes, we did need to talk. Buildings closed in all around us as we left the CIA offices behind and drove deeper into the city, but the further I went, the deeper that ache in my chest moved. He was taking me to the airport and within the hour, I'd be on a plane, leaving Alexi far behind. I closed my eyes and leaned my head back against the seat. I didn't want that, I didn't want to leave him, not without knowing the truth.

"Stop the car," I cried, opening my eyes and focusing on the driver.

My father's lawyer jerked his gaze my way. "What?"

I leaned forward, drawing the driver's attention. "I said, *stop the car.*"

The driver hit the turning signal and jerked the wheel amid a blare of angry horns from behind us.

"You can't get out here. Leila, let's discuss this," the lawyer spluttered.

But I was beyond discussing anything. I shoved open the door as he called out, *"I'll have to call Mr. Volkov!"*

"You just do that." I slammed the door behind me and stepped out on the sidewalk into the rush of oncoming pedestrians.

I tried to step around them, fighting my way through. Behind me, the lawyer roared, but I wasn't listening to him anymore. I was listening to that voice inside me, the one that was beating bloody fists inside my chest, the one that told me that, as much as I was hurting, I also needed the pain.

My pulse was pounding furiously, as I lifted my head and scanned the buildings, searching for Alexi's apartment. I had no idea where I was. Some buildings seemed vaguely familiar. So I kept walking, stepping in and out of the traffic as people crossed the street. I stopped, asking a woman who was walking her dog for directions, but the more nervous I became, the thicker my accent was. She didn't understand me, shaking her head and giving me a shrug before walking away.

Catcalls rang out as I passed a group of men. They whistled. One even followed as I hurried away. Panicked, I glanced over my shoulder and picked up the pace until I was almost running. A burn moved into my chest with the hard breaths. My phone started ringing, but I didn't need to look at the screen to know who it was.

I wasn't going to stop now, not until I saw Alexi, not until I knew the truth. Lies had stained my life, tearing me from my home and plunging me into a world I didn't understand. Tears blurred my gaze until I rounded a corner and winced at the sunlight. As the glare dulled and my focus sharpened, I saw Alexi's building in the distance.

I surged forward, stepping around those who walked too slow. By the time I reached the entrance, I was out of breath, my pulse booming inside my head. I licked my lips and rushed through the doors, glancing to the elevator. But I had no key, no way to get inside.

"Can I help you, ma'am?" the doorman rose from behind the counter.

"Alexi..." I gasped. "Alexi Kilpatrick."

His brow furrowed. "I'm sorry, but Mr. Kilpatrick isn't in."

"I know he isn't, I was with him before. Can you let me into his apartment?" I glanced over my shoulder to the doors, knowing that Theon would be here any moment. Then there'd be no more running, no more arguing. He'd haul me over his shoulder if he had to. Panic filled me at the thought.

"I'm sorry, ma'am, but I can't."

"*Then call him!*" I practically yelled. "*Call him and Alexi will let me in.*"

I was close to begging, close to running from the building before Theon could get here.

"One minute, ma'am." The doorman gave a nod. He ran to the counter once more, picked up a handset, and dialled a number. Seconds felt like hours before the call was answered. "Mr. Kilpatrick, there's a woman." He glanced my way.

"Leila Ivanov," I answered.

"Ms. Ivanov..." he repeated, listening to Alexi. "I understand. Yes, sir, I'll let her in right away."

I glanced over my shoulder, searching the streets outside as I hurried toward the elevator. "Yes, thank you." The rush of relief was instant, sweeping through me as we stepped into the elevator and watched the doors close.

I closed my eyes and gripped the railing as we rose upwards, all the way to the penthouse suite. I prayed Alexi made it here before Theon. The elevator came to a stop and we exited, heading toward Alexi's apartment. The doorman pulled out his keycard, slapping it against the reader before opening the door. "Ma'am."

I took a step inside as the door at the far end of the hallway opened. The sound of rushing footsteps was thunderous. The doorman glanced toward the sound, drawing my gaze as a soft *pop!* rang out.

I watched in horror as he stumbled backwards, blood blooming at his chest as he fell. The doorway was filled with darkness in an instant as three men wearing black rushed in.

A gun was aimed at me, coldness moving through me in an instant. "We've been waiting for you, Ms. Ivanov." The killer stepped closer, forcing me backwards as he stared into my eyes. "Now, you're going to be a good girl for us, aren't you? You don't want to know how bad it'll get if you scream."

THIRTY-SIX

Leila

"Where is the file, Ms. Ivanov?" he murmured, looking around the apartment.

"The file...what file?" A sickening feeling washed through me.

"Now, are you going to play those games with me?" He motioned with his hand and the two others came forward.

"No." I shook my head and stepped backwards toward the window as fear took hold. "I don't know of any file. I don't know what you're talking about."

"Are you sure?" He cocked his head before he glanced at the others.

Desperation punched through me as they closed in on all sides. I lunged, driving myself toward the bedroom...until one caught me around the middle.

He yanked me hard against him, growling in my ear, "I don't think so, mafia bitch."

I kicked and screamed, bucking against his hold and clawing his arms. *Fight...fight...FIGHT!*

His hand went over my mouth. Terror raged inside me, chilling me to the bone. I was lifted until my feet left the floor, then dragged backwards.

"I don't think you're telling the truth," the predator murmured, his eyes slowly lowering until they stopped on my breasts. "In fact, I think you're a lying little whore."

No...no...*no!*

He reached out, gripped the neck of my blouse, and yanked.

Buttons flew, peppering the floor, leaving me exposed...

His hand was on me, cupping my breast, kneading and squeezing. I bucked and twisted, screaming against his hand. "No!"

"Hold her!" he barked.

Cruel fingers slid under the lace of my bra as he yanked down the cup.

He was on me in an instant, gripping my hips and nuzzling my breast. A sharp pain came as he bit. I howled, thrashing and kicking. Still, I was no match for their brute strength.

"They said we could do whatever we wanted with you," he mumbled as he licked the sore spot where he'd bitten me. The warmth slightly eased the cruel throb at the peak of my breast. My body clenched in dread. "You know what I want to do?" he taunted me as his hand slid between my thighs.

"Gordon...boots," one of the others growled.

The ravager lifted his head and turned as the faint thud of steps grew louder...*and faster.* "Door," he commanded.

One of them moved *fast*, hurrying to slip behind the door as the lock snapped open and Theon rushed in.

Panicked breaths, then him. He was all I saw...his savage, unmerciful gaze, that face I'd known my entire life. My bodyguard...*my protector*.

"Get the fuck off her!" Theon roared as he raised his hand, taking aim.

My eyes were wide, a scream building in my chest. *Boom!* The sound shattered the stillness...and in an instant, my bodyguard slumped to the floor.

"No..." I whimpered around my attacker's hold. "No...NO, THEON!"

I screamed, bucking and fighting...until the fight slowly drained out of me. I couldn't look away, devastated with fear as I watched the one man I'd loved like a father bleed out on the slate gray floor.

My movements came slower, then slower still, until all the fight was gone.

The world seemed to dull, slipping away until there was nothing left...no pain...no terror, no feel of the hand over my mouth, or the sting at my breast.

Nothing but dullness...even as my attacker turned to me and the dark blur of the man behind the door came closer. My attacker spoke words I could no longer hear...words that faded into oblivion, words I no longer cared about. *Make this end*...that's all that filled me. *Make this end...make this end...make this—*

Crack! My attacker jolted forward, stumbling a step, before he hit the floor.

Theon's hand smacked the floor in front of me, the gun slipping from his fingers.

He stared into my eyes. There was only love for me there...only loyalty. *"Mia..."* he whispered before the end rushed in and stole the life from his eyes.

A low, terrifying sound filled my ears, like a wounded animal. The moan grew louder, burning the back of my throat and all the way down my chest. Movement rushed in through the open doorway. But all I saw was a blur...the gunman behind me slammed backwards. I jolted from the movement as his hand tore from my mouth.

"LEILA!"

The roar filled me. A face appeared in front of me. Blue eyes I should know...but didn't.

I didn't know anything. Not the feel of his hands as he grabbed my shoulders. Not the faces of the other men as they killed my attackers and dropped to the floor beside Theon.

*He's gone...*I tried to say. But the words never came. They just rattled inside my head, clinking and gnashing like shards of glass, cutting deep as they went.

"Fucking bastards!" The man with the blue eyes raged. "Who the fuck are they?"

Where's the file...

The man who held me stiffened and slowly drew his gaze to mine. "What did you say?"

Tears blurred as they rolled Theon over. But there was nothing left for me there, nothing but the ache in my chest that seemed to swell with every thud of my heart. Instead, I turned my head, diving into his ocean-blue eyes. "Where's the file...that's what they said."

There was a twitch at the corner of his eye, then a stillness...*no, a death.* He closed down, sliding that mask he wore into place as he asked. "Is that all they said?"

"Isn't that enough?" I whispered. "What file are they talking about, Alexi?"

He gave a shake of his head and stepped away from me...

But I wasn't done...I couldn't be done, not as one of my father's men picked up my protectors's body, lifted it over his shoulder, and walked toward the door. *"What goddamn...motherfucking file?" I screamed.*

THIRTY-SEVEN

Alexi

"Where is the file?" she screamed. The shrill sound rang in my ears. "*What goddamn motherfucking file?*"

I couldn't speak, couldn't answer. I couldn't give her what she wanted. I swallowed hard and shook my head, seeing the light dull in her eyes.

There was a look of resignation. Like a killing thing, like a knife between the ribs, a quick stab to the heart. One I never wanted to see.

Not from her...

Footsteps thudded from her father's men as they left the apartment, carrying Theon as they went. But I couldn't look away from her, couldn't stop the spark from dulling in her gaze, couldn't stop anything. My heart howled, thrashing inside my chest at the sight. She gave a nod, small and quiet, before she stepped away.

No!

"Leila, please..." I pleaded, but she was already moving, tugging her torn shirt into place as much as she could, before gripping it against her chest as she turned and walked away.

No...no...no...no...no.

I ground my teeth, my body rocking with the blow. A hammer slammed inside me. All I saw was her face as she'd lunged at the asshole trying to kill me on the island. Her face, twisted into a look of savagery as she risked her life to save mine.

And look where that had gotten her...

Look where *I'd* gotten her.

I took a step and stopped. Something was hard under my boot, dragging my focus down. A button glinted from the floor... another near it, and another scattered to the side. *Her button... the buttons they'd ripped from her.*

The sight rocked me. I stumbled with the blow, slowly lifting my gaze to her as she left my apartment. I could deal with Jager, I could handle seeing him in that bed with his head bandaged and tubes sticking out from his chest.

I could even handle seeing the smug fucking smile on Kardinov's face as Leila turned at the sight of him and buried her face into his chest. I could even handle feeling that foul, goddamn gaze from my father as he turned his attention to me, already calculating in his head if Jager was worth saving.

I could deal with all that...

But what shattered me...what made the floor slip out from underneath me, was that quiet, controlled woman as she clutched her fucking blouse closed and walked away in silence.

Her silence was a roar.

Her silence was a scream.

Her silence was death to me, because that's what it felt like...*a death.*

"*No!*" I lunged, driving my body through the apartment and out into the hall.

The doorman was on the floor, his eyes wide and blank. Blood seeped out from under his head to creep along the tiles toward the doorway. But I didn't care about him. All I saw was her as she stepped into the elevator behind her father's men, and disappeared from view.

I'd known...I knew the moment I saw her father's men step into the elevator, knew the moment I realized Theon wasn't there... knew as that sickening feeling flooded me when I'd found the desk in the lobby empty.

That desk had never been empty...not in all the years I'd lived here. I'd just known...

"*Leila!*" I roared, and picked up my pace, slamming my boots onto the floor as I ran.

But the elevator doors were already closing. Steel slammed shut in front of me. I punched the surface, watching through the gaps as the light faded and the elevator disappeared, taking her with it.

I lowered my head, my pulse thrashing in my ears as I pressed against the closed doors.

I didn't love her...I didn't love her. I didn't feel this fucking agony, this uncontrolled rage. This *hurricane* inside me...I didn't...I didn't...

I lied...

Agony ripped through my chest as I stood there, my forehead pressed against the cold metal. I wanted to tear the world apart and burn it to the ground. I clenched my fist and swung, driving the knuckles into the steel. *I can fix this...I can fix this...I CAN FIX THIS!*

But I couldn't...and she knew it.

Her hollow stare told me the truth. She was gone...*it was over.*

"No." I ground my forehead against the cold surface. I couldn't lose her... *I refused to lose her.*

This was all because of that bitch, that fucking betraying fucking cunt. I lifted my head as that cold feeling swept through me. *Give us the file, Alexi.* Hannah's voice rang in my ears. *Give us the file and we'll let you go.*

But she wouldn't let me go, would she? I glanced over my shoulder at the dead body of the doorman on the floor, then thought of the three others in my apartment. The three who'd come for the file. The three that looked so fucking familiar. Three I *knew* were connected to those who'd attacked the island.

They sure as hell weren't CIA.

I headed back to my apartment, stopping at the doorway and looking down at the familiar face that had greeted me every goddamn morning. "I'm sorry, Liam. I'll make this right."

I bent down, grabbed his ankles, and pulled him inside the apartment, leaving streaks of blood behind. A coldness came over me as I strode into the kitchen and ran a cloth under the tap before I returned. I moved fast, wiping up the blood from the floor, making sure there was no evidence of anything outside before I closed the door to my apartment and turned my attention to the three dead men lying around the living room.

Hate rolled through me as I crossed the floor, stopping at the bastard who'd had his hands on her. Images stabbed through my mind as I bent down and went through his pockets. His ID said Russian. *Vladamir Arranov.* I winced at the sight and went through the pockets of the others, pulling out their IDs.

Every one of them said the same. They weren't American. They sure as hell weren't feds.

Russian...

I was stuck on that, held prisoner by Vad's fucking voice as it rose inside my head. *You really want to know who she is? Then what we have to do is take a look at Russia.*

A change of guard...isn't that what he'd said? A change of guard and something about them leaving and coming here. *Where is the file, Alexi?* I flinched and pushed to stand up, looking down at the dead bodies on the floor.

Nothing made sense...

Except for one.

There was only one person this all pointed to. The woman in the center of it all...

Hannah.

I headed for the bedroom as cold detachment swept through me. It all came back to her...

Memories rose as I made my way into the bedroom, then into the closet, and stopped at my safe. It'd been too easy when she came onto me, too simple. A good, hard fuck with no strings attached. *That's what she'd said, right? No strings attached.*

Until the string became a noose and tightened around my fucking throat.

I pulled out my gun, and the silencer. I should've put a bullet in her head the moment she threatened me. I should've never let it get this far. I should've protected those I loved...those like Leila.

Finish the job.

My father's words rang in my head as I slipped on my shoulder holster and seated the gun against my ribs before I pulled on my jacket and buttoned it tight. My footsteps thudded, the sound reverberating as I headed out of the apartment and walked down the hall.

The red exit light glowed above the stairwell door, beckoning me as I slipped inside. The gloom blurred until my eyes adjusted, and I made my way up to the rooftop of the building. But I didn't step out the door to the lap pool and the grand rooftop spa. Instead, I knelt down in the darkness, breathing in the heavy scent of damp concrete. There was a cut in the wall in the corner of the stairwell, one you'd never see if you were walking past. You'd almost have to tear the damn building apart just to find it.

But I'd found it.

I knelt, gripped the edges of the block, and pulled it free. Behind it was a small gap, not wide enough to hide a gun, or a go-bag in case shit went south. But it was wide enough to hide a file...just one...but that was enough.

I pulled it out before placing the concrete block back, then dusted off my pants and grabbed my phone, typing the message: *I have what you want,* before hitting send.

Finish the job...

My father's words stayed with me as I walked back down to the penthouse floor and took the elevator all the way to the foyer. They were the words he'd demanded of Jager, the words that had turned a man into a monster.

Finish the job...

That's what I was going to do.

"I'm coming for you, bitch. This time we'll be done for good."

THIRTY-EIGHT

Alexi

I LIFTED MY GAZE AS THE ELEVATOR DOORS CLOSED. IN MY hand, my cell vibrated with a message. One I didn't need to look at, still I did, finding the words I expected.

Hannah: About time. Where do you want to meet?

I stared at the words as places rolled through my head. Somewhere private. Somewhere I could watch her...follow her. Somewhere I could finish this once and for all. I typed out: *The place where we fucked the first time.*

She'd remember the place. Dark, quiet. The park where we'd driven to, pulling up in the middle of the night. We couldn't even make it back to her place. Instead, we'd fucked on the hood of my car, her hands splayed wide, her panties around her knees, my headlights shining around us as I'd rammed myself into her over and over and over again.

I'd fucked her...when all the time, she'd been fucking me.

The elevator came to a stop. I stepped out and made for the garage, glancing at the doorman's desk as the phone rang and rang. The automatic doors opened. I headed for my car, pressed the button to unlock the doors, and climbed in.

The second I started the engine, the message came through.

Hannah: be there in 30.

I knew she would, she didn't even think about the repercussions of what had just happened. All Hannah cared about was the file, and the images contained within it. I pulled out of the garage and turned onto the street. I'd get to the park early, and find a place where I could hide and wait. My phone rang and Helene's number flashed across the screen before I answered.

"Helene?" Panic filled me.

"They brought him out of the sedation, just enough to test. They said he's showing promising signs, Alexi. They think he has a chance."

"A chance to survive, but not live," I answered sadly.

I knew what the doctors had said. Knew if Jager made it, there was an eighty percent chance of some kind of permanent brain damage. Eighty percent was a tough call.

"He *will* live, Alexi," Helene's steely tone filled the car. "Whatever happens, we'll take care of him."

I clenched my fist around the wheel. She was too good, too honest, too fucking loyal to belong to us. "Yeah," I answered. "We will."

"Okay, I'll keep you updated. Just, try not to let Dad get to you, okay? He doesn't mean what he says."

I winced at the desperation in her voice as I leaned forward. "Yeah, Helene, he does."

Time to fulfill your obligation. The bastard had actually said the words as we'd watched our brother get wheeled out of surgery. *Jager's gone now, you need to handle business.*

Handle business.

That's exactly what I was doing.

I glanced at the GPS, following the directions, until a dark blur caught my eye. A car followed in the distance. I hit my turning signal and pulled into a quiet street, and the car turned too. Maybe it was a coincidence, then again, maybe it wasn't.

My gun rubbed against me, the hard steel comforting as I glanced across the seat at the file. I leaned forward, grabbed it, and slid it underneath the seat. No one was getting anything until I decided. My attention was captured by the sight of that car, gripped by a tight sense of dread…I didn't see them coming, not the black four-wheel drive as it hurtled toward me…or the steely gaze of the driver right before it plowed into my car.

The impact was brutal. Glass shattered and steel crunched as I was thrown forward until the seatbelt snapped tight. My body flew sideways, slamming my head against the side as the four-wheel drive kept coming, pushing my car sideways and slamming me against the curb.

Stars collided. The world dulled to gray. Movement filled my eyes. But I couldn't focus…I couldn't fight, not as they yanked my door open, and dragged me from the car.

My knees buckled the moment I was upright. Still, I cocked my fist and swung. *"Get the fuck off me!"* But my blows went wild, driving into nothing but air.

They said nothing as they yanked something over my head, plunging my world into darkness. Plastic cuffs snapped tight around my wrists as the sound of a door opened and I was thrown inside a vehicle.

"What the fuck!" I screamed, bucking and fighting as that dull feeling gave way to pain. Deep, knot-like pulses slammed through my head. I winced and kicked, slamming my heels against the door as it swung shut.

The bark of Russian made my stomach clench tight. Hard breaths sucked the fabric against my mouth until I tasted the dye. "Who the fuck are you!" I screamed.

More commands were uttered before the four-wheel drive moved, throwing me forward before it came to a stop. Glass crunched under the tires...and it was a whole second before I realized...*the file was still in the car.*

"No," I whimpered. "No...no...no...no." I slammed backwards as the vehicle pulled away, leaving my wrecked car behind. "I'll fucking kill you! *Do you hear me...I'll fucking kill—*"

Hard steel pressed against my temple. I knew the feel of that metal, knew it intimately.

"Speak again and it will be the last thing you say."

My stomach clenched and my balls tightened. My mind was racing, trying to understand. Leila's face filled me, even as the words slipped free. "Did you shoot my brother?"

They didn't answer. One hard shove, and I was pushed backwards. My gun was taken in an instant. I kicked out, driving myself away. *"DID YOU SHOOT MY BROTHER?"*

Thump!

The blow to my head came, hard and savage, slamming me sideways until I slumped to the floor. Something wet trickled down my face and the metallic scent of my own blood moved in...and darkness followed close behind.

"WAKE UP."

The command slipped in, pulling me closer to the surface.

"Get him to his knees."

Someone gripped under my arm, fingers clenched, driving that pain deeper. My mind sharpened, pushing aside the blur...until I remembered.

The island...

Jager...

Leila.

That name hit me like a shot of adrenaline. I came to with a moan. "Get...get the fuck off me." My body wobbled as I was pulled up to my knees. I gripped my hands together tightly, trying to beat back the pinching numbness and work the feeling back into my fingers. "You touched the wrong woman...I'm going to fucking kill you. I'm going to fucking kill you. I'm going to—"

The cover was ripped from my head. But the darkness stayed, lingering, like I was blind.

The car door opened and the faded wash of the taillights flared, brightening my world in red.

"I think it's you who's touched the wrong woman," the man in front of me spoke. The cold, clipped tone...one I knew.

I jerked my gaze to his, watching as Maxim Ivanov stepped closer.

"You?" I muttered.

"You hurt my only child, put her life at risk...you allowed those...*animals* to hurt her." He took another step closer. "To touch her...put their filthy fucking hands on her." Hate raged in those eyes as he stared down at me.

Shadows welled in the dark circles underneath his eyes, making him look demonic in the glow of the taillights.

"I brought her here to protect her. I brought her here to keep her safe, and with one look, Alexi Kilpatrick, you've undone everything I fought for...*everything I betrayed for. EVERYTHING I BLED FOR!*"

I sucked in hard breaths as he raged. He wasn't a man in that moment, nor was he a beast.

He was a father.

"I fled my home, left my friends behind. I left them to die as that *bastard* moved in. I left them all *because of Leila.*"

I shook my head, my fingers still clenching as the pieces started to fall into place. "That was the reason you left so fast. Because you knew...you knew they were coming and you ran."

"I bided my time," he answered coldly. "I made sure those I loved were protected. The *island was supposed to be protected!*"

"They came. They came," I repeated, my mind racing. "The men in the apartment...those are the men you ran from?"

One nod, that's all he gave.

That's all I had time for.

"Kill him," he commanded.

His man moved quickly, drawing his gun and taking aim at my head.

"*Wait!*" I screamed, desperation driving through me. "There's more. So much more. There're things I haven't said. Things no one but my brother knows."

"The brother that was shot today?"

I nodded as anguish slammed into me. The brother that was lying in the hospital, all because of a— *"the file."*

Maxim lifted his hand, halting the execution. "What file?"

"The file the CIA wanted. The file that has images of Carter Benfold's execution."

The older man stiffened, those demonic eyes growing even darker. "The advisor to the president?"

"He refused to bow, refused to obey. The hit was ordered by—"

"Dominic Salvatore."

I gave a nod. Relief swept through me, even if I wasn't getting out of this, I needed someone to know. Someone to stop them. Someone to...*find the file.* "It's in my car."

"What's in your car?"

"The file." I lifted my gaze to his. "The file with all the images of the hit...it's in my car."

"Jesus," Maxim muttered as a look of disgust crossed his face. "You left a file with images of an execution in your goddamn *car?*"

"I wasn't intending on getting rammed," I answered.

Maxim leaned down, those dead eyes boring into mine. "What were you planning on doing with it, this so-called file that could singlehandedly take down the Commission?"

"Killing for it," I answered. "To keep it safe."

"And just who were you killing, Alexi? Who was after this file?"

This was it...this was my secret. The one I'd give him, right before he ended my life. "CIA Agent Hannah Davids."

"The CIA?" he stiffened. "The same CIA who took my daughter?"

I slowly nodded. "The same one. I had no idea. You gotta believe me, I had no idea she was undercover."

"She played you."

It wasn't a question, and there was nothing to correct. I'd been played, it was as simple as that. "Yeah."

"Get up," he demanded.

He gave his man a nod. "Get him loose, give him back his weapon."

"What?" I jerked my gaze to the guard as he bent down, flicked open his knife, and cut me free. My hands flopped forward. I rubbed my wrists, wincing at the sting. "What are you doing?"

"I'm going to get some goddamn answers, Alexi," he snarled. "*And you're coming with me.*"

THIRTY-NINE

Alexi

I STUMBLED TO MY FEET, STILL RUBBING MY HANDS. MAXIM just turned and strode toward the car as his bodyguard opened the door for him. He expected me to follow, without question or demand. His other guard moved closer, handing me my gun. I took it, striding forward to follow Ivanov into the backseat.

"Where?" He glanced toward me.

I licked my lips, the address filling me. "There's a park, corner of Eastgate South and First. It's dark, and quiet. She's probably gone by now."

"No, she won't."

The car started as Maxim's henchman talked on the phone and slid into the passenger's seat. Barely a second later, we were pulling away from the darkened road in the middle of nowhere and headed back for the city lights once more. His hitman muttered something in Russian as Maxim gave a nod.

I wanted to ask what was said, but my death was still far too close. I sat in silence, watching the night blur by, trying to keep my shit together, and probed the wound inside my head. Maxim never glanced my way, just kept that dead gaze fixed to the front. I'd been wrong about him, he wasn't some cold, heartless bastard. He'd run from his home to keep his daughter safe.

He seemed haunted, maybe even more haunted than me, if that was even possible. We drove into the city, familiar streets surrounding me on all sides, until we turned off and, instead of heading for the park where Hannah was waiting, we drove to the industrial part of the city, where floodlights illuminated a razor wire fence line.

I wanted to ask what we were doing there, but the moment we turned once more, I understood. The towing yard sat at the end of the street, with a towering fence line and a man in an office trailer at the front. Two tow trucks sat just inside the gates...one of them carrying my car. What was left of it, anyway.

The henchman climbed out, closing the door behind himself before he made for the guard shack, and rapped his knuckles on the glass window. It was yanked open and a slob of a man leaned out, barking at Maxim's soldier. But the male never reacted. I couldn't hear what he said, but whatever it was, it made the man behind the window flinch, then slowly raise his gaze to the car where we sat.

The window was closed, this time not as forcefully as it had opened, and before I knew it, the heavy male waddled his way out of the trailer and headed for the gate.

"You own this, don't you?" I didn't know why it had taken me so long to piece it together.

"Yes."

Of course he did. Maxim Ivanov hadn't just appeared one day in the city of New York. He'd infiltrated it, slowly and carefully, like roots taking hold in darkened corners. What else was he involved in? I didn't dare ask. The gate was opened and

Maxim's man strode in, made his way to the tow truck, and hauled himself up onto the bed, then climbed in through the smashed window.

The windshield was shattered, the headlight smashed in on one side. I looked away, swallowing hard. I could've died there, could've fucking died a number of times tonight...yet here I was, still breathing.

His man disappeared inside, searching the car before leaning across the passenger's seat, and reached down. It took him barely five minutes before he was climbing back out, my phone and the file in his hand.

He made his way out of the yard and climbed back into the car. But he didn't hand the file to me...instead, he handed it to Maxim. My gut clenched as he opened the file and went through the photos, stopping at the one behind this all. "Is this the only copy?"

"I don't know."

He met my gaze. "The only copy in *your* possession?"

"Yes, the only copy in my possession. I didn't want it in the first place."

"But you were going to give it to them...the government."

The way he said it made me feel like shit, like I was nothing more than the lowlife he expected when he looked at me. "No," I answered, holding his gaze, letting him see the truth in my eyes. "I was using it."

"To kill her...this agent whore?"

I swallowed hard, the words sickening. "Yes."

He gave a nod as the car pulled away. "Good."

Did it matter that my conscience screamed at the idea of that? That this was my last resort...that if I could just get her to see... get her to understand how dangerous this was...*how dangerous I was*...that I'd somehow make her change her mind.

We drove through busy city streets, pulling up not far from the park. His car idled and the silence inside was strained, until he handed me the file. "Go, make your deal with the devil, Alexi."

Just like that?

Just like that, he was letting me leave? My hands shook as I grabbed the file and my cell phone from the hitman in the front.

"Go." Maxim stared straight ahead, to where the headlights of his car splashed against the asphalt of the parking lot.

I yanked the handle and climbed out. Agony slammed into me, making me stumble. Still, I forced myself to keep moving, heading across the park to where we'd once parked all those months ago.

To kill her...that agent whore.

I didn't recognize myself anymore. Didn't feel, didn't think, didn't act. Didn't care. Not about her...not about me...

Only about Leila.

The memory of her as she'd walked from my apartment. She didn't scream at me, didn't rage. Just gave a careful nod and stepped away. That one movement hit me harder than any blow and more terrifying that a hurtling four-wheel drive headed my way. It was more final than a fucking bullet. One coated with my blood.

Headlights came on as a car door opened.

"About fucking time...*Jesus, what happened to you?*"

I cradled the file against my curled arm, hiding the gun underneath. "Fucking car accident."

"Christ," Hannah muttered, rounding the front of her car.

Through the glare of her headlights, I scanned her car. I could hardly see shit.

"Is that the file?" She glanced at my hand, I was sure she saw the gun, but she made no move for her weapon, just stared at the file as she took a step forward. "You did the right thing, Alexi. You did the right—"

Thwack.

She stumbled backwards, her eyes widening as blood bloomed on her chest. "What the..."

Maxim's man strode forward, leaned in through her open car window, and killed the lights.

"Who do you work for?" Maxim stepped closer in the dark, drawing her gaze.

She wobbled for a second, then crumpled, hitting the ground with a thump.

"Who...do you work for?"

"Fuck you, Ivanov," she groaned, dark drool slipping from the corner of her mouth.

A nod, and Maxim's man stepped forward, leaning down to drive his fingers into her chest.

She screamed with agony, thrashing and fighting, kicking and clawing. But it was useless. That man wasn't an assassin...he was a fucking truck waiting to mow you down. He grappled with her, lifting her to her feet to face his employer.

"Andrei?" Maxim murmured, watching the sparks ignite in her eyes.

"You think this is over? Right now, he's attacking whoever's left on the island. He's going to kill the Commander, and the Commission." Hannah smiled. "Then he's going to kill you and your bitch daughter."

She looked at me when she said the words, dragging the beast to the surface, making me lower the file and lift the gun. She'd come for Leila under the guise of espionage. But it wasn't the woman I loved who was the betrayer of this country...it was her.

I lifted the gun. "If it's between you and her, then I will *always* choose her."

"Fuck you, Alexi," Hannah growled, curling her lips. Something savage moved through her eyes. Something unhinged and desperate, right before she lunged.

FORTY

Leila

"She won't see you."

I stared at the wall as my father's voice reached me. The heavy boom of steps followed someone growling. That sound made my heart clench tight. Still, I didn't look away. I couldn't look away. Because it wasn't the pale green wall I saw in front of me, it was Theon's eyes as they slowly dulled.

"Alexi..."

I flinched at the sound of his name.

Boom...boom...boom. His fists beat against the door. "Leila," he pleaded, and my body tensed tight. "Leila, please...please open the door."

A soft *thud* came. I knew without seeing him that his head was pressed against the door. Lies would come. Lies and excuses, because that's all men like Alexi ever had to offer. I'd been so happy...so *damn happy*. I'd waited for him in that apartment, waited like an idiot for him to come. I'd waited, *smiling*, desperate to tell him that I didn't want to go back to that place with the ugly bricks and the towering gates.

I'd waited to tell him that I wanted to stay there, in that apartment overlooking the city, that apartment where I could see myself becoming my own person for the first time in my life.

But I couldn't go back there now. Not *ever* again.

Because that's where my nightmares now waited...that's where Theon lay.

I swallowed hard and turned my head, staring at the shadows under the door.

"I'm sorry," he murmured. "I'm so fucking sorry."

I turned away at the sound, pulling away from him, pulling away from everything. I didn't feel his *sorry*. I didn't feel anything, just emptiness.

"I killed a woman tonight." My heart lunged, slamming against my chest. I turned toward the doorway once more, listening to that bleak tone in his voice. "I killed her...and I'd kill her again."

I swallowed hard.

"I killed her not because I cared about me anymore. I killed her...because she threatened you."

I was moving before I knew, sliding off the end of the bed and striding toward the door. I didn't want to see him didn't want to know him. I didn't want to *ever* know Alexi Kilpatrick existed.

But he *did* exist.

He existed in my head. He existed in my heart. He existed in the memory of his touch and it was that memory that lingered. That cruel existence where he'd set my body on fire. I reached out and gripped the handle.

"I'm begging, Leila."

My pulse spiked with my hand on the door.

"I'll do anything, *kill anyone*. I'll kill—"

I twisted the handle and yanked open the door, finding him with one arm braced against the doorway and his head dropped low. He looked like a man beaten. A man so far removed from the Alexi Kilpatrick I knew.

He looked like a man who'd fallen.

He lifted his head. Blood matted his hair on the side of his head, and there were scratches on his cheek. But it was that haunted look in his eyes that gripped me. That look of a killer...that same look I saw in my dad.

"I will do *anything*," he repeated. "Just don't...don't shut me out."

"Theon was killed because of you." The words ripped out of me and a burn followed. "I was attacked...*because of you*."

He just stared into my eyes. Lost, so fucking lost.

He was a soul adrift in that moment. Tethered to one moment, one space, *one woman*.

Me.

"I hate you."

He didn't flinch, just lowered his hand and stepped inside, forcing me backwards as he quietly closed the door behind him. "I know."

"I hate *you*."

He flicked the lock and turned to me. "I know."

"I can *never* forgive you for what you've done." Even as I said the words, I knew they were a lie. I wanted to forgive him. *I ached to forgive him*. But how could I? How could I forgive a man who was a liar? Who, because of his lies, killed those around him..."

"She had me up against the wall, threatened to go to the Commission if I didn't give her the images of my brother and Dominic Salvatore killing a very prominent person." He stepped closer, his fingers working the buttons of his blood-splattered shirt. Blood that wasn't just his.

"But she was a liar. You weren't the one who was a spy, Leila. *She was.*"

She...*she*...only one face came to me. One name. One savage look of desperation. I knew the moment she said his name. Knew deep down, she'd fucked the man I was falling for.

"She was working with the Russians, using me to get to the Commission. I don't know how deep it went, or who else she was working for, but the same men who came after your family in Russia are somehow connected to the attack. But she won't come after you, not anymore."

She was the one he'd killed tonight.

The woman whose blood he wore.

How could I trust a man like that? A man who'd kill a woman to save another? *Could I ever trust a man like that?*

He dropped his shirt to the floor and kicked off his boots. This was the man who didn't undress first, right? The man who only wanted me naked...who wanted me...*because he didn't care for me then.*

The answer was obvious, and it hurt. Blood splatter marred his neck and his chest. He looked savage in that moment. Bloody and savage, a man unhinged. I didn't know this man. He wasn't the cocky, blonde, detached man I'd met on the island.

He'd changed...dramatically.

Sleek muscles moved as he stepped closer. He looked like a predator in that moment, a ravenous, desperate predator. "I will make you love me again," he promised. "I will make you hate and rage, and want me. I'll make you do all those things because without you, without *this,* there is nothing left for me. Not now. Not ever."

I shook my head and stepped backwards. "No."

"I will, Leila."

"No." I stepped again, until my legs hit the bed and there was nowhere else for me to go.

But this wasn't like the attack in his apartment. He was the one raw and desperate, his hands still cruel as they slid around my neck and drew me close. "I will make this right between us...and it starts now."

He lowered his hand, skimming the outline of my dress. I didn't fight him. I *couldn't* fight him as he stepped closer and lifted me, taking two steps to lay me on the bed.

"It starts now, Leila."

My body was limp, my mind frozen, as he placed me onto the bed, his hand around my wrist over my head. I wanted to feel something other than this iceberg inside me. But I was under the water, drowning in the cold and the rage. I closed my eyes. "I hate you."

"I know you do."

I clenched my jaw with the trail of his finger along the edge of my jaw, as the ache flared in the side of my face, a remnant from the men who'd hurt me, *the men who'd killed Theon.*

Rage lashed through me. I swung, hitting his cheek with a *slap.* His head snapped to the side, and there he stayed. I hated myself in that moment, hated that I was hurting a man already in pain. He *was* in pain, physically and emotionally. The tortured look in his eyes only grew deeper as he looked back at me. I clenched my fist as his fingers continued trailing down my jaw to my throat.

I swung again, only this time, he caught my arm, forcing it above me once more, until he held both my wrists in one hand. I arched my back, hating the way he touched me, hating the way his fingers trailed down until he skimmed the back of his fingers over my breast.

I bucked, dislodging his touch. "Get the fuck off me, you *lying piece of shit!*"

One hard breath, and he gripped my dress, yanking it down with a savage jerk. Fabric ripped before he yanked the strap of my bra down, until cool air licked my nipple, making it pucker under his stare.

"You do this and I'll never forgive you," I growled.

"I know."

I closed my eyes as his finger found my peak, shivering as it moved lower, to find the tear in my dress and pushed it aside. "No, Alexi...*no.*"

"I'm a weak man, Leila. Weak and pathetic." He pushed my thighs apart. "But weak men are dangerous. They'll do whatever they want...and they won't care about the consequences. You are my consequence. Your hate, your anger. That cold look in your eyes that tells me you're leaving me. I can't let that happen...not now...*not ever.*" He crested my panties, then slipped lower, making me stiffen as he touched my clit. "I'm so fucking weak when it comes to you."

I swallowed hard as he slipped his finger under the elastic. It took everything I had not to moan as he pushed inside me.

"You're so wet. So goddamn wet."

I couldn't fight it, unleashing a sickening, desperate sound, and jerked my head from side to side, bucking my hips to throw away his touch. But all it did was drive him deeper, all the way to the fire.

"Fuck, you feel good." He lowered his head.

His warm breath blew against my neck as he slowly thrust his fingers inside me. My thighs trembled, desperate to widen. I hated that he had that power over me. Hated that I was his to control. Hated that I screamed *yes!* as he slipped from my pussy and yanked down his zipper.

Then grabbed my panties and, with a brutal yank, tore them away. *"No!"* I bucked with the sound.

My wrists throbbed as he grasped my throat with his other hand.

"I'm going to fuck you, Leila, and you're going to come for me... whether you want to or not."

"Fuck you!" I roared, my breath panting, my eyes wide. I bucked and kicked, fighting him. *Fighting this...*

I scratched his back and kicked my legs as he shifted his weight, climbing between my legs. My tears blurred his face. It didn't matter. I knew this beast of man and as much as I hated him, I wanted him more.

"I love you, Leila. Like I've never loved anything else before."

I jerked my gaze to him. *"And I hate you, Alexi! I hate you with my entire being!"*

He thrust inside me, forcing every inch into me until I froze with the assault. But he didn't stop, slowly pulling out, only to thrust back in again. I wanted him to be savage. I wanted him to be cruel. A moan tore free as I held his gaze. I wanted this beast of a man to stay.

Because maybe...maybe he was different from the man I'd fallen in love with. Maybe this man wasn't the liar anymore. He fucked me, this stranger, dropping his head to roll his hips and drive himself in once more. Heat licked inside me with every merciless stroke. That fire rekindled, until the spark turned into a firestorm, one that raged. My body clenched, and desire hungered. Sparks of the inferno took flight.

"Come for me, Leila," the beast of a man demanded. "But know this, there's no leaving me...*not ever again...*"

FORTY-ONE

Leila
---

3 MONTHS LATER...

THERE WAS STILL no sign of Viktoriya. Bodies and blood were all we found when we went back to Russia once more. There was word of a sighting of her father, but even that wasn't confirmed. I pulled up outside the home I'd spent my entire childhood in and climbed out of the car.

Everything was different now. There was no Theon waiting to open the door. Still, there was another male at my side. I turned my head, finding the icy stare of the man who was once the man I loved, then became a stranger, and now he was...

What was he?

He turned and met my gaze, and those same cold eyes that stabbed me from my father looked at me from the man who shared my bed. A man I didn't love, a man I was a little afraid of. A man who knew no bounds when it came to protecting me...to loving me...to wanting me.

He held out his hand. "Ready to show me your room?"

I swallowed hard and nodded. "Ready."

He gave me the ghost of a smile, one that didn't reach his eyes, and for some reason, I was comforted by that. At least he tried.

"We'll find her," he promised.

He'd made promises before.

"We'll find her."

I gave a nod. We would find the woman who was like a sister to me, no matter what it took, because that's what it meant to be an Ivanov. Never give up...

Never give in...

Until you were as cold as ice.

FORTY-TWO

Leila

3 *MONTHS LATER...*

DAD: *I don't like you going out, Leila. Please reconsider, stay home where you are safe.*

I flinched as I stared at the message, then lowered my phone and tucked it under my dress.

"Everything okay?" Alexi asked, his voice a low murmur beside me in the limousine.

I gave him a soft smile. "Fine."

But those dark, brooding eyes saw right through my lie, one brow rising carefully. "Maxim?"

I swallowed and gave a nod. This was the third message saying the same thing. My father didn't want me out in public, not after the second attempt on his life in the last month. We were vulnerable, he said, we needed to be careful. So the last thing I should be doing was attending a lavish opening of an elite nightclub in the middle of the city with people all around me.

But that wasn't what Alexi wanted...

This is exactly what we should be doing according to the man sitting beside me. The man I now called *husband*. My fingers nervously twisted the white gold band inlaid with diamonds. A ring Alexi had placed on my finger months ago, but we still hadn't taken a honeymoon. Instead, I'd spent most of that time searching for my best friend...*Viktoriya*...

She was still missing, and every day we didn't find her was one day closer to never finding her. I knew that...so did Alexi.

We were at our most vulnerable, he said. Hiding behind our towering wrought iron gates and armed former Marines was a sign of weakness and, if there was something the Kilpatricks and the Ivanovs weren't, it was weak.

That I was beginning to learn.

The driver's door opened then closed. I tracked the movement behind the darkly tinted windows, hating how my trapped breath burned in my lungs, and flinched when the door opened beside me.

Warmth surrounded my hand as thick fingers slid between mine before Alexi crouched, moved in front of me, and stepped out of the car. He was my strength. He was my protector...but he was also a liar—a liar and a murderer—and someone who had betrayed me once before.

Only that was then...*right?*

I lifted my gaze as he climbed out and scanned the cars, waiting for our men who were in the black Explorer in front of us to move into position before he gave a careful nod and held out his hand for me. "Baby."

My pulse raced when he called me that. I didn't need threats against my life to make me feel weak. Alexi did all that on his own with one look fuelled with desire.

I took his hand, caught the long trail of the shimmering black designer dress, and stepped out. The cool night air hit me, cutting along the walkway and between the row of limousines, all pulling into the street behind us. I glanced at the wide concrete stairs that led up to the gleaming brand new building.

"Jacobs," I murmured to Alexi. "That's his name, right?"

He gave a ghost of a smile and nodded. "That's right."

Jacobs Enterprises. I was trying hard to fit into Alexi's world, first memorizing the five Mafia families who sat on the Commission and now those who had money. I gripped his hand as we headed to the wide stairs, stepping behind a group of others, who turned to stared.

Bodyguards dressed in black moved in around us, two flanked Alexi's side, but one moved in beside me and kept pace with my slower gait. *Davidov* was his name. The man my father had insisted on being part of our security detail. He was young, hungry, and Russian, just like me.

I glanced his way, met those dark green eyes, and kept climbing, turning my attention back to Alexi as we headed to the last few stairs. Music spilled through the gleaming glass doors that lined the lower floor of the sparkling Goliath of a building. The club was elite, expensive, and owned by a man Alexi called a friend. Someone he wanted to impress...someone I had yet to meet.

"Leila..." the thick accent carried. "Leila Ivanov."

I stopped walking and my hand slipped from Alexi's before he realized. On the other side of the railing that divided the stairs was a man...an older man who smiled as he stared at me. With steel gray hair and deep, dark blue eyes, he was flanked by three men. My heart clenched tight at the sight of him...and my insides turned to water.

If he thought the tight curl of his lips was disarming, then he was mistaken. Alexi scowled as he glanced at the guy, then stepped back against me.

"Leila, you forgot me already?"

"No, Lev," my voice was nothing more than a whisper. "I haven't forgotten you."

That cold, false smile stayed.

"It's Kilpatrick now." Alexi saw the fear in my eyes before he stepped closer. "I don't think we've been introduced."

But Lev Fedorov didn't even acknowledge that Alexi had spoken. No, he just levelled that chilling stare at me. "I'm sorry to hear about your father's troubles here in the United of States." His mispronunciation only highlighted how out of place he was here. "He might get the notion of returning home?"

A chill raced along my spine.

Only then did my father's dangerous rival turn his focus to my husband. Flanked by his own guards, the smile faded on the Russian oligarch. "Kilpatrick," he repeated. "The one who was in trouble with the CIA? That Kilpatrick?"

Alexi stiffened, and there was a twitch at the corner of his eye.

"I do hope you enjoy your evening, Leila," Lev murmured before he gave a slow nod and kept on walking down the stairs, the only one heading away from the thronged nightclub and the sounds of the invitation-only party inside.

Alexi just stood, watching the older man and his formidable guards as they walked away. Other partygoers moved around us, some muttering a snarl as they passed until Alexi jerked a glare toward them. Once they realized who they'd bitched at, they were quiet, only glancing over their shoulders as they hurried away.

Alexi just turned back to stare at Lev as he disappeared, then murmured. "Motherfucker." He turned to me. "Who the *fuck* is that?"

A shudder tore along my spine as I stared at the man who had not only savagely gone after my father, but was the sole driving force of us escaping to the United States...and now he was here...in this city—*at this exact party.*

The coincidence was terrifying.

I turned to Alexi, fighting the tremble in my voice. "I...I think..." *I want to go home...*

Home.

The place where I was protected.

The place where I could hide.

"Baby?" He stepped closer, lifting his gaze to the bodyguard next to him and motioned with his head.

The guard left, no doubt following Lev and his men to gather what information he could.

"His name is Lev Fedorov," my bodyguard murmured, then glanced away, probably embarrassed to have spoken out of turn. "Someone your father will need to be advised of."

"Fuck." Alexi looked at me, those blue eyes boring into mine. "Is he a threat?"

"Yes." The word slipped out. I gave a careful nod. "Very much so."

The sound of music drew my husband's attention. I knew Alexi well now. I knew him at his murderous, betraying worst, so I knew exactly what he was thinking.

"Let's go inside." He reached out his hand as another small group of elites approached the stairs and headed toward us. When he met my gaze, those blue eyes were just as chilling from my husband as they had been from my father's enemy.

I gave in, took his hand, and let him lead me up the stairs toward the the two bouncers standing in front of the club.

"Invitation," one of them commanded, but the older bouncer cut him a savage glare, unclipped the rope, and motioned us forward.

"Mr. Kilpatrick, sir," he muttered, then smiled as he met my gaze. "Mrs. Kilpatrick."

Alexi just nodded, gripped my hand a little tighter, and stepped forward. I caught the older bouncer's mutter. "Fucking idiot. Don't you know who that is?"

If he didn't, he was about to find out.

People didn't stand in Alexi's way, especially not in the last six months. If they did, they didn't stand for long. There had been rumors that he had something to do with the female CIA agent who went missing. But those rumors were quickly squashed after the attack on the island and the arrests which followed. Because no one in their right mind wanted to point fingers at one of the five Mafia families...especially not someone who was as ruthless as Alexi.

We made our way inside behind a group of women who stopped and stared at my husband. He was stunning in a black-on-black tuxedo, tall and strong, and those piercing blue eyes promised darkness and the kind of sexual hunger you couldn't just walk away from. Six months ago, I would've been concerned by all the attention, maybe even a little jealous. But that was before Alexi had used my name and family to save his life and before he'd fallen hard for me. I knew the demon my husband had been...knew him in all his vile, possessive ways. I also knew the fear in his eyes when he'd thought he'd lost me. And that fear remained, igniting in his stare now as he turned and met my gaze.

I don't give a fuck about them. The stare said. *I'm here with you...*his hand slipped around mine and his fingers slipped between mine. *Only you.*

I gave a nod as he led me toward the bar. He passed the trays loaded with flutes of champagne ready to be consumed, but not once did he make a move to hand me one. Instead, he rapped his knuckles on the bar, immediately drawing the bartender's attention. "Dom, a single malt. The good stuff Balor keeps under the bar too. Not that shit on the shelf."

"Sure, Mr. Kilpatrick." The guy nodded, glanced my way, and hurried to grab our drinks.

Alexi pulled me close against him, as though he sensed I needed the contact. I pressed my palm against his hard chest as I lifted my gaze and stared into his eyes.

I didn't voice my fear.

In my country, tears and breakdowns were a sign of weakness, especially in front of people. You didn't show that in public. I even struggled to show it in private. But I was learning, especially with Alexi. So, I held his stare and let him see past the icy exterior. I held his stare as the bartender placed our glasses in front of Alexi and waited.

My husband broke my gaze to give the guy a careful nod, and took the glasses. There was no way he'd take a glass from a tray for me. No way he'd trust anyone—not where we were concerned—not after all we'd been through.

I took a sip of my champagne and dropped my hand from his heat, turning to the party instead. But the fleeting excitement I'd had before was now gone, smothered under fear. What had Lev Fedorov wanted? Was that a threat...a *message*?

I reached for my purse, pulled out my phone, and sent my father a text: *Please, do not go out, stay home. Make sure Vladimir is close. I'll call you later* and hit send.

I wanted out of there, wanted far away from this party and the crowd. One look from Alexi and I knew he wanted the same. Instead, he scanned the crowd and stopped on a group of people sitting around a table up on a platform.

"Come on." He took my hand, led me away from the bar, and headed for the cordoned-off area, until we were stopped at the bottom of the stairs by a heavyset bouncer. "Sorry, sir. This part of the function is private."

"Then make it *un*private" Alexi demanded.

The bouncer just shook his head, which only pissed Alexi off. A dangerous energy seethed in my husband until a deep, booming voice came from the table above us.

"Let him through, Cole."

I lifted my gaze to the man who rose from the table, adjusting his jacket as he made his way down the stairs. His dark russet hair was clipped short, but there was an intensity in that dark stare, one that made me catch my breath.

"Balor," Alexi murmured, meeting the guy's gaze.

Balor Jacobs, billionaire and owner of Jacobs Enterprises, placed his hand on the bouncer's shoulder and nodded as the bouncer stepped aside.

Alexi glanced over his shoulder, then reached for my hand, the movement drawing Balor's gaze. He turned that brooding, cautious gaze my way and froze, one brow rising. His reaction wasn't lost on Alexi either, so he took my hand possessively and drew me against his side. "Balor, this is my wife, Leila."

"Wife?" He cut a glance at Alexi, then looked carefully at the plain white wedding band on his finger. There was a flicker of annoyance in his eyes as he turned back to me. "That is a shame indeed."

Alexi's chuckle was cold as we climbed the stairs to the platform. "As if you ever had a chance with someone like her."

"Oh, I dunno." Balor rubbed his chin.

"I forgot her former last name," my husband added, keeping his voice so low it was almost swallowed by the music. "Ivanov."

"Ivanov?" Balor flinched, and that pissed off look slipped away, leaving a careful, stony look.

I knew that look. I'd seen it my entire life. It was a look that spoke of an uncomfortable position, of a fear that I was even there. He jerked his gaze to the bouncer, and then to the people watching him from the table behind him. All of a sudden, I was made of glass.

"Please." Balor motioned to me. "Won't you join us."

I gave a careful nod, even if it was the last thing I wanted to do. My last name was the one you gave when doors were closed, or when you wanted to put the fear of God into someone. It was a name that was spoken carefully, or just not at all, as though my father was the Devil himself.

He was...in many ways.

Bloodthirsty and unmerciful.

He'd earned his reputation in ways that even I didn't want to know about.

But Alexi stopped short of joining the others at the table and turned to face him. "Tell me, Lev Fedorov. How well do you know him?"

Balor scowled. "Fedorov? I don't."

Alexi leaned a bit closer. "So why did he just low-key threaten me and my wife on your fucking steps?"

A flicker of fear sparked. "Threaten?"

"Yeah, fucking threaten," Alexi snarled.

Balor lifted his hand and motioned to someone making his way through the crowd. The man veered and headed our way, climbing the stairs to stop at Balor's side. The music changed, smothering his words, but I didn't need to hear him speak. I saw the nervousness in Balor's eyes as he demanded information from his second-in-command.

The poor guy just scowled and pulled away to look into Balor's stare, then he slowly turned to Alexi, and finally me. His eyes widened and he shook his head, as he turned to speak to Balor in a flurry of panic.

The owner leaned forward and spoke loud enough for Alexi to hear. *"He tried to get in without an invitation and was turned away."*

Alexi just processed that information, then leaned in himself. *"I want to know if that guy gets on your radar again."*

"Got it." Balor acknowledged. "Anything you need, Alexi, it's yours."

My husband just nodded, glanced at the party waiting at the table, then turned, pulling me with him. We were down the stairs in an instant, cutting our way through the crowd. I drained my champagne, just as he swallowed his scotch, and placed both our glasses on a waitress' tray as we headed for the door.

Our men closed in around us as we headed for the door, then outside to where our limousine was waiting. It wasn't until we were inside with the doors closed that I allowed the shudders to break free. "Oh, God...*oh, God.*" I closed my eyes. "This is bad, Alexi. This is really bad."

FORTY-THREE

Alexi

She shuddered beside me. Head down, her fingers twisted and wrung until her damn knuckles were white. I winced at the sight of the torture and reached out to take her hand in mine. "It's going to be okay. You believe me, right?"

Did she believe me?

Please, God, tell me she at least trusted that I'd take care of her.

No matter the cost.

The limousine pulled out from the curb. I met Sebastian's gaze in the rear-view mirror and gave him a small nod. We headed for home, leaving the party behind. Could I trust Balor to tell me the truth? The man was a fucking savage when it came to business. But alliances? That's where the man had to align with the right person.

The exclusive invitation proved that. My phone gave a *beep*, so I pulled it from my pocket, never once letting go of her hand.

Balor: Let me know if I can be of any assistance.

I tucked my phone back into my pocket and caught Leila's nervous glance at the movement. "I ruined your evening," she murmured.

"You did no such thing." I ran my thumb along the back of her hand.

My chest tightened and my pulse raced. The things I'd do to keep this woman and keep her safe knew no bounds. I wanted to protect her, to comfort her to *keep* her against me always. I lifted her hand but watched from the corner of my eye as our security detail moved in around us, the black Explorers getting into position, one in front and one behind us.

I'd take no risks where Leila was concerned.

Not after the last time.

The stain of that terror still lingered, blazing to life as we made our way back home.

Beep.

I pulled out my phone again and found Balor's latest message:

I'll check in with you tomorrow.

I shut down the screen and stared out at the night while my wife stared out her window, consumed by turmoil. My thoughts turned to that cold stare from Lev Fedorov, and a shiver raced along my spine. I didn't know what the Russian bastard was doing here, but I sure as hell would find out.

I grabbed my phone and punched out a message to my brother. *I need you to find out everything there is to know about Lev Fedorov,* then closed the screen down.

He wouldn't reply.

Not until he had something for me.

Leila's hand dropped from mine to the seat beside her, her nails pressed against the leather, white-knuckling the entire way home. Darkness waited outside. I turned my head, lost in my thoughts. There was a fucking lot to get lost in.

The sparkling lights of the city slipped away, leaving a blanket of darkness outside. Headlights bounced off the towering fence that surrounded our home.

The place was a fortress, but still, it wasn't enough.

To protect what was mine...

The car slowed and pulled into the driveway. We waited in silence. The rush of her breath barely reached my ears. I watched her, closed down, cold. Christ, how had we gotten so cold?

The gate rolled open and we pulled through. Movement came from the corner of my eye. The armed men patrolling the grounds watched us as we headed for the house and pulled up outside the front door.

I climbed out and breathed in the cold night air before I buttoned my jacket and rounded the rear of the car. She didn't move right away when I opened her door. Instead, she seemed to be lost in her thoughts.

"Baby."

Slowly, her head turned toward me, those piercing blue eyes so bright I could almost see the stars. I held out my hand. She took it and let me guide her out of the car toward the house.

The moment we were inside, she pulled away and headed deeper into the dimness to our bedroom. I unbuttoned my jacket as I strode to the kitchen, took it off, and tossed it on the end of the counter before I opened the cupboard and grabbed a glass.

Scotch, that's what I needed.

Something warm to chase the chill away.

I grabbed the bottle from the counter, unscrewed the top and poured, watching the amber liquid splash against the bottom. The sound of her steps faded as I swallowed, then I lowered the glass and turned my head.

She was slipping away from me.

I knew it.

I felt it.

I slid the bottle away and left everything behind when I turned.

I'd hold onto her the only way I knew...

FORTY-FOUR

Leila

My hands shook as I reached around for the zipper of my dress. The clasp slipped from my fingers with the shaking. I pulled away and clenched my fist, trying my best to still the trembling.

The one who was in trouble with the CIA. That Kilpatrick?

Lev's words echoed in my head. Alexi didn't realize the kind of violence that man was capable of, the sheer brutality someone like him carried from their command in the Russian Army. Lev Fedorov had fed on that kind of violence, consuming it until it was all he knew.

Even my father had been afraid of him.

I'd seen the newspaper stories. I'd heard what they whispered.

Now he was here...

The Monster of Ishiluk.

It'd been a town caught in the war's grip. A town Lev Fedorov was tasked to protect. But he didn't protect it...he destroyed it instead.

I clenched my hand and tried again, grasping the zipper as the heavy thud of Alexi's steps echoed along the hall.

"Let me help."

I closed my eyes at the brush of his knuckles along my spine. My breath caught, just like it always did at his touch. "You don't have to."

"I want to."

The slow slide of my zipper came before he pushed my dress off to crumple to the floor at my feet.

"I want to take care of you, keep you safe, fed, sated."

His fingers slipped into the waistband of my panties and slowly slid them down.

"Alexi..." I whispered, feeling his body shift behind me as he knelt.

"Shhh."

His heavy hand pressed between my shoulders, forcing me to bend over. "Enjoy this, my love."

My hands went to the bed to brace myself as he kissed the top of my ass, then moved down. That is how it was with us. When he was worried, we fucked. When he was angry, we fucked. When he was awake...we fucked.

His tongue licked along my center, dragging slowly all the way up.

"Christ, you taste good."

I fisted my hands in the satin bedding.

"So goddamn good."

His fingers followed the slick trail his tongue had left behind, parting me before he pushed them in.

"My beautiful wife." He finger-fucked me slowly. "Say it."

Heavy breaths consumed me, just like the strokes of his fingers had. "I'm your wife, Alexi."

Warmth pressed over my core, his tongue pushing in. He pulled away long enough to growl. *"Again."*

I rocked backwards, driving against him. My blood raced as my desire took over. Because I needed Alexi far more than he needed me. "Your wife," I gasped. "I'm *your wife.*"

He rose swiftly and the clash of his belt buckle jarred the room. I opened my eyes at the thud of his pants as they hit the floor, and tried to brace myself for what was coming.

But there was no preparing for Alexi...not when he was like this. His hand went around my throat, gripping hard enough to let me know he was in charge. But he never hurt me. He knew better than to do that. Especially after last time.

"I can't get enough of you," he grunted in my ear.

His other hand went to the inside of my thighs, pushing my legs wider apart. One hard thrust and he was inside me.

My breath tore from my lungs at the impact. I grabbed hold of his arm, steadying myself as he drove all the way inside.

"I will never get enough of you, Leila. Do you understand me? Never. Get. Enough."

I just closed my eyes, giving over to him. His hard thrusts were brutal, his grip around my throat, controlling. But he did something to me when he was like this, barely a man and mostly a beast. My body craved that desperation and hunger hummed inside me, building in intensity, until I met those invasions with my own desperate cries.

"Harder," I cried, holding onto him. "Alexi, *harder.*"

And he did, grunting as he used every inch of that powerful body to drive me upwards. *Oh, God, that's it.* I clawed his arm. *That's...*

He pulled out and dragged me with him to the bed.

"Won't let you slip away from me, baby." He rolled me until I was underneath him.

Those dark eyes were almost black in the shadows of our bedroom. Still, I felt the heat of that stare as he looked down, then grabbed the strap of my bra and pulled it low. His head lowered and his tongue licked the tight peak of my breast.

"You can't escape me," he murmured against my nipple. "Do you get that?"

I nodded, but the movement was lost on him. He was focused on my body, trying to tether me to him the only way he knew how.

I reached down, slid my fingers through his hair, and nuzzled his mouth harder against me. Teeth grazed sensitive flesh. I shuddered at the contact, needing that deep flare of pain. He shifted his body, positioning himself between my legs.

I opened for him, my pulse racing as he slid inside. My breath caught. A trapped moan tore free. He lifted his head at the sound, holding onto my gaze as he slid out and then thrust back in.

"*Oh...*" I whimpered.

Which only made him thrust harder. He rose like a god, looming above me, driving the hunger through me until my core pulsed and my body quivered. Still, it wasn't enough for him. He grabbed my wrists, imprisoned them above my head, and slammed his hips against mine.

My climax hit me in a rush, making my thighs tremble and my heart stuttered. With a roar, he came, grunting as he filled me with warmth. The hard rush of our breaths filled the space. There wasn't anything else now, just him and me...and this.

The mattress bounced as he fell beside me. I couldn't think, couldn't speak, just lay there as he pulled me against his chest and wrapped his arms around me.

"I'll keep you safe," his whisper was a rush against my ear. "I promised you that before, and I'm promising that again now. I'll keep you safe, Leila, if it's the last thing I do."

I closed my eyes, soaking in that heady rush until he gave my forehead a kiss and rolled away.

He didn't stay, he never stayed, just climbed out of the bed, slowly dressing as he watched me and then, before I knew it, he left. I lay there in the dark, then dragged the bedding down until I slipped underneath. I knew where he was, where he always was. In his study, pacing the floor, finding out who meant us harm...

And plotting revenge.

FORTY-FIVE

Alexi

I stopped outside our bedroom door. My heart was pounding and it wasn't because of the sex. It was fear. Fear I tasted in the back of my throat. Fear that held me in a chokehold. I winced and pressed my fist against my chest, then kept moving.

That's all I could do for her...

Hunt.

I kept walking and grabbed the bottle and the glass from the kitchen counter as I made my way through the house. My footsteps echoed in the expanse of the place. I'd built it because I could protect us here. I could defend us from those wishing us harm...

But I couldn't protect us from the fear that invaded her head, or the goddamn Russian oligarch that decided to crash the one fucking party we'd attended in months just to threaten her.

"*Fuck,*" I snarled and shoved open the study door before flicking on the lights.

The muted amber glow filled the room. I left the door open in case she needed me, and rounded the desk. The lights from the monitor were harsh as I switched it on and sat. I punched in my details, bringing up the information from the two teams of mercenaries I had searching for Viktoriya Korolev.

I scanned the list of information, from the places they'd searched, to the details they'd found. I knew she was being held captive by a brutal trafficking ring that haunted the outskirts of the city.

How they'd found her, I didn't know...

But I had a suspicion.

One I'd tracked all the way back to Russia and the brutal comrades Leila's father had left behind.

Those men weren't just powerful, they were fucking ruthless and cunning, as well. If they'd come after the Korolevs...then they'd come after us.

That same choking feeling gripped me tighter. I grabbed my phone and punched out a message to the new head of my security detail.

Make sure we double the patrols. I want every inch of this place guarded at all times.

Then I pressed send, and glanced at the gun on my desk. There were three in this study alone.

Four in the bedroom.

At least ten more scattered throughout the rest of the house.

I'd even had a panic room installed that would protect us for a week, at least, from anything short of a bomb.

But I couldn't be here with her all the time, and the thought of that made me fucking terrified.

I scanned the rest of the information the teams had sent me, then closed down the program. They were closing in. They knew names, dates...and were tracking a female cop that'd been abducted while off-duty. I leaned back in my chair. It wouldn't be long now...not long until we found her.

What then?

I winced and glanced toward the door.

I didn't know. But what I did know, if Viktoriya was found dead, then Leila would slip even further away from me...and I couldn't have that. Not now. Not after all we'd been through.

Beep.

I glanced down at my phone, to find a text from Jager.

Trouble at the club. You'd better get here.

"What now?" I whispered, rising. I grabbed my gun, slipped it into the waistband of my pants, and headed for the door.

I went to the bedroom first, stepping inside to find Leila still mostly naked, curled up on her side. Her breaths were even, and she had a serene look on her face. Nightmares still plagued her, so I needed to deal with whatever this was and be back before she woke.

Hurry...

The word echoed as I turned from her and left. As I climbed into the Lexus, I typed out a text to my head of security.

Craig, I'm needed in the city. I'll be home as soon as I can.

Then I hit send.

Guilt filled me as I backed out of the garage and headed toward the gate. By the time it started to close behind me, I was already punching the accelerator, pushing the sleek car hard.

If Jager couldn't deal with this, then it must be bad.

He didn't text me, not like that.

That alone made me fucking nervous.

Headlights cut through the dark as I headed for the city. By the time I pulled into the group of clubs called Jupiter's Calling, my stomach was a fucking rock. Red and blue lights flashed outside The Den. I didn't need a fucking blow-by-blow to know what had happened.

Goddamn Dornan.

I pulled the car over and parked as patrons and dancers spilled from the club. "Goddammit."

The roar of the crowd grew louder as I shoved open the door and climbed out. I scanned faces, searching for my brother amongst the shadows, and caught movement heading toward me.

The crowd parted.

People stared, as they always stared.

My brother wasn't just gruesome to look at, he also carried an air of brutality, one that no one wanted to be part of.

"What the fuck happened?" I yelled, fighting the roar of pissed off partygoers.

"Mac is what happened. Him and his fucking buddies."

He glanced over his shoulder as a team of agents pushed through the crowd. Mac Dornan led the pack. He turned his head, searching the pissed off, slightly intoxicated horde, and stilled the moment he found me. There was a gleam of satisfaction in his eyes as he held up his badge. "No more partying here, people. Go on now, head on home."

"Oh, come on!" someone called out. "This is *bullshit!*"

"Bullshit indeed," I muttered, holding Dornan's stare.

"I don't care where you go," the CIA officer answered, still holding my stare. "As long as it's not here."

I tightened my jaw and stepped forward, until I was stopped by my brother's hold on my arm.

"Not here," Jager murmured.

I sucked in deep breaths. The goddamn bastard was a thorn in my fucking side and had been since the fallout. Heat rushed to my cheeks as Dornan and two other men headed my way.

"Alexi," Dornan called as he carved his way through the crowd.

"Dornan," I muttered, glancing at the two other agents by his side.

He turned his head and looked at the agents. "Meet Peters and Newman with Alcohol, Tobacco, and Firearms. They're going to be staying here for a while." He turned back to me. "Think of them as your very own licensing agents."

"We're fully licensed," I forced through gritted teeth. "A simple check of our licensing would show that."

"You were, until we found two young females passed out beside the bar of an apparent overdose."

A nerve twitched at the corner of my eye. He and I knew this had *nothing* to do with our fucking licenses and *everything* to do with his former partner, Hannah Danvers.

The agent who'd tried her best to turn me into giving evidence against one of the most powerful families who occupied a seat on the Commission.

An agent who was dead...

I should know.

I'd killed her.

Dornan stepped closer. Hate sparkled in his stare as he stopped close enough to breathe my same fucking air. "I promised I'd destroy you," he murmured. "This is me making good on that promise."

I sucked in another deep breath. "You're wasting your time, Dornan, I told you before."

"You don't know anything about Hannah."

"That's right."

"So why the hell don't I believe you?"

I swallowed a flare of panic and fought to stay in control. He didn't have a goddamn thing on me. I knew that, yet I couldn't stop that rush. Threats were one thing...closing down my fucking club was another.

"You won't get away with this," I snarled.

That fucking gleam in his eyes brightened. "I already have, motherfucker," he countered. "This is only the start. You want this to stop? Then you know what to do."

I shook my head.

"Peters," Dornan called. "He's all yours."

FORTY-SIX

Alexi

I watched the crowd disperse outside the club under Dornan's orders. Most left, but there were still a few who lingered.

"Let's get this over with," I muttered to Jager.

I headed toward the front doors, stepping around a group who'd stayed.

"Alexi?"

I turned at my name and a familiar brunette came toward me, wild black hair, big eyes, and a seductive smile. I searched my memory for her name.

"I was hoping to see you tonight," she started as I cast a panicked glance to Jager. *Help?*

He just gave a smirk and kept on walking, leaving me behind. I had no choice but to meet her stare. "And here I am."

She slid her hand over my chest, then slowly slid it down my stomach. Stunned, it took me a second before I grabbed her wrist and stopped her as she went for my belt. There was something eerily familiar. Still, the action pissed me off, slapping me hard with the way I'd fucked around.

But that was before...

Before *Leila*.

"I'm married," I growled and gave her hand a shove.

"That's not a problem for me." She pinned me with that ravenous stare. "We had fun before."

I shook my head. "Not anymore."

"Oh?" Her brows rose as she gave a shrug. "Your loss."

I gave a hard chuff as I turned away. "I doubt it."

"Asshole," she snapped as I kept walking, heading into the club and the battle that waited for me.

Fucking some random piece of ass wasn't a loss in the slightest. But losing Leila...

I knew what betraying her felt like. I'd almost ruined what we had once, and that was something I'd never do again. Not even if I was tempted...and I was *never* tempted.

"I want to see the inventory of the stock on hand, as well as all the relevant licenses," Special Agent Peters commanded, glancing up from his notepad as I approached.

"Of course," I muttered, making my way across the dance floor to the door at the rear of the club.

The asshole just followed, keeping one step behind. I could feel the bastard's breath on the back of my neck as I unlocked the office door and stepped in. He was after more than liquor licenses, that was obvious. I scanned the office as I switched on the light.

But if he expected a breakdown of all our fucking enterprises laid out for him, then he was severely mistaken. I crossed the floor, opened a cabinet under my desk with my key, and pulled out the folder I needed.

Four different certificates were spread out on my desk. "As you can see, we're all certified and up to date."

The asshole slowly made his way over to glance down at the certificates. He barely looked at them, just shoved the first one aside.

"The young women," he murmured.

Heat rushed to my cheeks. "There was no way they obtained those drugs on our premises."

"Even so." He met my stare. "Your staff needs to be more aware of their patrons."

"And they will be." I stepped closer. "But closing down our club on our busiest night of the week seems a little...excessive."

He gave a shrug.

I knew then this had been Dornan all along.

Motherfucker.

He turned away, barely giving the certificates a second glance. He seemed far more interested in anything else he could find, which was exactly...*nothing.*

My brother's heavy footsteps resounded. I lifted my head as he filled the doorway, six foot five of pure menace. The agent stilled, lifted his gaze, then muttered, "Excuse me," as he tried to pass him in the doorway.

But Jager never moved, just lifted his gaze to mine.

He was the one who should've been running the clubs and the shipments interstate. But he wasn't. Instead, he was lucky to be alive after taking a bullet to his goddamn head. It had left him disfigured and scarred...both qualities that made him terrifying.

He just met the agent's stare and lifted his gaze to me. "Do you want me to get the crew in for closing?"

I looked at my watch, it was barely one a.m. We should be taking in a thousand a minute right now, yet here I was, giving my brother a nod to end the night.

"How long are we closed?" I asked.

"Twenty-four hours," Peters answered.

"Of course, take out not just one night, but two."

The asshole merely gave another shrug and continued to glare at my brother. But Jager couldn't care less, just waited for me to nod before he turned away.

"Twenty-four hours," I murmured. "Not a second longer, right?"

Peters stilled in the doorway. "That's how long it takes us to complete the relevant checks...unless you wanted to...*speed things up?*"

Speed things up? I swallowed the icy shiver that raced along my spine. The bastard was trying to set me up, knowing full well one whisper of a bribe and Dornan would be all over my business. He wanted nothing more than to expose me and my family.

Right now, that was the last thing I wanted.

"No." I held his stare. "If that's how long it takes, then we'll wait."

A slow nod of his head and the bastard walked away. I clenched my jaw as I stared at the certificates spread across my desk. All for nothing, every single second of this.

Rage ripped through me.

How long would I have to deal with this fucking fallout?

For as long as it takes...

The words rose inside my head.

As long as it takes.

I slid the certificates back into the folder and stowed them away in my desk before relocking it. By the time I walked out, the ATF agents were already gone. I stared around at the empty club and the bartenders cleaning up for the night before I turned away and went to find Jager outside.

Headlights flared as the agents' dark sedan pulled out from the curb and drove away.

"They'll be back," I growled. "Next time, they won't leave until they've ruined us."

"I know," Jager answered. "And there's not a damn thing we can do to stop it."

That icy shiver of rage plunged deeper until it was all I could feel. Movement drew my gaze...that raven-haired beauty was leaning against a white Lexus, watching me with a desperate stare.

They were all fucking wolves, just waiting to tear me apart any way they could.

"Do you have this?" I asked Jager.

"Yeah," he answered, following my gaze to where she waited. "And I'm already onto the Russian."

I gave my brother a soft clap on the shoulder and turned away, heading for my car. That desperation stayed with me as I climbed inside and started the engine. In the rear-view mirror, the woman watched me as I pulled out and drove away.

My past was a demon I just couldn't seem to shake. No matter how hard I tried.

I focused on the streets as I drove through the city, then out the other side. City lights gave way to endless darkness. I drove down the familiar road and spied the towering fences of my compound.

I pulled up outside the gates and stared at the dark house in the distance. In an instant, my heart started pounding. I clenched the wheel as the gates slowly opened, and saw that my hands were shaking. Heat raced across my face, making me feel like I was going to be sick.

"Jesus fucking Christ," I muttered, shoving the car into gear and driving through. "That's all I need is a fucking heart attack."

I wasn't having one...that I knew.

Life wouldn't let me off that fucking easy.

I pulled up outside the garage and parked.

But I couldn't get out, not yet.

All I could do was stare up at the house I'd had built as I tried to get myself together. I'd thought escaping that fucking island would be the hardest thing I'd ever do. But this shit was harder. The constant waiting. The constant watching. The constant doubting.

I didn't like it.

It wasn't me...

Not anymore.

I yanked the handle and climbed out, pressing the button to lock the car. I needed to get a handle on this, need to find a way out from under the boulder. Dornan, my family...and now that Russian fuck who'd decided to threaten my goddamn wife.

I climbed the stairs, punched in the code for the security system, and pushed open the door. Leila was still asleep when I stepped into the bedroom. But she was on her back now, arms thrown out, her brows creased and her forehead shining.

She was sweating.

Panicked.

I kicked off my shoes, unbuttoned my shirt, and stepped out of my pants. The image of the dark-haired beauty surfaced. But she was no one compared to this. I slipped under the covers and slid across the bed to curl my body around hers.

"I'm here, baby," I crooned, reaching to brush some hair from her face.

Her eyelids fluttered, and her lips parted, her breaths were fast and panting. She was dreaming...no, she was running. Her jaw flexed and the tendons in her neck corded. I was fixed on the panicked jump of her pulse.

I didn't like it.

Not at all.

I tugged down the sheet to find her bare body. I reached down and slid my hand between her thighs.

"No." She thrashed her head, fighting me.

I knew this fight well.

Something shifted inside me as I moved down the bed, kissing the top of her breast, then the jutting bones of her ribs before I moved to her hip. "Let me take care of you."

Purpose filled me. She was the change, the only fucking change I needed. I kissed her body, moving over to the top of her mound. I knew the moment she became aware of me. Still, she didn't open her eyes, leaving me to move lower, kissing and licking.

She tasted like us.

My come, her desire.

I slid my finger along her crease, spreading her open until I licked her clit. She responded, just like I knew she would. That tiny tremble was a telltale sign. I moved lower, sucking harder until I dragged that little nub into my mouth.

A small moan rumbled in the back of her throat. I licked lower, closing my mouth over her sex. She was so still, so utterly still. But her body responded, getting wetter, so fucking wet. I gently thrust my finger in, careful not to hurt her.

Her hips moved ever so slightly, pushing against me as I sucked and fucked her.

"That's it. Give over to me."

Her head tilted up as she looked down at me, and I was mesmerized by those blue eyes, transfixed by her beauty as she thrust against me, until she closed them. Her teeth pinned her lower lip, biting down as her spine arched...and that moan became a cry.

I licked her desire, swallowing until I felt the weight of her hand on my head as her fingers slipped through my hair.

"Alexi," she whimpered.

I always wanted to hear my name like that.

Desperate.

Needy.

Loved.

FORTY-SEVEN

Leila

I THINK YOU SHOULD COME HERE. ALEXI ISN'T SAFE. NOT right now.

My father's words rang in my head. I paced the floor and watched Alexi stride from the gym at the rear of the house, wiping the sweat from his brow with a towel. He stopped at the kitchen, those dark eyes finding me as he cracked open a bottle of water. "Everything okay?"

I forced a smile and turned, lifting my phone. "I've been summoned."

He said nothing, just glanced at the phone, then finally said. "Is that right?" He swallowed, drinking half of the bottle before he finally lowered his hand. "And you want to go."

"I don't really have a choice where my father is concerned." I strode toward him. "Neither of us do."

He rounded the counter to me. "You always have a choice, Leila."

Heat rushed to my cheeks as the memory of this morning came rushing back. I'd felt his presence when he'd left to go to the city, even as I slipped back to sleep. But it was the moment I'd awoken to the feel of his mouth between my thighs that roared to the surface of my mind.

I was so vulnerable with him.

So utterly weak.

He took whatever he wanted with every graze of his fingers and every lick of his tongue. Just like he did now as he captured a drop of water on his bottom lip. My breath caught...and it wasn't lost on Alexi.

There was a twitch at the corner of his mouth as he moved closer and leaned down to whisper against my ear. "If you look at me like that, Leila, you're not going anywhere except back to bed."

Desire slammed into me.

He'd had me more times than I could count, in every room and every position...and yet, it still wasn't enough. I closed my eyes, inhaling the heady scent of him.

Beep.

I flinched at the sound and looked down at my phone.

Malik: I'll be there in five minutes.

"Unfortunately, there's no getting out of this one," I murmured. "My father's driver is on his way."

"His driver, huh?" Alexi pulled away, that devilish gleam dying away in his eyes. "I don't think you should be going anywhere, not after last—"

I shook my head.

I refused to be a prisoner again. I'd had enough of that growing up, confined by towering walls and armed men. I might still be that small child in need of imprisoning in my father's eyes, but I refused to be that to Alexi. "You know Malik. He isn't reckless, he'll be careful."

I'd barely managed the words before his own phone started vibrating in his hand.

"Besides." I nodded. "You're busy. It'll give me an excuse to stay out of your way."

"Baby," he muttered, scowling at his screen. "You're the only one I want in my way, believe me." He lifted his phone. "Yeah?"

I watched him step away, knowing instantly it was Jager he spoke to.

"You've got to be kidding me. That guy just won't leave it alone, will he?" The sound of his footsteps faded as he headed for the bedroom. "Okay, yeah. Let me shower and I'll be in."

Looked like that solved the issue for the both of us.

I grabbed my purse, checked my phone, and headed for the living room window, just in time to catch the glint of sunlight as it bounced off my father's black Mercedes. Alexi still hadn't returned. The thought of going to him surfaced as Malik pulled up outside.

My husband was busy with the clubs anyway.

I doubted he'd even notice I was gone.

I inhaled hard and headed for the door, stepping through as Malik opened the car door for me.

"Leila." He smiled. "Lovely as always."

I couldn't help but return the smile with one of my own as I slipped into the car. "You are far too sweet."

He was...he was also professional, gently closing my door before he climbed back in behind the wheel. Silence filled the space, leaving me to clasp my seatbelt in place and ease back against the seat.

I turned my focus instead to the world outside as we passed through the gates and headed toward the city. I liked it out here. In a way, it reminded me of home. Towering green pine trees looked like the thick blanket of forest that surrounded our home in Russia.

I slid my sunglasses in place and let my mind drift. But it wasn't our home I thought of...it was my best friend, Viktoriya. She'd been abducted from her home and had last been tracked to somewhere in the US. Alexi had men looking for her...but every day that went by, my hope of finding her faded a little more. The thought of losing her was like losing myself.

I closed my eyes and leaned my head back against the headrest, my thoughts swallowed by the stabbing ache in my chest. Slowly, the sounds of traffic intruded. I opened my eyes as we slipped onto the on-ramp and headed across the city. Cars flew past, as did the familiar sights, until we veered off, headed past the built-up part of the city, and headed south.

Car horns blared.

We were sandwiched in.

Huge trucks dwarfed us. I glanced up at the driver as Malik murmured. "There's a detour up ahead."

The sun glinted off glass, blinding me for a moment as he leaned to the side, to find the lane we were in closed off.

Malik glanced into the rear-view mirror and cursed as the truck beside us honked his horn.

I jumped at the sound and gripped the seat as we turned with the flow of traffic, then turned again. Malik flicked on the GPS, shifting his gaze from the screen to the signs in front.

"Is everything okay?" I murmured.

"Absolutely," he answered with confidence. "I just need to figure out a way to get us back on to the main road.

I glanced at the highway signs falling away behind us, then tried to relax. Wherever we were, Malik would figure out a way to get us heading back to my father's estate. But as we hit another detour sign, I grew nervous.

"Goddamn," Malik snapped, braking hard as we came to yet another detour.

I flinched and widened my eyes at the sudden outburst. My father's driver had never spoken like that before, and he'd never been so volatile, especially in my presence. A sudden jerk of the wheel drove me sideways. I slammed my hand out, unleashing a cry as a sudden horn blare came from behind us.

But there was nowhere to go, the road was blocked ahead, and a truck was mere inches from our bumper. There was nowhere for us to move. I looked around before fixing my gaze on Malik, who suddenly jerked his gaze to the rear-view mirror.

The blur of black came from both sides of the car. In my side mirror, I caught movement, then fixed my gaze on four masked men dressed in black and carrying automatic rifles as they flanked the sides of the car.

A scream ripped free as Malik shoved the car into reverse. "Hold on, Leila!" he roared before we hit with a crunch.

Crack...crack...crack!

The sound of gunfire was deafening. I screamed again as I folded forward and clung to the seatbelt.

BOOM!

The sound of shattering glass filled the air. But Malik already had his gun in his hand. With a roar, he shoved his arm out the window's hole and opened fire. Shouts followed, terrifyingly brutal screams as men in masks yanked on the handle of my door. I lunged, grabbed my purse, and fumbled for my phone.

My fingers shook as I stabbed the screen to enter my code.

Boom!

The crack of gunfire continued. Still, I pressed the number for Alexi's phone, but could only listen to it ring as the door beside me was jerked open and the men dressed in black reached in.

"No, you don't," one of them growled as he grabbed me by the hair and wrenched me backwards.

I kicked out, screaming. If they thought I was meek and mild, then they had no idea what was coming for them. I swung around, pulled my foot up, and drove my heel into the middle of his chest. My attacker let out a hard grunt and stumbled backwards when my stiletto punched into his chest. But I was already scrambling for the front seat of the car, desperate to get out, with my phone in my hand. My first call had been disconnected when they'd grabbed me, and now my finger slipped across the screen, but still, I found Alexi's number and pressed call.

"Get the fuck back here." My attacker grabbed another handful of my hair and dragged me backwards.

Agony lashed across my scalp. I grabbed hold of the passenger seat, but my hands slipped as I was torn away and pulled from the car. Behind me, the faint sound of Alexi's phone rang…and rang…and rang.

"Get off me! Malik! MALIK!" I roared as I tripped and fell, desperately searching for my protector.

Crack!

CRACK!

My father's driver opened fire and hit my attacker in the center of his chest.

"LEILA, RUN!" he roared.

I couldn't see him, but I heard the sickening boom that silenced him.

Blood drained from my face at the sound of the gunshot. Under the car, I saw Malik's body hit the ground. Blood ran from a bullet hole in the center of his forehead. I sucked in an all-consuming breath, but before I could unleash the scream trapped in my throat, a hand clamped over my mouth.

FORTY-EIGHT

Alexi

"Play it again," Dornan muttered behind me.

Auggie lifted his gaze to me as the pain in the ass Special Agent leaned closer, snarling in the security guard's face. "I said, play it again."

I gave a slow nod, saying nothing. Dornan could demand all he fucking well wanted. There wasn't damn thing Auggie would do without my express consent. He knew better...all my staff did.

So Auggie turned back and rewound to the moment the two women who'd started all this pulled the drugs out of their purses outside the women's restroom and decided to get royally fucked...and me along with them.

"So you can very clearly see, they didn't purchase those drugs on my premises," I murmured, desperate for this entire thing to be over.

The sonofabitch said nothing.

Anger flared as I fixed on his fucking pissed off expression. I wanted nothing more than to lunge across the security room and wrap my fucking hands around his neck and strangle the bastard. But I didn't. Instead, I stood there like a fucking chump and took the asshole's wrath.

Beep.

I looked down at my phone to a text from Leila's father.

Alexi, Leila hasn't arrived. My men are out looking for her now. I'll let you know what happened.

"What the fuck?" I snarled and stabbed the icon beside his name.

"What is it?" Dornan asked.

I turned away, ignoring him, and listened to Maxim's ringing phone before he finally answered. "What do you mean she hasn't arrived? She left over two hours ago."

"And she hasn't arrived." The icy tone of his voice echoed down the line. "Don't worry. I have my men involved."

"Don't worry? Don't worry!? SHE'S MY GODDAMN WIFE!"

"What's happening?" Dornan demanded behind me as I headed for the door.

"I want details, Maxim, where she was, who she was with. I want to know exactly what happened and by Christ, you better tell me right fucking now."

I stalked along the hallway, heading back to my office, and listened to his unflinching fucking tone tell me exactly what had happened, from the loss of communication...to the fucking disappearance of my wife.

"I will let you know once I have any more information."

"Don't fucking bother." I snatched my jacket from the back of my chair and turned around to find Dornan in the middle of my office doorway.

I hung up on my father-in-law and headed out, slamming into the fucking pain in my ass as he stared. "Not now, Dornan."

He stumbled backwards. "Hey," he growled, then grabbed my arm, wrenching me around.

I lunged, grabbed his shirt, and shoved him back against the wall as reality slammed into me. "I said not the fuck now! Do you *hear* that?"

Hard breaths consumed me as I suddenly realized what I was doing. I pushed him away, staring at the crumpled fabric, before I turned and strode away. My damn hand shook as I lifted my phone and pressed the number for the only other person I trusted in this world.

"Yeah?"

"They took her," I forced the words out as I stepped out of the club and into the harsh sunlight. "They fucking took her, Jager. I want her back. I want her found."

He was suddenly alert. "Who?"

"That's what I want to know. I want her back, then I want revenge, brother. Give her back to me…so I can cut the hands off every motherfucker who touched a hair on her head."

The heavy thud of his steps mirrored the pounding of my heart. Agony tore through my chest. I reached out, slamming my fist against the roof of my car as the world grayed.

BOOM…

BOOM…

BOOM.

The deafening sound swallowed everything else. Jager's voice tried to push in...but I couldn't hear a damn thing over the panic.

"Alexi!" My brother's voice snapped in my ear, wrenching me out of the goddamn spiral that was taking me under.

"Yeah." I sucked in a breath. "I'm here."

"The driver, was he one of yours?"

I shook my head. "No. Malik, one of her father's."

"And he picked her up from your house to go where?"

"Her father's." The moment I said the words, the clear blue eyes of that motherfucker roared back to me from last night.

A chill coursed down my spine. "I think I know who has her." My voice was bitter, so cold. I lifted my gaze, then yanked open the driver's door and climbed in behind the wheel. "That Russian motherfucker from last night."

"Tell me how you know that?"

"Call it a very good fucking hunch."

"Are you willing to stake her life on that? Because if I waste a single second getting her back, then it could cost you everything."

My breaths raced. I lifted my gaze as Dornan stumbled from my club, then looked around until he found me. I didn't know...I didn't kn—

I'm sorry to hear about your father's troubles here in the United of States. He might get the notion of returning home?

That heavy Russian accent slammed into me. The way he'd looked at her...the way he'd looked at me. "Yeah." I leaned forward and started the car. "It's him."

"Then I'll start with the GPS in her father's car. Keep your phone close. You'll hear from me soon."

I didn't need to answer, because he was already gone. I shoved the car into gear and punched the accelerator, heading for the city. Horns blared And cars tore past as I raced by. My damn hands shook as I gripped the wheel, imagining her at the hands of that motherfucker.

I'd kill him if he hurt her.

I'd fucking *kill* him.

My phone had barely vibrated before I snatched it up and answered. "What do you have?"

"I'm sending you the GPS location of the car. I'm on my way, but you might get there faster."

I pushed the Audi harder. "Guaranteed."

A second later, my phone vibrated again. I glanced at the screen, then punched the details for the map and narrowed in. "What the fuck were they doing at the Cross?"

"Hell if I know," he answered. "But I'm heading there now."

The engine of his motorcycle roared to life in the background. He'd get there...and fast.

"Find her, Jager." I gripped the wheel and punched the accelerator even harder. "Whatever it takes."

I tossed my phone to the passenger seat, then fixed my focus on the road as I raced deeper into the city. Twenty minutes fighting the traffic felt like time in Hell. I turned the wheel and braked hard at the detour sign. "What the fuck?" I snarled.

Cars were stopped mid-flow. Horns blared as they tried to reverse and turn around. Crunch! Others collided as I stared at the frozen lane of traffic ahead. "Come on!" I screamed, pounding the wheel.

Until that heavy punch came to my chest once more.

I glanced at the phone on the seat, then grabbed it.

The car's GPS location was straight ahead...

I glared at the traffic, then that red blinking marker on the map, and slowly a sickening feeling washed over me. I killed the engine and climbed out. Horns blared all around me and pissed off drivers yelled out their windows.

But I ignored them all and kept walking to where the drivers stood outside their cars and stared.

Crunch.

I looked down, catching the glint of broken glass, and in an instant, the past came rushing back. The island. The attack. We'd barely escaped the last time...

I moved without thinking as I caught sight of the back of the black Mercedes. The car doors were open and bullets had punctured the trunk and shattered the rear window. Heads turned as I neared and one of Maxim's men came closer.

"Mr. Kilpatrick." He lifted his hand to stop me.

But I kept walking, pushing past him to the open back door of the vehicle, and stared inside. Glass was scattered everywhere. I could almost taste her fear. I caught sight of her phone on the floor of the car.

She didn't have it.

She didn't—

"The driver?"

"On the other side," Maxim's man said carefully.

I gave a nod, stepped away, and rounded the rear of the car. I didn't want to look, but I had to see for myself. Polished black shoes, immaculately pressed pants...and a bullet hole in the middle of his forehead.

"If there were witnesses, they're long gone," the guard said.

"Of course there were."

The faint sound of a motorcycle was growing louder in the distance. I turned as my brother wove through traffic, pulled up beside the car, and took off his helmet.

I rounded the car to stand beside him. "She's gone, and the driver is dead."

Those cold eyes met mine. "Lev Fedorov," I murmured. "I want him found, Jager. He needs to be found, we need to get her back, and he needs to be bleeding."

I left him behind as I strode back to my car, grabbed my phone, and hit the number for Balor.

It only rang twice before it was answered. "Alexi." He sounded flustered.

"Lev Fedorov," I snarled as I started the engine. "What did you find out?"

"Not much," he answered. "Arrived in the States a week ago and he's staying at some place up in Develin Hills."

"Where?"

"The address?"

"Yeah, the goddamn address."

His voice turned careful. "Alexi, has something happened?"

"You could say that," I answered as I shoved my car into reverse and punched the accelerator, backing until I slammed into the car behind me. "The bastard has taken my goddamn wife."

FORTY-NINE

Leila

Pain pounded in the back of my head. I wanted to stay down in the darkness, where nothing waited. But that agonizing throb wouldn't leave me alone. *Pulse...pulse...pulse...*

I winced, sucked in a deep breath, and released a moan. Light flooded in as I cracked open my eyes. The moment I did, that gnawing ache in the back of my head grew fangs. I sucked in a hard breath, fought through the wave, and opened my eyes a little wider.

There was light.

Light, and a room I didn't recognize.

I blinked and carefully turned my head, taking in the room inch by inch. There was a door in front and one to my left. I was slumped on a sofa in some kind of sunroom, with the light streaming through the windows to my left. Blue sky was all I saw. That sight spurred me on. I tried to move, but my hands wouldn't budge.

I jerked forward until my muscles strained and a dull ache tore along my arms. Footsteps echoed, drawing my gaze. Panic followed, making my pulse race. Through the blur of my vision, a door opened and someone stepped into the room.

"There she is."

I flinched at the sound of that voice as Lev Fedorov came closer...and bent down in front of me. Deep, unflinching blue eyes were fixed on me.

"Are you in pain?"

I said nothing, just glared at him.

He never noticed, just lifted his hand to brush the hair from my face, just like Alexi. Only this time, I jerked away and snarled, "Don't touch me."

He stilled, his hand hovering in the air before he finally lowered it. I licked my dry lips and swallowed, trying to wet my throat. "Where am I?"

"Safe," he answered coldly.

I searched the room, trying to find anything I could use to get free.

"Are you in pain?"

I jerked back to him, ready to scream into his face...until I saw the flicker of desire in his eyes.

I knew that look...that *hunger*. I saw it every day in the eyes of my husband. I licked my lips once more and sank down into that stony part of my nature. "Yes." I whispered, holding his stare.

He was uncomfortable, looking away...*men*.

"My arms. I think they...I think they hurt me when they pulled me from the car."

He flinched, that stare empty now. "I apologize for that. It was... unavoidable." There was a moment of hesitation before he leaned forward and reached around me.

I closed my eyes and held my breath as he pressed against me. His muscular body was too close. Pressure built in my lungs as he released the cuffs around my wrists, but I couldn't hold it forever and, as the cuffs released, the air left my body...and the *stench* of him invaded.

He pulled away, letting my arms drop to my sides until I cautiously lifted them and rubbed the muscles. But he wasn't done, lifting that fucking hand to my cheek once more. "You always were such a beautiful woman, Leila." His tone turned chilling. "Too beautiful for the American scum."

He pulled away then, changing in an instant as he rose.

"What do you want from me?"

Crack!

The sound of gunfire erupted.

"What I've always wanted..." he answered. "Your father on his knees."

My stomach clenched as I jerked my head toward the doorway.

"It's time to find out where your father's loyalty lies, Leila. With his daughter...or his country."

"No." I shook my head as Lev took a step backwards. *"No! Don't do this! You don't have to do this!"*

Panic filled me as he turned and made for the door. I did the only thing I could. I lunged from the seat. My body moved far too slowly, still weighed down by the pounding at the back of my head. Still, I hit him with my full weight, driving him forward.

He wasn't expecting it and slammed facefirst into the wall before he swung around.

"You fucking *bitch!*" His fist was in my hair in an instant, yanking me as he stumbled.

My pent-up breaths unleashed in a scream. The room blurred as I was thrown around, stopping my shrill cry. Footsteps came from beyond the door, then a voice roared, followed by the *crack...crack...CRACK* of gunshots.

I needed to buy time, needed to keep him here any way I could. So I grabbed his hand on my head and yanked my foot upward before I drove it out, catching him in the side of his knee.

Crunch.

He released my hair in an instant and grabbed his leg instead, unleashing a howl of agony as he staggered sideways. I didn't wait, just jerked my gaze to the door and drove myself forward.

"NO!" Lev roared.

Crack!

I flinched at the gunshot and stopped. My hand slipped from the door handle as I stared at the hole in the wall next to my head, then slowly turned to find the gun in his hand.

"You." His lips curled, exposing his teeth. "Are not going anywhere."

I shook my head and slowly lowered my hand. "Easy."

He jerked the muzzle toward me. "Move away from the door, Leila."

But that roar came once more, only this time closer. I knew instantly who it was...*my father.*

Lev turned toward the sound. "Move," he growled and stepped carefully forward.

He was going to kill him, I knew that now. My father may not have been perfect, he might've been cold and distant and at times terrifying, but he was the only father I had. Tears blurred my vision as I shook my head. "No."

Fedorov scowled and limped forward. "Move away, now."

I shook my head, my words careful. "You'll have to kill me."

"If that's what it takes." He took aim at the center of my chest.

Cold plunged all the way through me until, through the door, my father spoke. "Leila...do what he says."

I shook my head, and those tears that had welled in my eyes fell, sliding down my cheeks.

I was trapped between them, unable to move.

"This is between me and your father," Lev urged.

"No, it's not," I whispered. "Not when you use me as collateral."

Lev glanced at the door behind me, then limped forward, grabbed me by the arm, and tried to yank me away from the doorway. "I said...*move.*"

But I resisted with all I had, refusing to budge until, with a crack, the door shoved inward, slammed into me and knocked me out of the way.

My father charged into the room, moving faster than I'd ever seen before. He was a blur before he slammed into Lev. They were all fists and fury. My father screamed as he punched, over and over again...

Bang!

I flinched and cried out.

I was frozen as I watched my father raise his head to look at Lev and whisper, "No."

I shook my head when my father stumbled backwards, his hand clasped over the blood seeping through his white shirt, and Lev turned to me and raised his gun. "Your father is over…" He sucked in a hard breath. "Now it's your turn."

FIFTY

Alexi

"Answer the FUCKING PHONE!" I roared as I listened to the tone ring and ring and ring, before I stabbed the icon and ended the sound.

Streets blurred as I pushed the Audi harder than I'd ever pushed it before. Balor had come through with the address, texting it to me as I received a voicemail from Maxim.

I have her location and I'm on my way. This is a feud between me and Lev, Alexi. Stay out of it. I'll call when my daughter is safe.

"Stay the fuck out of it?" I clenched the wheel tighter, everything else blurring except for my rage.

She was my wife...

She was MY goddamn wife.

This is how it was always going to be with him, always one step out of focus, always controlling her every goddamn move. He was stifling, controlling, completely unable to let her find happiness. He didn't want his daughter married to me, that was obvious.

This was going to be just another way to get her to move back in with him.

And away from me.

"Over my fucking dead body," I snarled and pushed the car harder as my phone vibrated.

I glanced at the screen, hitting the speaker as I answered.

"How far away are you?" Jager's bike howled in the background.

"Coming up on it now," I answered, scanning the exclusive houses carved into the side of the hill.

"Wait for me," Jager urged. "Alexi, do you hear me? *Wait for—*"

I ended the call. There was no way I was waiting a second longer.

I jerked the wheel at the sight of Maxim's car parked on the edge of the road. The doors were open, his men gone. Panic filled me as I pumped the brakes, slowed hard, and pulled up in a screech of tires. My gun was in my hand in an instant as I fumbled for the door handle, yanked it open, and jumped out.

All I cared about was finding her alive...

Everything else could wait.

I lunged along the walkway toward the imposing front door of the house, which stood open. Feet were lying in view, with polished boots and black trousers. I pushed in, finding the splayed legs of a guard I didn't recognise...dead.

A cough jerked my gaze from the body in the entrance. I lifted my gun and advanced, glancing at what looked like the living room to my right.

"*NO!*"

I jerked my gaze upwards at the sound of Maxim's roar. My heart was pounding, clenching tight until agony roared through me, driving me deeper into the house. I pushed further found a set of stairs, and climbed fast, toward the sound of fists and grunts of fury.

CRACK!

The steps were a blur as I caught a low fucking murmur. "Your father is over...now it's your turn."

"The FUCK it is!" I howled, lifting my gun as I charged into the room.

I didn't see anything but him, not even my wife. All I saw was the *threat*. One I had to end in an instant.

Bang!

The gun kicked in my hand by reflex. For a split second, panic filled me, but I was already turning to her, finding those wide, terrified blue eyes and the scratches on her cheek, already darkening to a bruise.

She was hurt.

She was fucking hurt!

My jaw clenched as I turned back to that bastard who stood over her father and charged further into the room.

Bang!

"You touched my goddamn wife!"

Bang!

"You touched what's *mine!*"

Blood spilled from the bullet holes in the center of his forehead. He crumpled in a heap on the floor next to her father. I glanced at Maxim and couldn't help but wince. The dark, spreading stain on his shirt drew me.

"Fuck!" I barked as I charged toward where he lay on the floor.

Flecks of blood flew through the air and landed on his cheek as he spluttered. I shoved the Russian piece of shit aside and knelt beside Maxim, kicking the gun out of Lev's dead hand by habit.

"Leila," Maxim whispered.

My wife was scurrying forward in an instant, falling to her knees beside her father. "Papa," she whispered, sounding so fucking small. *"Papa, no!"*

"Alexi!" Jager howled my name. *"ALEXI!"*

The heavy thud of his steps resounded a heartbeat later on the stairs.

"Up here!" I yelled. *"Get a fucking ambulance!"*

My brother charged into the room, drawing my gaze. I met that savage stare, then gave a slow shake of my head. He turned his focus to the man in my arms as, beside me, my wife unleashed a sob and hugged her father as he slowly died.

There was no saving Maxim, not even if we'd had the most experienced paramedics on standby.

"Papa..." she cried.

Beep.

My phone vibrated in my pocket. But I couldn't look away as my wife held the body of her father against her. Her head was bowed and her body shuddered as she sobbed. All I could do was place my arm around her shoulders.

"Call his men," I murmured to my brother. "We need to be gone before the cops arrive."

The last thing I needed was Dornan up in my fucking face with my wife's Russian Mafia father lying dead in front of us. I'd never see her again if he got here before we could disappear.

"Baby," I urged, grasping her arm and gently pulling her away. "We have to go."

She shook her head, sobbing. "No."

My soul was torn between giving her peace or protection.

In the end, the answer was simple.

She could hate me all she wanted to for this...*after*.

I rose, then bent down and pulled her hands from her father's body. She bucked, screaming, and beat on me with her fists. *"PUT ME DOWN! ALEXI...ALEXI!"*

I handled her as gently as I could, lifting her against me. She bucked, fighting like I knew she would...until the fight went out of her, and I turned and headed for the door. I carried her out of that house as she clung to me and sobbed.

My car was still there, the driver's door wide open. I could still taste the panic as I'd yanked open the passenger door and eased her in. She was still when I pulled the seatbelt across her, that numb, empty stare fixed on nothing.

"I'll take care of you," I promised, brushing my thumb across her cheek. "I promise."

FIFTY-ONE

Leila

5 DAYS LATER...

THUD.

I flinched and tightened my hold on Alexi's hand as the dirt hit my father's casket. The priest dressed in ornate Orthodox robes kept talking, speaking in earnest about a man he didn't know. A good man. An honest man. My father had been anything but.

Still, he'd protected me when I'd needed it. He—my throat thickened as the memory of those last few moments returned. He was brave and honorable...when it came to me. Alexi shifted at my side, just enough to pull me harder against him.

Thud.

I flinched once more as the priest looked at me and gave me a solemn smile. A slow nod and he turned toward the men who'd protected my father and the scattering of acquaintances he'd gathered in the few months he'd been here in this country. Violence followed us, no matter where we went. It clung to us like a stain. No matter how hard we scrubbed or how many continents we travelled, we just couldn't escape.

I closed my eyes as movement came around me...and those who'd come finally left.

We couldn't escape.

Not on an island in the middle of nowhere, and not here in a city surrounded by armed men. There was no fleeing, no hiding, no...*running.*

A shudder tore through me, making my knees tremble.

"I'm right here." Alexi gripped me tightly. "Use me."

He was the only one I had now. The only one who was as violent and as viscious as those who meant me harm. Lev might've been killed...but there were more of his kind out there, dangerous men who'd stop at nothing to bring my family name to its knees. And I was the only one left to defend it now.

The only one *left.*

I turned, finding Alexi's intense stare. He was the only one I had now. The only person who'd love me, protect me...defend me.

Use me...

His words resounded in my head as, slowly, those who'd come to mourn left us. I stared at the casket as dirt slowly fell in.

"Do you want to stay?"

I shook my head. "No."

"Want to get out of here?"

An ache spread across my chest. I couldn't move...couldn't breathe—

"I have a surprise, "Alexi murmured. "I've been keeping it, waiting for the right time."

He tugged my hand, gently pulling me away. I tore my focus from the gravesite and met his stare. He gave me a smile, but it wasn't one filled with sadness, like the priest's. It was mischievous and hopeful. "What are you doing, Alexi?"

He gave a shrug, smoothly leading me away. "You'll see."

I had no choice but to follow him. My heels sank into the soft ground once more as we made our way back to the car. There was no driver waiting, just us. Alexi unlocked the car and opened my door, holding my hand until I slid inside.

I glanced across the green to where the groundskeepers had set to work filling in my father's grave as Alexi climbed in behind the wheel and started the engine.

"I think you're going to like this." He shoved the car into gear.

"Do you?" I answered as we pulled away from the curb and headed along the expansive drive.

There was no wake to be held for my father. No celebration of his life. Only the private mourning of those he'd left behind. It was the way he'd wanted it.

Move on, sweetheart, were his last words for me, delivered by his attorney along with a list of all the properties, shares, and money he'd left behind.

I was wealthy by any standards. Extremely wealthy...and before I found Alexi, I was alone.

Alexi drove, and I drifted away. It didn't matter what he had planned, I just wanted to go home, to stare out into the forest that lingered at the edge of our estate, remembering a time when I'd felt almost whole and sink into his arms.

But Alexi didn't take me home.

Instead, he drove across the city.

"Do you remember Marcus Baldeon?"

Baldeon...I tried to remember. My stomach clenched first before it hit me. *The island.* "Yes."

Alexi glanced my way. "He had a brother, an older one, Lucius."

"Okay." I frowned, confused as to why he was telling me this. He turned along a road. Even from here I could see the opulent two and three story houses.

"Apparently, he was ambushed by one of his own men and taken captive, roughed up pretty bad, held in some filthy backwater place in the middle of nowhere for a weeks." He pushed the car, driving along the street. "He barely escaped, it was only because of a woman who risked her life to save his."

I jerked my gaze to Alexi as he slowed the car, then turned into a driveway guarded by a massive, towering fence, one that screamed *Mafia*.

"She was ruthless, apparently. Somehow amongst it all..." the gate slowly opened, leading us to a long driveway.

I saw her first, standing there at the end...her long brown hair swept away by the wind. My heart leaped. Reflex took over, making me grab the door handle.

"Easy, baby!" Alexi barked braking hard and reaching over to grab me.

But I was pushing the door open before I knew it and shoving from the car. The tears that had threatened to fall at my father's funeral rose swiftly to blur my sight. But I saw her...I saw her, and she saw me.

"*Leila!*" she cried out, lunging for the car.

I just made it past the front before we collided. My arms wrapped around her as my face buried against her neck. "I thought you were dead... *Viktoriya...I thought you were—*"

"I know," she wept, too, her arms tightening around me.

The *thud* of a car door sounded before the heavy footsteps sounded.

"Alexi." Came a deep, unfamiliar murmur.

"Lucius," Alexi answered.

I pulled back to stare into her eyes. There was sadness there, deep, resounding sadness. The kind I saw in my own eyes in the wake of my father's death. I swallowed the tang of my tears and brushed the hair from her face, then lifted her chin. "You're stained, too?"

She knew what I was saying.

Of course she did. She gave me a careful nod before turning her gaze to the man who stood at her side. "Leila, this is Lucius."

I met his gaze. He was stained, too, that was easy to see. The bruises on his face were yellowed, just barely visible, and he held himself as though he was still in pain, but he was trying his best to hide it. Still, I saw it. I dropped my arms from my best friend and moved toward him, wrapping my arms around him instead. "Thank you...thank you for bringing her back to me."

He never moved, standing still. From the corner of my eye, Alexi gave a small nod. Only then did the man touch me, wrapping his arms around me.

"You're very welcome. But I think you have this whole thing the wrong way around. Viktoriya is the one who saved me. I was just an idiot in her way of escaping."

"Not in the way," she denied as I pulled away.

I looked down, swiping the tears from my eyes before moving to Alexi's side. "That sounds like the sister I know," I chuckled, giving her a smile. "How long have you been here?"

"A couple of weeks," she answered, her smile fading. "I wanted to reach out, but it wasn't safe. The men who took us, they attacked us again when we tried to hide here."

I jerked my gaze to Lucius, finding the truth in his stare. "And now?"

"Now they're dead," he answered in that stony tone I knew so well.

It was the same tone Alexi had when he was protective. I moved closer to him, sliding my arm around his waist, then I stared. Love burned in his stare. Powerful, dangerous love. The kind that would keep me safe. The same look I saw in Lucius when he looked at my best friend.

"What now?" I asked.

"I dunno about you," Lucius answered. "But I'm ready for a scotch at ten a.m. and to spend the day with newly gained friends. How does that sound, sweetheart?" he asked Viktoriya.

I'd never seen my best friend blush before. But she did now, smiling as she held out her hand.

He took it, lifting it to his lips.

"A drink sounds wonderful," I answered. "As long as you have vodka."

"Only the best." He gave me a smile as he turned toward the house.

But Alexi waited, that mischievous grin growing wider.

"I love you for this," I whispered. "And a million other things."

He pulled me closer, tilted my chin up, and kissed me softly before murmuring, "As I love you."

Printed in Great Britain
by Amazon